AN

"I wonder what kind of tree this is?" Miss Denny asked. "Don't the blossoms have a lovely smell? It's positively heavenly."

"They're orange blossoms," said the Duke. "They do smell divinely, don't they? I believe it is the custom to use them for bridals in France."

He spoke the word "bridal" with quiet significance. Miss Denny gave him an alarmed look, started to speak, then hesitated. "How interesting," she said at last.

"I wish I could believe you really thought so," said the Duke sadly. "But I am not a fool. I am perfectly aware that for the past month or so you've been doing your best to discourage me. I have no doubt that if I were to ask you to marry me this minute, as I came here on purpose to do, you would refuse me."

Miss Denny found her voice almost wholly suspended by a lump in her throat. She swallowed hard and nodded. "Yes, James."

"Of course I knew you must say so. The question I would like to ask is—why?"

"Why?" repeated Miss Denny.

"Yes, why? Right from the start it seemed to me there was something between us, and for me, at least, it's only gotten stronger as I've come to know you better. I love you, Judith Denny, with all my heart—and I wish with all my heart you loved me back. Do you truly not?"

Before she could answer, the Duke put his hands on Miss Denny's shoulders and drew her toward him. Miss Denny's eyes widened with surprise. She knew it was her duty to protest or turn away, but instead she merely shut her eyes and surrendered to his kiss . . .

Books by Joy Reed

AN INCONVENIENT ENGAGEMENT

TWELFTH NIGHT

THE SEDUCTION OF LADY CARROLL

MIDSUMMER MOON

LORD WYLAND TAKES A WIFE

THE DUKE AND MISS DENNY

Published by Zebra Books

THE DUKE AND MISS DENNY

Joy Reed

Zebra Books
Kensington Publishing Corp.

http://www.zebrabooks.com

ZEBRA BOOKS are published by

Kensington Publishing Corp.
850 Third Avenue
New York, NY 10022

Zebra and the Z logo Reg. U.S. Pat. & TM Off.

First Printing: July, 1998
10 9 8 7 6 5 4 3 2 1

Printed in the United States of America

Dedicated to
Janet Dalton
with gratitude for her support and encouragement
and for the invaluable precepts I learned
in her classes

Chapter I

When Miss Judith Denny first arrived at her sister's house in St. James's Square, she was as green as grass and as rustic as a cow-byre. So at least her sister informed her, and as a renowned society hostess and acknowledged leader of fashion, Lady Spicer ought to have known.

"You must not be seen abroad until we have you looking a good deal more *à la mode*," she decreed, as she showed Miss Denny into the luxurious guest bedchamber prepared for her reception. "I mean to take you to my own dressmaker tomorrow, so we can see about ordering new dresses for you as soon as possible."

"I shan't need a new bonnet, anyway," said Miss Denny, proudly displaying the modest straw bonnet which she had just removed from her head. "I bought this one only a few weeks ago. Don't you think it's pretty, Fanny? I trimmed it all myself."

With difficulty, Lady Spicer repressed a shudder. "I'm sure it does very well for you at home," she said, as tactfully as she could. "But you must know, dear, that fashions in London are vastly different from those that prevail in provincial places like Winfield. You will certainly need a new bonnet before I take you out in public. Several new ones, actually, for it is not at all the thing for a lady to appear in the same hat or bonnet day after day.''

Over the next few days, this and a great deal of other worldly advice was imparted to the wide-eyed Miss Denny. For the most part, Lady Spicer found her an apt pupil, although Miss Denny did balk at having her soft golden-brown hair cropped in the fashionable mode.

"I am sure yours is all the crack, Fanny, but it's so short! And how fair it has become." Miss Denny surveyed with innocent wonder her sister's close-cropped golden locks. "Back in Winfield, your hair was used to be almost as dark as mine. You must have spent a great deal of time in the sun."

Lady Spicer gave a discreet titter of laughter. " 'Tis not the sun, child. I have my woman bleach my hair, so as to make it more in the mode. That is also why I must keep it cut short,'' she added, with a rueful glance in the mirror. "The bleach makes it so brittle that I must have it cropped every few weeks if I don't wish my head to look like a haystack."

Miss Denny, remembering her sister's former luxuriant tresses, thought this was rather a steep price to pay for *à la modality*. She had no wish to be rude, however, and so merely said politely, "Short hair looks very nice on *you,* Fanny. But if you don't mind, I'd as soon keep mine as it is."

"Of course, my dear. You are a bit young to adopt such an extreme fashion anyway. We will only have your hair cropped a bit in front, so as to make a few little light curls about your face, and I'm sure you will do very well."

Lady Spicer made this speech with the air of one granting a generous concession, but in truth she was not sorry to see her sister opt for a less striking style than her own. Having struggled hard for some years to attain her current position as a leader of fashion among the *ton,* she had no wish now to see her younger sister outshine her. Although there was little danger of that, Lady Spicer reflected, as she surveyed Miss Denny's small, slight figure. The danger was more whether such an insignificant-looking young lady could be made to present an appearance that would do her, the modish and dashing Lady Spicer, credit.

In truth, Miss Denny bore scant resemblance to her statuesque sister. She was of rather less than average height with a thin and still lamentably girlish figure. Her hair was abundant and glossy with health, but since its color was an indeterminate shade between blonde and brown, this could not be counted any great advantage. Her eyes were likewise brown, and Lady Spicer could only thank her lucky stars that she herself had inherited her mother's clear blue orbs rather than her father's more ordinary dark ones.

As for Miss Denny's other features, Lady Spicer admitted them to be good, but her face was too thin and her brows too level and strongly marked to suit the current mode of beauty. The overall effect, while agreeable, was not at all striking. Lady Spicer, secure in her own superior attractions, could envy her sister nothing but her fresh-from-the-country complexion. And since she had hopes that the *Eau de Ninon* which she had recently ordered her dressing woman to buy might repair the ravages wrought in her own complexion by irregular hours and fashionable dissipations, she was able to survey with complaisance her sister's transformation into a young lady of fashion.

This transformation took place gradually over the space of the next couple of weeks. It was accomplished for the most part without too many difficulties. Once permission had been reluctantly obtained from the principal party, for instance, there was no difficulty at all in providing Miss Denny with a new and suitably fashionable coiffure. The hairdresser was called in, and in the space of only an hour or two, Lady Spicer's *protegée* emerged with her hair charmingly coiffed in clusters of curls about her face, with her back hair left long to be braided atop her head or dressed in a knot at the nape of her neck, just as her own taste and the demands of fashion might dictate.

It took a little longer to assemble the wardrobe of new dresses, hats, slippers, and other accoutrements necessary to a young lady making her debut in society. But thanks to Lady Spicer's unflagging energy and nearly bottomless purse, this too was accomplished in an amazingly short time. What proved more difficult was inculcating Miss Denny with the attitude proper to a young lady making her first appearance among the *haut ton.*

Lady Spicer did her best. She lectured her sister endlessly on all the nuances of polite behavior. Under her own tutelage and that of her dressing woman, Miss Denny was drilled on the proper way to acknowledge an introduction, accept a compliment, or decline an invitation to dance. She practiced her curtsy and her dance steps; she learned to manage a fan, a shawl, and even a hoop skirt, for this last antiquated garment was still required wear for young ladies appearing at the Queen's Drawing Room ceremony. This signal honor was to be Miss Denny's, and Lady Spicer tried hard to impress upon her what an honor it was, but Miss Denny showed herself singularly ungrateful for the pains taken on her behalf. The first time she beheld herself in the glory of full court dress with its embroidered petticoat, trained overskirt, and headdress composed of ribbons, feathers, lappets and pearls, she burst out laughing so hard that the dressmaker, who was bustling about adjusting the drape of the overskirt, looked mortally offended, and Lady Spicer, greatly vexed, was obliged to speak to her sharply.

"But it's so ridiculous, Fanny," gasped Miss Denny, plucking at the stiff swags of fabric on either side of her torso. "I don't mind wearing my waist under my armpits in the usual way, but with a hoopskirt underneath—! Surely you must see how foolish it looks?"

"Nonsense, my dear, you look charming. Perhaps it is a trifle odd to wear hoops beneath a high-waisted dress, but—"

"A *trifle* odd? Oh, Fanny!"

"I beg you will have a little conduct, Judy," said Lady Spicer sternly. "The dress is just as it should be, and it looks perfectly elegant. I'm sure it ought to, considering how much it costs me! But you don't seem the least bit grateful for it."

"Well, you know I didn't ask you to spend a penny on me, Fanny," said Miss Denny candidly. "To be sure, it is delightful having so many new dresses, and I'm much obliged to you for buying them for me. But this one is so ghastly! It seems to me a great pity to spend money on a dress that doesn't become one, particularly when it is such an expensive dress." Miss Denny looked critically down at her lace and pearl encrusted petticoat. "I'll wager I could make a dozen dresses for the cost of this underskirt alone."

"Don't be foolish, Judy," said Lady Spicer sharply. She signed for the dressmaker to unfasten the buttons securing the dress down her sister's back. When the woman had removed the dress from Miss Denny and carried it away to make the necessary alterations, Lady Spicer spoke again in a reproving voice.

"You must know I don't begrudge spending money on you, Judy. Indeed, I have quite enjoyed having something new to occupy myself. But I must beg of you to conduct yourself a little better, especially when there are other people about than you and I. You will be making your bows only next week, and it is vital that you should present a good appearance. If you were to laugh out loud in that foolish way when you are at St. James's, it would prejudice all your chances right from the beginning and bring disgrace upon me as well as you."

"Well, you know I didn't ask to go to St. James's either, Fanny," returned Miss Denny. "Mind you, I should like very well to see the Queen and the Princesses, but the idea of cutting a dash in society doesn't much appeal to me. I think I'd be just as happy going on as we have this last week or two, with shopping and sight-seeing and walking in the park."

This heretical speech shocked Lady Spicer, but then she remembered how complete was her sister's naïveté, and smiled indulgently. "You will think otherwise when you have had a taste of what society has to offer," she predicted. "I can assure you that dancing at Almack's is a deal more enjoyable than walking in the park! But the thing is, Judy, that you will not be given a voucher to Almack's if you do not conduct yourself properly. You have one or two rather—well, rather rustic tendencies, don't you know, which I have been wanting to caution you about. Now will be as good a time as any to do it."

"What rustic tendencies are those?" inquired Miss Denny. Her sister observed with disapproval that she looked more amused than offended.

"Well, just now, for instance, when you were laughing about your court costume. I daresay it *is* rather foolish to wear a hoopskirt beneath a high-waisted dress, but hoops have been customary wear at court for hundreds of years. Just because the fashion is now for high-waisted dresses is no reason why the custom should be suspended."

"If it looks ridiculous, I'd say it's plenty of reason," said Miss Denny, with a smiling glance down at her hooped petticoat. "If the fashion changes, then so should the custom."

"Well, that's not how society works, my love. There are plenty of social customs that have no apparent reason behind them, but well-bred men and women still follow them, and if you go around ridiculing the ones you think odd, you will only make yourself look provincial. And that brings me to another point, Judith. That comment you made earlier, about being able to make up a dozen dresses for the cost of your court petticoat, had much better been left unsaid. No lady of fashion would dream of making up her own dresses, or of counting the cost of her attire either, for that matter. If you say such things in public, people will think you the most perfect rustic."

"Do ladies in London never make their own dresses?" inquired Miss Denny with surprise. "I know you need not, Fanny, but not everyone is as rich as you, surely."

"Oh, I am sure there are women of the *ton* unfortunate enough to have to do their own dressmaking, but none of the *haut ton*," said Lady Spicer with lofty conviction. "And if there were, you may be sure they would not admit to it."

Miss Denny reflected on this for a moment or two. "That seems to me very odd," she said at last, in a disapproving voice. "If one is clever with a needle, it appears to me that one ought to be able to receive credit for it. There's nothing unladylike about sewing, after all. Why, when you were still living in Winfield, Fan, you know you made all your own dresses, and I'm sure no one thought any the worse of you for it. Indeed, I remember people always complimenting you on how nicely you sewed."

"Take my word for it that London is different," said Lady Spicer with asperity. "And I would be much obliged to you,

Judy, if you would hold your tongue on the subject of my making my own dresses in Winfield. If such a thing were to get about here in London, I should be utterly undone. Indeed, it would be better if you refrained from speaking of Winfield at all. Nothing more surely makes one look rustic than to always be talking about the place one came from, especially when it is an obscure little place like Winfield."

"Well, if I may not talk about hoopskirts, or dressmaking, or Winfield, what am I to talk about?" demanded Miss Denny, in a tone half amused and half exasperated.

"Why, anything, my child, so long as you show discretion in your choice of subjects. You may talk about the latest play, or the latest party, or the latest *on-dit,* and be sure of being right."

Instead of looking enlightened by this speech, Miss Denny merely looked puzzled. "The latest what?" she said. "What was that last thing you mentioned, Fan?"

Lady Spicer sighed deeply. *"On-dit,"* she said. "An *on-dit* is a story—an item of gossip. It comes from the French, you know. You will find it is quite the fashion to sprinkle one's conversation with French phrases."

"On-dit," repeated Miss Denny, committing the phrase to memory. "I'm afraid my French is rather rusty, Fan, but I'll do the best I can."

Lady Spicer smiled at this further example of her sister's naiveté. "A very little will suffice, my dear," she said. "I'm sure you know as much French already as most people in society. Most members of the *ton* don't really speak the language, but merely use an occasional French word or phrase to be fashionable. You'll soon pick up the phrases that are current, just as you'll soon pick up the latest gossip."

Miss Denny looked as though she thought this unlikely, but was too polite to say so. Lady Spicer did not observe her dubious expression, but went on with a cautionary air.

"Speaking of gossip, mind you don't go repeating any *on-dits* that are actually scandalous," she told Miss Denny. "It would be most inappropriate for a girl of your age and position to be telling warm stories. It's a lamentable fact, but though people will often applaud a girl for doing something daring or provocative, they invariably think less of her afterwards. Gentlemen are particularly prone to behave in this respect. And that brings me to the chief subject I wanted to discuss. I beg you will listen closely, my dear, for what I have to say is of the utmost importance.''

Miss Denny folded her hands in front of her and fixed her eyes on her sister with an obedient but somewhat wary expression. "You know, of course, that your main reason for being here in London is to make a good marriage—'' began Lady Spicer.

"Indeed it is not! My main reason for being here is to bear you company, Fanny,'' protested Miss Denny with a look of indignation. "That's what you wrote in your letter, at any rate. You said you were lonely and wanted me to come to Town this spring and stay with you for a few months. And when Mama said I might come, I am sure she said nothing about marriage.''

"Yes, but you may be sure she is hoping you will meet some eligible gentleman while you are here. Naturally I am happy to have your company for the Season, Judith. Indeed, that alone would be reason enough to have invited you. But as long as you are here, I see no reason why we cannot kill two birds with one stone. I was lucky enough to meet Sir Geoffrey at one of the Winfield assemblies, but the chances of your being equally lucky are very small. So long as you are living in Winfield, you cannot hope to do better than marry Stanley Hibbert, or one of the Smith boys, perhaps.''

This bleak prophecy did not impress Miss Denny so much as Lady Spicer had hoped. "Well, you know, Fan, Stanley Hibbert is really very nice,'' she said cheerfully. "And though I wouldn't much care to marry one of the Smith boys, only think what a pleasure it would be to have Mrs. Smith as one's mama-in-law! One would have a constant source of amusement in living with such an absurd creature.''

"I beg you will be serious, Judy,'' said Lady Spicer in exasperation. "You can do much better than marry Stanley Hibbert or one of the Smith boys. You're not a beauty, of course, and your portion is no more than adequate, but our family is a very old and respected one, and I flatter myself that we may see you achieve a good match if only you will apply yourself.''

"Apply myself?" exclaimed Miss Denny, with another burst of mirth. "How does one apply one's self to making a good match, Fanny? Am I to pick out a suitable gentleman, hunt him down, and marry him willy-nilly? The last I heard, gentlemen still had *some* voice in the matter of whom they married.''

Lady Spicer frowned upon this levity and again begged her sister to be serious. "What I mean by applying yourself is simply that you should comport yourself like a lady and make a good appearance when you are in company, Judith. Merely by being a little on your guard all the time and thinking before you speak or act, you can avoid a great many blunders. And there are a few simple rules I can give you that will assist you even more in achieving a social success. Pray pay close attention, my love, while I review them with you.''

Miss Denny composed herself to listen, but could not resist murmuring under her breath, "Just like learning one's catechism.''

"The first rule is that you should rid yourself of this habit of always laughing and making foolish jokes every time you open your mouth,'' said her sister severely. "Gentlemen have the greatest dislike of bouncing, giggling, hoydenish girls. It is necessary that you should acquire dignity, polish, and an air of quiet self-possession.''

"Dignity, polish, and self-possession,'' repeated Miss Denny, with a slightly incredulous air. "Well, I'll try, Fan, but I tell you fairly it'll be a struggle.''

Lady Spicer patted her shoulder with condescending kindness. "You will find it grows easier with practice,'' she said. "I was as green as you when I first came to London, but I flatter myself now that there are very few situations that see me at a loss. I'm sure you can become equally *au fait* if you try, for despite your levity you're an intelligent girl and don't want for sense.''

"Thank you," said Miss Denny meekly, with only a faint quaver of laughter in her voice.

"You're welcome, love. I think you'll find the results repay the effort, for to achieve a true social success your behavior must be impeccable. And that includes your behavior in women's company as well as men's." Lady Spicer lowered her voice to a confidential murmur. "In fact, I would counsel you to take greater care in the company of your own sex. Be pleasant to all women, young and old, but don't trust any of them further than you can see them."

Miss Denny regarded her sister with incredulity. "But surely that is not how *you* go on, Fanny," she said. "You must have friends whom you trust, after living in London all these years?"

Lady Spicer laughed rather bitterly. "No, I assure you! I made the trial a few times in the beginning, but found it did not pay. One's friends remain one's friends much longer if one does not try them too far."

"No wonder you said you were lonely in London," said Miss Denny, regarding her with a mixture of astonishment and compassion. "I can see now why you wanted me to come visit. You know you can always rely on me, Fanny, no matter if I am a complete rustic."

Lady Spicer was touched by this avowal, but she found the pity in her sister's voice irritating. She turned the subject aside with a little laugh. "Of course I know I can rely on you, Judy. And you can always rely on me—just don't make the mistake of relying on any other woman. Not on your maidservant, to be sure: servants' gossip has ruined the reputation of more women than I can name. And don't, I beg of you, make the mistake of becoming confidential with other girls your age whom you meet in society. They may—I hope they *will*—be friendly toward you, but the plain fact is that they are your rivals, competing with you toward the same goal. And if they think they can better their chances of success by ruining yours, you'll find they won't hesitate to do so."

Miss Denny was looking rather repelled, but all she said was, "I see."

"As for the other women you may meet—married women

like myself, and older women past the age of being married—pay them the utmost respect, but talk and behave as circumspectly as possible in their company. Some you will find quite pleasant and well-disposed, but the greater number make a pastime out of picking faults in the comportment of girls like you. The only way you can be sure of doing no wrong is to be on your guard with them all the time."

"I see," said Miss Denny again. In a hesitant voice, she added, "It all sounds rather unpleasant, Fanny. I wonder you care to go into society at all if everyone is as hateful as you say."

Lady Spicer received this with an indulgent smile. "But everyone is *not* hateful, child. Indeed, most of the members of the *ton* are exceptionally charming. They represent the very best that society has to offer, and if they have their faults—well, that is merely human nature, and no different from the society of Winfield or any other place."

Miss Denny looked unconvinced, but Lady Spicer had already continued with her lecture, not waiting for any further response from her sister. "Among the patronesses of Almack's, of course, it will behoove you to take special care," she told Miss Denny. "I cannot too strongly stress the importance of making a good impression on them. It would not be overstating the case to say that your entire future rests in their hands."

This was too much for Miss Denny. "Oh, but that is nonsense, Fanny," she protested, torn between indignation and laughter. "What can they do to me, after all? If worst comes to worst, I can always return to Winfield!"

"Yes, and marry one of the Smith boys, and spend the rest of your life fretting about the price of tea and the difficulty of keeping good servants," said Lady Spicer scathingly. "If that is the future you want, Judy, then of course there is nothing more to be said. But if you wish for something more, you must strive to make a good impression on the patronesses of Almack's."

"We shall see," was all Miss Denny said. She said it rather rebelliously, however, and Lady Spicer thought it better not to press her point further, but to continue with her instruction.

"The rules for dealing with gentlemen are a little different than for dealing with ladies," she told her sister. "When you are conversing with an eligible gentleman, the most important thing to remember is to adapt yourself to your company. Gentlemen can be divided into several rough categories, each of which requires different treatment."

"Indeed?" said Miss Denny, looking politely incredulous.

"Indeed, yes," said Lady Spicer firmly. "The first group consists of young gentlemen who, like yourself, are new to society and who may be a trifle shy and backwards in company. With these you must be extremely encouraging, even to the point of being forward. Show yourself interested in their conversation and flattered by their attentions. Never miss an opportunity of demonstrating how much you enjoy their company. Encourage them to talk of themselves. All gentlemen enjoy talking about themselves, and nothing more should be necessary to ensure your sucess with this group."

Here Lady Spicer paused, but Miss Denny had nothing to say to this proposition. Lady Spicer continued, therefore, in her best elder-sister voice.

"These same rules also apply to a large extent when you are speaking to gentlemen who are—shall we say?—a little past their prime. Older gentlemen like to fancy themselves still attractive to young ladies, and if you only flatter and flirt with them a bit, you will be sure of winning their good opinion."

Miss Denny looked so revolted by this advice that Lady Spicer hurried on, purposely ignoring her sister's expression. "This brings us to the third and most important group, the gentlemen who are neither young nor old, but who fall between the two extremes. These consist of men who have been on the town a few years—men of fashion and consequence, oftentimes, such as the members of the dandy and Corinthian sets. These are the men whom you will doubtless find most attractive, Judy, yet at the same time you will find they present the greatest challenge to any lady seeking to attract them. The most desirable men are so used to pursuit and flattery that the tactics which succeed with younger or older men merely bore them."

"It sounds a hopeless business," said Miss Denny, in a

carefully restrained voice. "If they are so hard to please, I should be inclined myself to merely ignore them."

"That's it exactly," said Lady Spicer, pleased to find her pupil so ready of comprehension. "You must seek to pique their interest with a show of disinterest. Don't seem too eager for their company, or too flattered by their attentions, especially when they happen to be one of those rare gentlemen who possess not only fortune but good looks, and perhaps a title as well. In fact, you may take it as a rule that the more eligible a gentleman is, the worse you should treat him."

"Indeed?" said Miss Denny, looking incredulous once more.

"Indeed, yes," said Lady Spicer with a vigorous nod. "I can say so from my own personal experience, for you must know that there were dozens of girls on the catch for Sir Geoffrey. They used to pursue him in the most shameless way when he attended the Winfield assemblies, but it was I who caught his interest, simply because I paid him no more heed than any of my other beaux."

"But surely there was more to it than that," protested Miss Denny, regarding her sister with pained surprise. "Perhaps your paying him no great heed served to pique Sir Geoffrey's interest at first, but he never would have asked you to marry him if he had not come to care for you sincerely, Fanny. And I am sure you must have cared for him, too, or you never would have accepted his proposal."

Lady Spicer gave a brittle laugh. "Oh, well! That is all ancient history now and has nothing to do with what we are discussing. We are merely talking now about capturing a gentleman's initial interest. Some degree of attachment to the gentleman one seeks to marry is of course natural and desirable, although I have known a great many women who have dispensed with it and seem to get on pretty well—as well, perhaps, as those of us who fancied ourselves in love with the men we married. But there will be time enough for us to concern ourselves with that later on, when you have succeeded in attaching a suitable *parti*. For now, we must concern ourselves merely with appearances and with making a good first impression. Let us see you practice your curtsy for the Queen."

Correctly taking these words to mean that the lecture was over, Miss Denny hurried to comply. The rest of the day was spent practicing her curtsy, refining her conversational skills, and trying to decide whether plain or rosetted slippers were most suitable to make her bows to Royalty.

Chapter II

As might be expected, Miss Denny thought a great deal about her sister's advice in the days that followed.

An observer might have supposed her to have little time for thinking, for Lady Spicer kept her busy morn to night with dress fittings, shopping, and practicing her social graces. But most of these activities were rather passive, or at best only intermittently absorbing. Even in the midst of such enjoyable pastimes as choosing gloves and slippers at Remmington's, or discussing with her sister whether satin coquings or bands of crepe would be a better trimming for her second-best pelisse, Miss Denny found her thoughts returning to the subject of their earlier conversation.

Her feelings on the subject were extremely mixed. On one hand, she had been deeply shocked by some of the counsel her sister had given her. Having lived all her life in the limited society of Winfield Parish, where everybody knew everybody else and where her father, a man of firm, open, and upright character, presided over the parish church as rector, she not unnaturally recoiled from hearing her sister preach a gospel so contrary to that which she was accustomed to hearing from the paternal pulpit. If Lady Spicer did not actually counsel deceit, she certainly counseled hypocrisy, along with a policy of greedy self-aggrandizement that would have been roundly condemned by the Reverend Thomas Denny.

So much Miss Denny was sure of, yet at the same time she could not bring herself to utterly discount Lady Spicer's advice. Ever since childhood she had been in the habit of looking up to her older sister as a fount of worldly wisdom. Now that they were both grown up, of course, the six years' age difference between them no longer seemed so vast, and their relationship was conducted on a more equal footing than had been the case when they were children. But even at the advanced age of nineteen, Miss Denny could not quite forget the awe she had felt toward her sister in childhood, when Fanny had seemed an impressively tall and adult figure whose authority was only slightly less imposing than her mother and father's. A respect for Fanny's authority still lingered now, making it hard for Miss Denny to disregard her counsel.

This respect was no doubt increased by the aura of wealth, splendor, and success that clung to the present-day Fanny. Upon first arriving in London, Miss Denny had been frankly dazzled by her sister's opulent lifestyle. Lady Spicer's town home was large, luxurious, and furnished in the first style of elegance. Whenever she wished to leave it, she had several new and expensive carriages to carry her, all drawn by the finest blood cattle and attended by liveried footmen not one of whom was less than six feet tall. She had a Frenchwoman to dress her and a vast and varied wardrobe of rich gowns whose number she increased almost daily. She had a male chef in the kitchen, with an assistant baker and confectioner to serve under him and any number of inferior kitchen and scullery maids. She had unlimited credit at the shops she patronized and was waited on with the utmost deference whenever she and Miss Denny dropped by to make some purchase.

Altogether, it was hard for Miss Denny to dispute with such an exalted personage as her sister had become. Fanny had clearly done well for herself, and since she did not hesitate to ascribe her success to the worldly principles she had imparted to Miss Denny, Miss Denny was inclined to think there must be something in them and that she was being foolishly scrupulous to make objections. Yet at the same time, she was becoming aware that her sister's lifestyle, for all its obvious advantages, was not without drawbacks.

It was clear, for one thing, that relations between Lady Spicer and her husband were less than ideal.

Miss Denny had come to London supposing that she would find Sir Geoffrey and her sister the same affectionate couple she had seen wed in Winfield Parish Church five years before. But in fact Sir Geoffrey and his wife now seemed to live wholly separate lives. When Lady Spicer spoke of her husband, which was seldom, there was a note of bitterness in her voice that shocked and distressed her younger sister.

What Sir Geoffrey's feelings might be in return, Miss Denny had thus far had little opportunity to discover. Sir Geoffrey had, it was true, dined at home on the day of Miss Denny's arrival and had made her welcome in an awkward but perfectly friendly fashion. "Glad to have you here, Judy," he had told her, a smile lighting his rather heavy countenance. "Fanny said you was coming down for a visit. I suppose you mean to cut a dash in society, hey?"

Miss Denny had laughed and shaken her head. "Not at all, Geoffrey. Fanny wishes me to, I find, and so I shall do my best to gratify her, but in truth my aspirations stretch no further than seeing the lions at Exeter Exchange and perhaps attending a performance or two of the theater."

"We ought to be able to see to that program all right," said Sir Geoffrey with enthusiasm. "I tell you what, Judy: if you like, I'll take you around to the 'Change tomorrow afternoon. We can see the lions, have a bite to eat at the Clarendon, and then go on to the theater afterwards."

Miss Denny was just about to accept this invitation with pleasure when her sister spoke up sharply. "Really, Geoffrey! You must know that Judy is already engaged for tomorrow afternoon. Madame Lanford is coming by to see about fitting her for her presentation dress. And as for going to the theater tomorrow evening, it's out of the question. Judy must not be seen in public until we have had time to make her more *à la mode*.''

Sir Geoffrey's face assumed a stubborn expression. "I don't see why," he said. "She looks fine to me just as she is."

"You know nothing about it," said Lady Spicer crushingly. "It would be doing her no favor to let her be seen abroad looking like a dowd, Geoffrey. Making a good first impression is crucial to achieving social success."

"Not everybody thinks social success is the be-all and end-all of life, Fanny," said Sir Geoffrey, cutting into a filet of veal with a savage air. He spoke so low that Lady Spicer did not hear him, however, or at least was able to pretend that she did not. There was no further conversation between the two for the rest of the meal, apart from such commonplaces as "Can I give you a wing, Fanny?" and "If you please, Geoffrey, I beg you will give Judith and me some of that custard."

Miss Denny was made very uncomfortable by this exchange. She hoped fervently to witness no more such mealtime quarrels during her stay in St. James's Square. In this hope she was gratified, though not for the reasons she might have wished. After that first evening, Sir Geoffrey had chosen to dine at his club, and Miss Denny scarcely saw him apart from occasional encounters on the stairs or in the breakfast parlor. When on the fourth night of her stay she innocently remarked on her brother-in-law's absence from the dinner table, Lady Spicer frowned and thinned her lips in a manner that Miss Denny knew betokened extreme irritation.

"Oh, you must know that Geoffrey has the greatest dislike of French cooking, Judy. We have one of the finest chefs in London, yet he prefers to dine on vulgar beefsteak and fried potatoes at his club rather than take dinner in his own home!"

"Well, and what is wrong with beefsteak and fried potatoes?" said Miss Denny practically. "You know we often used to eat those dishes at home, Fanny. And I am sure you used to enjoy them as much as any of us."

"That is because I knew nothing better," said Lady Spicer in a testy voice. "I will not be made the laughingstock of

London by serving beefsteak and fried potatoes at my dinner table!''

Miss Denny perceived that this subject was a sore point with her sister. ''I can see you might not want to serve such a plain dish at a formal dinner with guests,'' she said, striving for a diplomatic tone. ''But could you not order it when you and Geoffrey dine alone, Fanny?''

Lady Spicer looked at first as though she were going to return a short answer. But after a tense moment, her face relaxed into a tolerant smile. ''Oh, Judy, you always were the diplomat of the family,'' she said with a shake of her head. ''I remember that when we were children, you were always able to talk the rest of us into making up our quarrels when we fell out. But indeed, you shall not reconcile me to serving beefsteak and fried potatoes at my dinner table. Good God! I expect Pierre would give notice at once if I dared order such a common dish.''

It was on the tip of Miss Denny's tongue to say that she herself would rather run the risk of losing her chef than of alienating her husband. But she saw that no good could come of voicing such a remark. Clearly matters between Sir Geoffrey and his wife had deteriorated beyond the point where a simple concession on the subject of beefsteak could be expected to do any good.

Inwardly Miss Denny grieved over this unhappy state of affairs. Being herself of a happy, peace-loving disposition, she liked those around her to be happy and peaceful, too, and it was clear from what she had seen and heard that her sister and Sir Geoffrey were far from this ideal state. Whether this was Sir Geoffrey's fault, as her sister seemed to feel, or Fanny's own, Miss Denny was not prepared to say, but as an experienced diplomat she suspected there were faults on both sides. In all probability an outsider could do little to help, but she resolved to do her utmost to further the cause of conjugal harmony whenever an opportunity should arise.

Her first opportunity came some days later, about a week and a half after her arrival in London. Having seen Miss Denny fashionably coiffed and gowned and instructed in the rudiments of polite behavior, Lady Spicer pronounced her ready to show herself in public for the first time. The setting she judged most suitable for this first outing was Hyde Park during the hour of the fashionable promenade.

"No doubt we shall find the park still rather thin of company, but that is all to the good," she told Miss Denny as she tied on her bonnet and pulled on a pair of elegant gray kid gloves. "There will undoubtedly be some of my acquaintance there, and I can show you about and make you known to a few people before you are called on to make a formal appearance in society. I think it is always easier at balls and assemblies if one knows a few people beforehand."

Miss Denny could easily see how this was so and readily agreed to her sister's plan. Under Lady Spicer's careful scrutiny, her hair was dressed, and she was arrayed in her best new carriage dress, a bronze green merino trimmed with three narrow flounces.

The dress was worn with a matching pelisse and a charming hat ornamented with quilling and foxtail feathers. Miss Denny, surveying herself in the glass, was surprised to see how really well she looked in this garb. Lady Spicer was surprised, too. Her sister might not be a beauty, but there was a pleasing neatness to Miss Denny's slender figure and a lively charm to the small face beneath the quilled hatbrim that made her very attractive. Lady Spicer had to damp down an incipient pang of jealousy by reminding herself that her own toilette of gray plush and ruby poplin would undoubtedly cast her sister's into the shade.

As the two of them were waiting in the front hall for Lady Spicer's barouche to be brought around, Sir Geoffrey came down the stairs.

"Good afternoon, Geoffrey," said Miss Denny, smiling up at him. "You behold me on the threshold of my first foray into the fashionable world. Fanny means to take me driving in the park this afternoon. I am quite stiff with fear, for I am sure I shall say or do something wrong, and then there will be nothing for it but for me to return to Winfield in disgrace."

"Oh, not at all, not at all," protested Sir Geoffrey, looking shocked. Then he discerned the jocular tone of his sister-in-law's speech, and his shocked expression changed into a belated smile. "But there, you're joking, of course. No need to fear you'll do anything amiss while Fanny's there to tip you the wink. Besides, you look so dashed pretty that nobody'll care what you say or do anyway. Both of you look pretty," he added, looking from Miss Denny to his wife with approval. "You'll take the shine out of all the other ladies in the park, see if you don't."

"Thank you, Geoffrey," said Lady Spicer with an indulgent smile. "I fear you are partial, however. Judy certainly looks very well, but for my part, I ask nothing more than that I should play the duenna's role with a tolerably good grace."

"You a duenna? Pooh, nonsense," scoffed Sir Geoffrey. "You may have been on the town a few years, but everybody knows you're still the handsomest woman in London."

Miss Denny was pleased to see the two of them upon such friendly terms. It seemed to her a pity that they should be called on to quit each other's society just when they were getting along so nicely. On an impulse she turned again to Sir Geoffrey.

"Why don't you accompany us to the park, Geoffrey?" she asked. "I would appreciate your support during the coming ordeal, I assure you. And there is plenty of room in the barouche for three."

Sir Geoffrey looked pleased but doubtful. "Well, I don't know," he said, rubbing his chin. "I'm afraid I'd just be in the way, Judy. All the beaux will be wanting to get a look at you, y'know, and it stands to reason they won't care to have another fellow around while they're whispering pretty compliments in your ear. And the fact is that I half promised Simon Desmond I'd go with him to Tatt's this afternoon."

Miss Denny thought Sir Geoffrey looked as though he wanted to be talked out of this engagement, but Lady Spicer broke in with a trill of mirthless laughter. "Oh, be sure Geoffrey has no wish to spend time with us, Judy! He will undoubtedly be much happier with his friends at Tattersall's. Come along now, and let us be on our way. The barouche has been waiting these five minutes."

As Miss Denny followed her sister out to the barouche, she reflected unhappily on the failure of her scheme. Instead of mending matters between Sir Geoffrey and Lady Spicer, she had only made them worse. Yet if she mistook not, Sir Geoffrey had been close to accepting her invitation to drive in the park. This seemed to show that he, at least, was well-disposed to a reconciliation. It had been Lady Spicer who had thrown cold water on the whole enterprise.

Was it possible that Lady Spicer did not want to be reconciled to her husband? No, it was not possible, Miss Denny assured herself, stealing a look at her sister's discontented face. No sister of hers could be so cold-hearted as to turn her back on a husband who still obviously cared for her. And if Fanny had not reciprocated Sir Geoffrey's feelings to some extent, she would not be looking so unhappy now. It stood to reason that a person one cared nothing about would have no power over one's emotions.

"You know, Fanny, I think Geoffrey really wanted to come with us this afternoon," she ventured tentatively. "If you had not been so short with him, I feel sure he would have canceled his engagement and come."

Lady Spicer's response to this speech was not encouraging. "For my part, I care nothing what Geoffrey does with himself," she said coldly. "Why should I? He has made it clear he cares nothing for what I do."

"What makes you say so? I would have said myself that he cares for you as much as ever," said Miss Denny, hoping desperately that she was not overstating the facts.

Lady Spicer showed no disposition to believe her in any case. "If Geoffrey does care, he has an odd way of showing it," she said, picking viciously at the plush trimming of her pelisse. "He scarcely ever goes into society with me, but prefers to spend all his evenings at White's with his friends. And if we do go to a party together, he goes off to the cardroom almost as soon as we get there, and I never see him again all evening."

Miss Denny, struggling but game, was just attempting a defense of her brother-in-law's conduct when Lady Spicer hushed her with a frown. "No more now, Judy, I beg of you.

We are in the park now, and here is Sally Jersey waving me to pull over. She is one of the patronesses of Almack's, you know, so mind what I told you and be on your best behavior." With a smile magically supplanting the frown on her face, she greeted the dark-haired woman in the barouche opposite. "How do you do, Sally? I see you, too, were tempted out by this lovely spring weather. What a charming hat you are wearing, upon my word!"

Miss Denny looked with interest at Lady Jersey. She was a handsome woman in her thirties with glossy dark curls and a decided air of fashion. The hat which Lady Spicer had admired was so loaded with cherries, plums, and other orchard produce as to resemble a fruitmonger's cart in Miss Denny's eyes, but Lady Jersey received the compliment with complaisance and complimented Lady Spicer in turn upon her own headgear. As she spoke, however, her eyes flickered several times to Miss Denny. Lady Spicer, observing her curiosity, soon begged leave to perform an introduction between them.

"Sally, this is my sister, Miss Denny, who will be staying with me this Season. Judith, this is Lady Jersey. You must know that she sets the styles which the rest of us attempt to follow."

"My dear Fanny, I am silenced, upon my word! How can I respond to such praise?" said Lady Jersey with a trill of laughter. But she soon showed herself equal to the challenge. In a burst of volubility, she complimented Miss Denny on her looks; observed that she was not very like her sister; promised to send her a voucher for Almack's; hoped she was enjoying her stay in London; and finally departed without having given Miss Denny a chance to do more than nod and smile in return.

"Well, Fanny, I don't think you need fear I said anything amiss on that occasion," said Miss Denny with a gurgle of laughter, as their barouche moved out of earshot of Lady Jersey's. "If everyone talks as much as Lady Jersey, I shall have no difficulty getting along in society!"

"Yes, Sally does talk a great deal. But you must not depend on everyone else you meet being so conciliating, Judith. Here, for instance is Mrs. Drummond Burrell. She is another of the patronesses of Almack's, but very different from dear Sally Jersey. I am glad we need not depend on her for your voucher! I daresay she will give us no more than a nod, if she condescends to notice us at all.''

Mrs. Drummond Burrell, a haughty-looking dame seated in a phaeton beside another lady, did deign to nod to Lady Spicer, but Miss Denny she only favored with a cool stare. Miss Denny was just meditating on the anomaly of such treatment coming from one known to be an arbitress of polite behavior when Lady Spicer uttered a low exclamation.

"What is it, Fanny?" asked Miss Denny.

Her sister's eyes were fixed on a gentleman astride a bay hack who was approaching the carriage drive. With noticeable diffidence, she said, "I think—I believe it is Lord Henry Nathorp." In a more natural voice she added, "And that is Thomas Bradford who has just joined him—the gentleman on the chestnut mare. I must be sure to introduce Mr. Bradford to you, Judith. He is a charming gentleman and quite eligible, too. By all accounts his fortune is very considerable."

"And what about the other gentleman?" said Miss Denny. She had not been acquainted with her sister for nineteen years without learning to read her voice. There had been a certain quality in Lady Spicer's voice when she spoke Lord Henry's name that put all her sisterly instincts on the alert.

"Lord Henry? I suppose I must introduce him to you, too, if he insists on coming over. Yes, it's clear he means to, along with Mr. Bradford. How vexing, to be sure. Henry can be amusing company, but I would rather not have you make his acquaintance, Judith. His is not the kind of society that can do you any good."

Although Lady Spicer made this speech in a matter-of-fact voice, her cheeks had grown noticeably pinker during the time she was speaking. Miss Denny did not fail to observe this phenomenon. With sudden suspicion she looked again toward the gentleman on the bay hack.

He was a handsome gentleman with dark hair and a lean, hawklike face. He was smiling as he approached the barouche, but it was a cynical, thin-lipped smile that left his eyes cold and untouched. Miss Denny disliked him on sight. She watched with hostility as he took her sister's hand in his and bowed over it.

"At last I find you, Fanny. Rumor has whispered that you have been in Town these three weeks, yet not one glimpse has been vouchsafed me, your most ardent worshiper. I think you might have permitted me a private audience, seeing that you have denied the *ton* a public one."

"Don't be nonsensical, Henry," said Lady Spicer, achieving a very creditable laugh. "I have no doubt you found objects of worship a-plenty while I was otherwise occupied."

"None that could compare to you. You eclipse all lesser beauties as the sun does a candle's feeble light."

"You are a consummate flatterer, Henry," said Lady Spicer, with the suggestion of another blush. Withdrawing her hand hurriedly, she directed Lord Henry's attention toward Miss Denny on the opposite banquette. "Let me make you known to my sister, Henry. And you, too, Tom," she added, smiling at the other gentleman, who had just joined Lord Henry beside the barouche. "Judith, this is Lord Henry Nathorp, and this is Mr. Thomas Bradford. Henry, Tom, this is my sister Miss Denny, who is staying with me for the Season."

Both gentlemen professed themselves delighted to make Miss Denny's acquaintance. Miss Denny was inclined to doubt Lord Henry's professions on this score, for he spoke in a bored tone that seemed to indicate he was merely performing a polite duty. But Mr. Bradford, a long-limbed gentleman with a pleasantly homely face, engaged her in conversation for several minutes and seemed genuinely interested in learning her opinion of Hyde Park and the other sights she had seen since arriving in London.

Miss Denny had no trouble holding her own in this conversation. By nature untroubled by shyness or reserve, she responded readily to Mr. Bradford's inquiries, only taking care not to betray too great a pleasure in his apparent interest. Although there was nothing very formidable about Mr. Bradford's intellect or person, he seemed to qualify as an eligible *parti* in Lady Spicer's eyes. Lacking any other guide, Miss Denny had decided to accept her sister's advice with certain reservations, and she was mindful now of the treatment to be accorded eligible gentlemen. When Mr. Bradford took leave of her and Lady Spicer a few minutes later, therefore, she merely returned a polite smile to his assurance that he had enjoyed talking to her very much and hoped they would soon meet again.

She herself would have enjoyed the talk more if she had not been so concerned with what was passing between Lord Henry and her sister. Although she strained her ears to hear their conversation, for the most part it was pitched too low for her to make out what they were saying. On one occasion, however, she distinctly heard Lady Spicer say, "Not here—not now, Henry," and throw an nervous look in her direction.

Lord Henry soon after excused himself and rode off to speak to another acquaintance. His place was immediately filled by another gentleman, who was succeeded in turn by a party of ladies in an old-fashioned landaulette who stopped their vehicle alongside the barouche to engage Lady Spicer in conversation for a few minutes. So it continued the whole time they remained in the park. Lady Spicer's acquaintance was evidently vast, and by the time they left Hyde Park Miss Denny's head was spinning with the effort to remember the names of all the people she had met that afternoon.

"Mr. Lowell. Mr. Savage. Lady McKearney and the Misses McKearney," said Lady Spicer, kindly lending her assistance to this endeavor. "Sir Stephen Willis was the blond gentleman in the tilbury, and Mr. Ramsey the dark one driving a curricle. And of course Mr. Bradford was the first gentleman you talked to right after we arrived in the Park."

"Along with Lord Henry Nathorp," said Miss Denny, with a direct look at her sister.

There was a faint tinge of color in Lady Spicer's cheeks, but she returned the look composedly enough. "Yes, Lord Henry," she said. "A charming flirt, but a sad gamester and not altogether a respectable character, I fear. I would advise you to avoid his society, Judith, insofar as you are able."

"It seems to me I might say the same to you, Fanny," said Miss Denny bluntly.

The soft color in Lady Spicer's cheeks grew deeper. "Don't be ridiculous, Judy," she said. "Our situations are not at all the same. As an unmarried girl, you are obliged to be very discreet in all your behavior and especially where gentlemen are concerned. A married woman like me has more license. Indeed, it is quite the thing for a lady of fashion to have her flirts. And since Lord Henry is notoriously hard to attach, it adds greatly to my consequence to be seen with him."

"But doesn't Sir Geoffrey mind?" said Miss Denny. "It seems to me that if Lord Henry has as bad a character as you say, then your husband might not like your flirting with him."

If Lady Spicer did not actually toss her head, she still managed to convey the sentiments which such a gesture would have contained. "I do not know what are Geoffrey's feelings on the subject. I doubt he grudges me Lord Henry's company, however. If he does, he has never shown any signs of wishing to take Henry's place." She then seemed to regret having spoken so warmly, for her next speech was made with an air of forced gaiety. "And perhaps that is just as well, for you know, Judith, it is not at all the fashion for a married couple to live in each other's pockets. As I said before, it is quite the thing for married women to have their flirts—and married men, too. Why, I daresay Geoffrey has his own flirts, if we only knew it." And having made this statement, she changed the subject and began to talk brightly and perseveringly about the beautiful display of daffodils in the park.

Miss Denny made no attempt to divert her, but inwardly she began to feel a good deal of uneasiness on her brother-in-law's account. It even crossed her mind fleetingly that Lady Spicer, duenna though she claimed to be, might stand in need of a duenna herself.

Chapter III

Having made her first public appearance and enjoyed a modest success, Miss Denny now began to prepare for the second and far more important appearance that would formally introduce her to society.

This was not the Queen's Drawing Room, although that event certainly marked her first formal appearance among the members of the *haut ton*. But as Lady Spicer explained, the Drawing Room itself was little more than a ceremonious form, useful of course as a credential to one's social standing, but doing little in terms of introducing one to the people who really mattered. It would be at the ball Lady Spicer was holding in the evening of that same day that Miss Denny would come under the full fire of public scrutiny, and where her behavior would determine whether she were to be a wild success, an abysmal failure, or—more likely—something in between.

Ceremonious form or not, however, the Queen's Drawing Room had to be gotten through first. Miss Denny did get through it, and with an unexpected degree of success.

"I was all in a quake for fear I should disgrace myself by laughing out loud. For really we looked quite ridiculous,

Fanny—a whole room full of us, loaded down with plumes and hoops and jewels in the middle of the afternoon.''

"It is quite customary, I assure you," said Lady Spicer. The two sisters were in the midst of changing their court dresses for balldresses, and Lady Spicer was giving a few touches to her sister's toilette before attending to her own. "One always wears full dress for court functions," she continued, as she smoothed the floss trimming on Miss Denny's corsage. "And one also wears one's best jewels—or even hires better ones for the occasion."

"I am sure it is *customary.* It just seems rather odd, that's all. But I forgot all about it when it was my turn to curtsy to the Queen. For you know, there she was, sitting with all her ladies—and it just struck me all at once how tiresome it must be for her, to have to pretend as though she were interested in a troop of perfectly strange young ladies when really she was probably wishing us all at Jericho so she could go about her business. So I just smiled at her as I curtsied—and she smiled back, and said I had a sweet face, and asked where I was from. It was quite odd to be having a conversation with the Queen, just as though she were anyone else!''

"You may well say so," agreed Lady Spicer in a reverent voice. "I never expected the Queen would speak to you, Judy. It was a great honor for her to single you out as she did."

"I suppose so. But I'm glad it's over now, and I need never wear that foolish gown and hoopskirt again. I like this dress much better." Miss Denny looked down at her costume with calm satisfaction.

She was wearing a robe of rose-colored sarcenet, open over a white satin petticoat. The dress had short puffed sleeves, a modest square neckline, and a trimming of floss silk. Miss Denny's soft golden-brown hair had been dressed in curls around her face, with a circlet of roses adorning the knot atop her head. Long white gloves, flat slippers of white satin, and a short necklet of pearls completed the outfit.

Lady Spicer, surveying Miss Denny, told herself complacently that her sister's appearance was just what it ought to be. She might not be a beauty like herself, but she really looked remarkably well. And when she was smiling, as at the present moment, there was something so altogether taking about her that it was no wonder Royalty had been moved to smile back. Lady Spicer, comfortable in the assurance of her own superior beauty, was able to take vicarious triumph in her sister's success and look forward to a similar success this evening.

Miss Denny, for her part, was also looking forward to the evening ahead. At the same time, however, she felt a trifle nervous about appearing as focus of attention at such a large gathering (for there had been no less than four hundred cards of invitation sent out, fully three hundred of which had been accepted). Then, too, most of the people she would meet that evening would be strangers to her and disposed to be rather critical if Lady Spicer were to be believed. Altogether it was an alarming prospect. Miss Denny was pleased as much for her own sake as for her sister's when, upon entering the ball-room, she beheld Sir Geoffrey's tall, heavy-set figure standing near the orchestra gallery.

"I am so glad you are going to be here, Geoffrey," she said warmly, giving him her hand. "I feel quite daunted at the prospect of meeting so many strangers this evening. But with you and Fanny to support me, I trust I shall rub through well enough."

"To be sure you will," said Sir Geoffrey heartily, taking her hand and bowing over it. "You'll find your feet in no time, see if I'm not right. By Jove, don't you look pretty! A regular beauty, 'pon my word."

"Thank you, Geoffrey. But you know I can never be counted a beauty while Fanny is standing by. She always was the handsomest in our family, and I never saw her in such looks as she is tonight."

Miss Denny made this speech, hoping to deflect Sir Geoffrey's admiration to her sister, who was indeed looking magnificent in a toilette of white lace over satin. Sir Geoffrey threw his wife a look, hesitated, then muttered something under his breath in which the words "fine as fivepence" alone were audible. It was not what Miss Denny had hoped for, but it served well enough, for Lady Spicer smiled graciously.

"You look very fine yourself, Geoffrey," she told him. "I'm sure you will do us great credit tonight." To Miss Denny, she added, "Don't be nervous, Judy. Geoffrey and I shall keep an eye on you to see you don't go wrong. And if you only remember everything I have told you, I have no doubt you will do very well."

The guests began arriving soon after this. For the first hour, Miss Denny remained at her sister's side, being introduced to countless people and receiving their compliments and congratulations. This was not a difficult business, she found, for she had little to do beyond smiling, curtsying, and saying, "Thank you," and "I am pleased to make your acquaintance." But the repetition soon grew boring, and she was glad when the orchestra began to tune their instruments in preparation for the start of the dancing.

Miss Denny's first partner was introduced to her by Lady Spicer. "Judith, allow me to present to you Mr. Manville," she said, indicating a gangling young man with a shock of fiery red hair who blushed violently and executed a clumsy bow. "He is eager to solicit your hand for the first dance." In a whispered aside, she added, "You must know that the Manvilles are related to the O'Henrys—this young man is actually Lord O'Henry's heir. An Irish title, of course, but there's money behind it, and the Manvilles are very good *ton*."

Miss Denny, rather discomposed by this disingenuous introduction, merely smiled and curtsied. Mr. Manville, blushing more violently than ever, bowed again. "Like very much to dance with you, ma'am, 'pon my word," he managed to stammer out with some difficulty. "Beg you'll do me the honor of standing up with me."

"I should be very happy to," responded Miss Denny, her heart going out to him in his difficulties. She could have no doubt that Mr. Manville fell in the first of the three categories of gentlemen her sister had spoken of and was new to London and London society. His manner plainly betrayed his youth and inexperience. As they went out to take their places on the floor, she smiled at him kindly. "My sister tells me your family is allied to the O'Henry family in Ireland," she said. "Are you from Ireland yourself?"

"N-n-no," enunciated Mr. Manville with difficulty. Making a further effort, he added, "Been there a few times to visit, though. Pretty country, Ireland."

"Yes, I have heard it is very beautiful. They raise a great many horses there, don't they? I remember my father saying once that the best horses come from Ireland."

Mr. Manville brightened. "Yes, Ireland's a great place for horses," he said, gasping a bit at the effort of speech but sounding more comfortable than before. "My uncle's got the most famous stables. You never saw such nags in your life, 'pon my word. D'you like horses, Miss Denny?"

"Very much," said Miss Denny, with perfect truth. "I have a horse of my own at home—actually a pony, I'm afraid, and getting rather long in the tooth, but I love him dearly."

Mr. Manville responded sympathetically, and with only an occasional stammer retailed the story of a roan mare whom, he said, he had felt just the same about. "I like horses," he added, stating a self-evident fact. "I'd a deal rather spend my time in the stables than doing the pretty at parties like this. Meaning no disrespect to you, ma'am, of course," he added, turning bright red once more as he realized his words might be construed as an insult by his companion. "Mean to say, I've enjoyed talking to you very much, but I'm no good at these affairs. I can't talk, I can't dance, and I never can remember anyone's name."

Miss Denny instantly contradicted the first and second of these statements, although with the third she had nothing but sympathy. "It *is* very difficult remembering people's names, isn't it?" she said with a sigh. "I'm sure I don't remember a tenth of the people I've been introduced to this evening. I suppose it will grow easier with time, but for now it makes things very uncomfortable."

"Yes, doesn't it?" said Mr. Manville with fervor. In an unexpected burst of gallantry, he added, "But I'm certain I shan't forget *your* name, Miss Denny. Mean to say, you're the nicest person I've met since coming to London."

Miss Denny, both touched and amused, thanked him gravely
for the compliment. Mr. Manville turned bright red once again,
but was so much emboldened at having successfully complimented a young lady that he invited Miss Denny to go out
driving with him the following afternoon. "If you've nothing
better to do, that is," he added, with a return to his former
bashful manner.

"I would like very much to go out driving with you," Miss
Denny assured him. "I don't believe my sister has any plans
for me tomorrow afternoon. But if she does, we will simply
arrange to go out another day instead."

Mr. Manville stammered out his thanks, and as soon as the
dance was over he escorted Miss Denny back to her sister.
Lady Spicer was deep in conversation with a stout dame wearing
an aigrette and an impressive set of emeralds. This lady she
introduced to Miss Denny as Mrs. Rupert Manville, Mr. Manville's mother. Miss Denny acknowledged the introduction
politely, then asked her sister if she were free to go out driving
with Mr. Manville the following afternoon.

"Yes, quite free, my love," said Lady Spicer, smiling. "I
am sure you will have a delightful outing. Mrs. Manville has
just been telling me what a notable whip her son is."

Mr. Manville, blushing, disclaimed this statement. As he and
Miss Denny were settling the time and place they would meet,
Miss Denny overheard Mrs. Manville murmur to Lady Spicer,
"A charming girl, to be sure. My Rupert seems quite taken
with her. What is her portion, do you know?"

Lady Spicer's reply to this question was pitched in a voice
too low for Miss Denny to hear. Mrs. Manville's response,
however, was unfortunately audible. "Oh, well, so long as she
has her ten thousand pounds. Ten thousand is not a fortune,
of course, but quite a respectable portion—quite respectable,
indeed. Rupert might do much worse for himself."

Miss Denny was much shocked by this conversation. As
soon as Mrs. Manville and her son had made their *adieux* and
moved off, she took her sister to task. "Fanny, you know I
have not a portion of ten thousand pounds! Eight thousand was
what Papa gave when you married Sir Geoffrey, and I am sure

he cannot afford to do more for me. Indeed, he may not be able to do as much with James's election bills to settle and Cecil to go up to Eton next year. You ought not to have lied to Mrs. Manville about it.''

"Don't be a goose, Judy," said Lady Spicer, her color a little heightened. "It was not a lie, only a tiny exaggeration. You must know that everyone exaggerates when talking about girls' portions, just as they do about gentlemen's fortunes. And I am sure eight thousand is almost the same as ten thousand. If it meant the difference between your marrying Mr. Manville and not marrying him, I doubt not that Sir Geoffrey would be willing to make up the difference.''

As so often when she was talking with her sister, Miss Denny was torn between anger and amusement. "Since I have only danced with Mr. Manville once, Fanny, I think it is a little premature to be talking about my marrying him," she said hotly. "And I would not dream of asking Sir Geoffrey to pay a penny of my marriage portion. Whatever Papa can give me when I marry is what I will have, and if a gentleman were willing to let a few thousand pounds make a difference in the way he felt about me, I would not want to marry him in the first place.''

"You know nothing about the matter," began Lady Spicer in a vexed tone. Then, abruptly, her tone changed, and she gave Miss Denny a bright artificial smile. "But let us not argue about it any more at present, Judy. Here comes Mr. Blessington, a gentleman I most particularly wanted to introduce to you. Good evening, Mr. Blessington," she said, hailing the stout, elderly gentleman who had just come up to join them. "I am delighted to see you here this evening. You have not yet made the acquaintance of my sister, have you? Judith, this is Mr. Blessington; Mr. Blessington, this is my sister Miss Denny.''

"Pleased to meet you, Miss Denny," said Mr. Blessington, baring a set of patently false teeth in a hideous grin. Miss Denny judged him to be some years older than her father and was thus rather surprised when he followed up his greeting with an invitation to dance. "I'd be very much honored if you'd stand up with me, 'pon my word, Miss Denny.''

Miss Denny looked to her sister for guidance. Lady Spicer laughed and gave her a little push in Mr. Blessington's direction. "To be sure, child. Go on and dance with Mr. Blessington. You need not wait on me."

"I thank you, sir. I should be very happy to dance with you," said Miss Denny politely. Inwardly, however, she was concerned at the idea of making so elderly a man undertake such a vigorous exercise as dancing. As they took their places on the floor, she could not refrain from asking, "This will not tire you too much, I trust, sir?"

"Tire me?" said Mr. Blessington, drawing his brows together. "Why should it tire me?"

Miss Denny saw that it had been the wrong thing to say. Mr. Blessington obviously considered himself still in the prime of life, a thing she might have guessed from his sprightly manner and determinedly youthful attire. Belatedly she recalled Lady Spicer's advice on the treatment of elderly gentlemen. The idea of flirting with Mr. Blessington was decidedly repellent, but there was no reason why she could not treat him with the same friendliness she had accorded to Mr. Manville.

So she smiled and said, "I am judging by myself, I suppose. You must know that I am just up from the country, and such late hours as you keep in London are new to me. I am beginning to adjust now, I hope, but still I shall probably have to have a cup of strong coffee later in the evening if I do not wish to fall asleep on my feet."

Mr. Blessington smiled, obviously mollified by this speech. "Ah, you'll soon be trotting as hard as the rest of us," he said, giving her hand a little squeeze. "Why, I was up till dawn t'other day, playing hazard at Watier's. Put away the best part of three bottles of malmsey while I was doing it, too, but you see I'm not a penny the worse for it. I dare swear I've as hard a head and as sound a constitution as any man here tonight," he finished boastfully.

"How fortunate for you," said Miss Denny politely.

Mr. Blessington said gallantly that he counted himself the fortunate one, to be dancing with such a pretty young lady. He reinforced these words with another squeeze of Miss Denny's hand. Miss Denny disliked this, but since his manner was more avuncular than anything else, she was able to bear with it pretty well and to listen with the appearance of interest while Mr. Blessington regaled her with further tales of his prowess at the gaming table. She was quite relieved when the dance was over, however, and she was once more restored to her sister.

"What did you think of him?" Lady Spicer asked, when Mr. Blessington had bowed himself off.

Miss Denny wrinkled her nose expressively. "I thought him an extremely silly old man. I am afraid he gambles a great deal and drinks far more than is good for him."

"Ah, but that is only because he is a widower," said Lady Spicer. "If he were to marry again, I am sure his wife might soon put a stop to his excesses."

There was a note of significance in Lady Spicer's voice as she spoke these words. Miss Denny stared at her. "Fanny, you cannot mean you think *I* might marry him!" she exclaimed. "An old man like that?"

"Not if you dislike it, love, to be sure," said Lady Spicer, coloring slightly. In a self-justifying tone, she added, "Mr. Blessington is tremendously rich, however, and very well-connected. I'm sure his wife would find herself very comfortably circumstanced. And then, too, he's a widower, and widowers are always easy marks, I have observed. I have no doubt that the first girl who sets her cap at him will win him."

Miss Denny had a great many things to say in reply to this speech, but she got no chance to utter any of them. Lady Spicer's attention at that moment was captured by an arrogant-looking dame in a helmet headdress who had just entered the ballroom. Beside her was a handsome dark-haired young lady whose features clearly proclaimed her the daughter of the other. Lady Spicer greeted the two of them with effusive smiles.

"My dear Lucretia! How delightful to see you. And Lady Emily, too! I am delighted that the two of you decided to attend tonight. Let me make you known to my sister, if you please." Turning to Miss Denny, she said impressively, "Judith, I would like to present you to Lucretia, Marchioness of St. Stephen, and to her daughter, Lady Emily DeVere. Lucretia, Lady Emily, this is my sister Miss Denny.''

"I am pleased to make your acquaintance,'' said Miss Denny, curtsying to them both.

The Marchioness, having surveyed Miss Denny through her quizzing glass, accorded her a slight nod, then turned again to Lady Spicer. Lady Emily's response was a still slighter nod, after which she stood gazing off into space while her mother conversed with Lady Spicer.

Miss Denny was rather daunted by this behavior, but since she was left *tête-à-tête* with Lady Emily, she felt compelled to try to make conversation with her. "I believe we have met before, ma'am,'' she said with a friendly smile. "Were you not at the Queen's Drawing Room this afternoon?''

Lady Emily withdrew her gaze from the chandelier she had been studying and gave Miss Denny a brief, cold glance. "Yes, I daresay,'' she said indifferently, and returned her gaze to the chandelier.

Miss Denny was nettled. As she was revolving in her mind various responses she might make to this snub, the Marchioness suddenly turned from Lady Spicer to address her daughter in an eager whisper. "My dear, I see Ashland is just arrived! We must not be backward in paying our respects.'' And having cut Lady Spicer off in mid-sentence and bestowed no more than a nod on her by way of farewell, she and her daughter set off across the room with a haste in marked contrast to their stately entry.

Lady Spicer took this behavior quite in stride. "The DeVeres are very aristocratic, you know—the very top of the trees,'' she told Miss Denny. "I'm sure I did not look for them to attend at all tonight. Lady Emily is very handsome, isn't she?''

"Yes, and very ill-mannered,'' said Miss Denny. This earned her a half-hearted rebuke from her sister. But Lady Spicer's attention was soon diverted by an effeminate gentleman with a gushing manner who came hurrying up to her, eager to discuss with her the scandalous behavior of a mutual acquaintance. Miss Denny, having been introduced to this gentleman, was left temporarily to her own devices while he and her sister engaged in a lengthy, low-toned gossip about persons and events unknown to her.

She amused herself by looking around the room to see what had caused the Marchioness and Lady Emily to go hurrying off so abruptly. At last she spied them, fluttering in great excitement about the ballroom doors. The cause of their excitement appeared to be a tall fair-haired gentleman who had just entered the ballroom and who was standing in the doorway, looking about him with an air of negligent interest.

Chapter IV

Miss Denny eyed the gentleman curiously. He was impressively tall with a lean figure accentuated by the severe tailoring of his black evening clothes. His hair was a very pale blond, closer to silver than gold in hue and worn longer than was the mode. His face was decidedly handsome, with a firm chin, aquiline nose, and humorous mouth. This last was very pronounced as he stood in the doorway, quietly surveying the crowd around him with a faint smile on his lips.

At that moment he was assailed by the Marchioness and her daughter. They attacked him, one on each side, uttering cries of delight and smiling in a way that startled Miss Denny, who would not have supposed two such haughty ladies could abase themselves to such a degree. She watched curiously as the one-sided interview continued. It was clear from the ladies' manner now that they were beseeching some favor from the fair-haired gentleman. He listened with the appearance of polite interest, but when they were done he merely shook his head, made a brief, smiling reply, and strolled away. The Marchioness and Lady Emily were left to gaze after him with a crestfallen look on their faces.

Miss Denny could hardly keep from laughing out loud. She

recollected herself in time, however, and turned away hastily. She had no wish to be caught gaping like a rustic at the fair-haired gentleman. Indeed, she reflected guiltily that she should not have been staring at him at all, though she was not sorry she had witnessed his encounter with the Marchioness and Lady Emily. It had been very satisfying to see those two arrogant dames snubbed just as they had snubbed her a few minutes before. She wished she could thank the gentleman for revenging her, but that was out of the question, of course. So she merely turned away and tried to interest herself in the conversation that was still going on between Lady Spicer and her scandal-loving acquaintance.

Miss Denny was yet destined to cross paths with the fair-haired gentleman, however. His progress across the room took him close by where she and her sister were standing. The press of people in the room was very great at that point, and as he stood courteously aside to let an elderly lady pass through the crowd, his sleeve brushed slightly against Miss Denny. As luck would have it, one of the fringes of her shawl became entangled in his sleeve buttons. Miss Denny, feeling the tug, turned around and found herself face to face with her avenging angel.

Her first impression was that he was even better looking than she had initially thought him. His eyes were very clear and blue, and there was a hint of rueful amusement in them as he looked down at his entangled sleeve.

"How clumsy of me," he said, in a voice that was low, pleasant, and unmistakably well-bred. "I do beg your pardon, ma'am. If you will have a moment's patience, however, I believe I can extricate myself without injuring your fringe. Ah, there we are." He gave Miss Denny a friendly smile. "I do trust no damage was done?"

Miss Denny's first impulse was to return his smile and disclaim any injury to her shawl. She was in charity with him anyway for having snubbed the Marchioness and her daughter, and her charity was increased by the courtesy of his manners on the present occasion. But just in time she remembered her sister's cautions about dealing with eligible gentlemen.

This was clearly a supremely eligible gentleman, to judge by the Marchioness and Lady Emily's behavior. It was necessary therefore that she treat him very harshly if she wished to have further dealings with him. And Miss Denny found she did wish to have further dealings with this gentleman—more than any other gentleman she had seen that evening. So instead of smiling, she merely gave him a cool stare, nodded, and turned away, twitching her shawl over her shoulders with an offended air.

The Duke was left staring at a slim back encased in a rose sarcenet gown, a cluster of golden-brown curls, and the edge of a rosy cheek that seemed a shade more rosy than before. He stood gazing fixedly at these sights until recalled to a sense of his surroundings by an indignant voice at his elbow.

"Here, Ashland, what d'ye mean by giving me the cut indirect? I've been trying to get your attention this half hour. Have you suddenly gone deaf and blind, that you can't recognize your friends?"

"Not at all," said the Duke. He withdrew his gaze from Miss Denny's back, to regard the speaker of these words, Mr. Charles Ormand, a slim dark gentleman with a pair of lively gray eyes and a foppish air. "I am not in the least blind or deaf, Charles. And it is quite impossible that you should have been trying to get my attention for half an hour. I only entered the room a few minutes ago." Having made this statement, the Duke promptly returned his gaze to Miss Denny's back.

"Well, I'm sure it seemed like half an hour," asserted Mr. Ormand. He observed the direction of the Duke's gaze and followed it curiously. "What're you staring at, Ashland? You look the most perfect mooncalf, standing there gawking as if you'd lost your wits."

With an effort, the Duke once more withdrew his gaze from Miss Denny. "No, my wits, such as they are, are still with me. At the moment, however, they are exercised by a considerable puzzle. I cannot think what I have done to make an enemy of that young lady over there."

Mr. Ormand regarded Miss Denny with interest. "Who, her?

What makes you think she's your enemy? Looks a nice enough sort of girl to me.''

"So too does she to me," said the Duke. "But the fact is that not two minutes ago, she dealt me the most crushing setdown.''

Mr. Ormand let out a crow of laughter. "No, did she? Demme if I don't go and shake her hand for it! High time somebody did snub you a bit, Ashland. It'd do you good to take a few knocks like the rest of us.''

"Perhaps, but I don't feel I deserved this particular knock," complained the Duke, regarding Miss Denny with perplexity. "It was not a mere brush-off, Charles, but an undoubted snub. And I cannot think what I did to deserve it. I am quite sure I have never said or done anything personally to offend the young lady—in fact, I'm fairly certain I've never set eyes on her before. Do you know who she is?''

Mr. Ormand surveyed Miss Denny with a wrinkled brow. "Let me see. I'm pretty sure I've seen her somewhere or other before. Aye, I've got it! No wonder she looked familiar. She's Fanny Spicer's sister, the gal Fanny's giving this party for tonight. I remember Fanny introducing me to her earlier this evening. Pretty little thing, just up from the country—Miss Denny, that's her name.''

"Miss Denny," repeated the Duke, contemplating Miss Denny's back with a frown. "And you say she is Fanny Spicer's sister? That still doesn't explain why she should snub me. I have always stood on decent terms with Fanny Spicer, though I don't consider her one of my particular friends.''

Mr. Ormand shook his head. "Perhaps Miss Denny's a revolutionary and disapproves of dukes on principle," he opined with a mischievous grin. "Or maybe she saw how you snubbed Emily DeVere and her mother when you came in and was revenging her sex for the insult. Or maybe she mistook you for somebody else. That'd be a blow to you, wouldn't it? His Grace, the noble Duke of Ashland, mistaken for somebody else! Why don't you go over and ask her?''

Although this suggestion was put forward in jest, the Duke took it quite seriously. "Do you know, Charles, I believe I'll do just that,'' he said. "Come over and perform the introductions for me, won't you?''

Much to the Duke's vexation, however, he found that this plan could not be put into immediate execution. While he and Mr. Ormand had been talking, the third dance had begun, and Miss Denny had been hailed by her old acquaintance, Mr. Manville, who was eager to engage her company for another dance.

"Indeed, I'd consider it a great favor if you'd stand up with me again, Miss Denny. You see I remember your name,'' he added with a shy grin. "You were good enough to say you didn't mind my dancing before, so I thought I'd see if you'd be willing to have another go at it.''

"Certainly,'' said Miss Denny with unfeigned pleasure. Her pleasure had little to do with the prospect of dancing again with Mr. Manville, however. She would have been glad of any excuse that put distance between her and the Duke. Ever since she had turned her back on him so brusquely, she had been careful not to look again in his direction, but she was uneasily conscious that he was still there, looking at her and perhaps wondering at her rudeness. Although she had merely been following her sister's instructions, her conscience told her that she had treated the fair-haired gentleman unjustly, and the idea made her very uncomfortable. It was with a sensation of relief that she took Mr. Manville's arm and accompanied him onto the floor.

The Duke was not pleased to see his quarry whisked off beneath his nose. "Who's the red-haired hobbledehoy?'' he demanded, looking after Miss Denny and her partner in some dudgeon.

Mr. Ormand consulted his capacious memory once again. "Believe it must be young Manville,'' he volunteered. "O'Henry's heir, you know. I heard he was in Town, but haven't been introduced to him yet.'' With a sly smile, he added, "Miss Denny seems to like Irish peers better than English ones, don't she, Ashland? Mean to say, she and Manville look to be getting on like a house afire.''

"Indeed,'' said the Duke, surveying Mr. Manville with displeasure. "I must say I wonder at Miss Denny's taste—but *chaçun son goût,* as the French say. Let us go get a glass of punch and wait for the dance to be over."

It seemed to the Duke a most interminable dance. He and Mr. Ormand stood near the edge of the dance floor, conversing in a desultory way and watching the couples taking part in the set. They were occasionally interrupted by a greeting from some male acquaintance and more often by the coy advances of some female one intent on engaging the Duke's attention. Several ladies made determined efforts to get him to dance, but the Duke fielded these quietly and expertly, remaining smilingly deaf to hints and innuendoes and politely excusing himself on the score of fatigue when the hints turned to open importunings. When one particularly persistent lady had finally been sent to the rightabout, Mr. Ormand shook his head.

"Don't see how you stand it, old man," he told the Duke. "Must be hellish to have to put up with that sort of thing every time you step out in public. If it were me, now, I'd have broken down and married one of 'em years ago, just to be rid of the rest. Mean to say, even if she turned out to be a complete harpy, it'd still be a deal more peaceful than being hunted day in and day out by every matchmaking mama in Town."

The Duke smiled slightly but made no reply to this speech. "I think the dance is almost over, Charles," he said instead. "Prepare yourself to introduce me to Miss Denny, if you please."

Miss Denny, meanwhile, had been doing her best to subdue the pricklings of her conscience by chattering with great animation to Mr. Manville. Being possessed of a sunny and sanguine temperament, she was reasonably successful in this endeavor, and by the dance's end she had almost convinced herself that her behavior had not been so bad as she had originally thought it.

She still could not help thinking she had been wrong to snub the fair-haired gentleman's friendly apology, but he had probably thought little of the incident one way or another. It was highly unlikely that she would have had further dealings with him in any case. And so, having rationalized the situation in this comfortable manner, Miss Denny was dismayed to perceive the Duke standing near the edge of the dance floor, regarding her with a steady, unsmiling gaze.

"Oh, dear," said Miss Denny, in a voice of foreboding.

"Something wrong, Miss D?" asked Mr. Manville, regarding her solicitously.

Miss Denny shook her head mutely. She told herself that it was mere accident that she and the fair-haired gentleman should meet again so soon, but this explanation did not satisfy her. There was something ominous in the gentleman's demeanor as he stood at the edge of the dance floor, surveying her with that somber, unblinking gaze. It was almost as though he were waiting to confront her as she came off the floor. It was not he who confronted her first, however, but rather a thin, dark, dandified-looking gentleman whom she vaguely remembered having been introduced to her earlier.

"Your servant, Miss Denny," said the gentleman, sweeping her a graceful bow. "Daresay you don't remember me, but your sister introduced us earlier. Charles Ormand, at your service."

"To be sure, Mr. Ormand. I remember you very well," said Miss Denny in a faint voice. Her eyes were fixed on the fair-haired gentleman who stood behind Mr. Ormand, still surveying her with that disquietingly steady gaze.

"There's a friend of mine I'd like to introduce to you," said Mr. Ormand, turning to the gentleman behind him. "He's very eager to make your acquaintance, ma'am, I do assure you. This is his Grace, the Duke of Ashland—also Earl of Barrington and Longworth, and Viscount Montfort, and a whole slew of other titles I can't be bothered to remember. Ashland, this is Miss Denny."

"I am very pleased to meet you, Miss Denny," said the Duke, bowing with ironic civility.

Miss Denny said nothing but dropped a deep curtsy. The Duke, looking down at her critically, saw that she had brown eyes, a thin little face, and a rather undeveloped figure: a pretty enough girl, as Mr. Ormand had said, but nothing out of the ordinary. There was, however, an extraordinary expression on her face as she looked up at him now. The Duke wondered what she was thinking. There was no way to find out with Mr. Ormand and Mr. Manville standing around; it would be necessary to get her by herself before he could question her on the subject. "Would you care to dance this next dance with me, Miss Denny?" he said, bowing a second time.

Miss Denny shook her head, still surveying him with that peculiar expression. The Duke was incredulous. This mousy-looking girl was snubbing him a second time! "I beg your pardon, ma'am," he said in a voice sharp with chagrin. "If you are already engaged, then of course I will not importune you."

Something suspiciously like a smile flitted across Miss Denny's face. When she spoke, however, her voice was very serious. "It's not because I'm engaged that I cannot dance this next dance with you, your Grace," she said, looking up at him earnestly. "It's because this next dance is a waltz."

"A waltz?" said the Duke, at a loss to understand her meaning.

"She can't waltz because she ain't been given the nod by the patronesses of Almack's," explained the knowledgeable Mr. Ormand. "Remember my sisters complaining about the same thing when they first came out."

"Oh," said the Duke, digesting this. Mustering a smile, he looked down at Miss Denny once again. "Well then, Miss Denny: if you cannot waltz with me, perhaps you will allow me to take you to the refreshment room and get you a glass of punch? I'm sure you could use it after your exertions on the floor."

"Your Grace is very kind," said Miss Denny in a voice devoid of expression. Turning to Mr. Manville beside her, she said in a very much warmer tone, "Thank you for the dance, Mr. Manville. I enjoyed it very much, I assure you. And I shall look forward to seeing you again tomorrow when we go out driving."

Mr. Manville, who had been staring open-mouthed at the Duke, recovered himself enough to bow and stammer his thanks. He then took himself off with great alacrity. Mr. Ormand, having accomplished his task, likewise took himself off; and the Duke took Miss Denny's arm and began to lead her toward the refreshment parlor. She went docilely but did not speak one work during the five minutes or so it took them to traverse the crowded ballroom. When the Duke looked down at her, he observed on her face the same peculiar expression he had noticed before.

"Is something amiss, Miss Denny?" he asked, unable to restrain his curiosity any longer.

She nodded, her lips quivering. "I am trying not to laugh— or to cry," she said in an unsteady voice. "Oh, dear, I *am* in the suds! To think I have snubbed a duke!"

The Duke was pleased by this open admission of guilt. "You admit, then, that you did deliberately snub me earlier?" he said, looking down at her keenly.

"Yes, but I didn't mean to, your Grace. Oh, dear, whatever will Fanny say? I have a strong notion she will be quite vexed when she learns I have snubbed a duke in her ballroom. What a blunder, to be sure! I might as well have fallen on my face when I made my bow to Queen Charlotte this afternoon—or insulted one of Almack's patronesses—or stepped on the Prince Regent's toes."

She spoke with such a mixture of drollery and despair that the Duke could not help smiling. "Oh, I don't think it's as serious a matter as all that," he said. "Indeed, I am quite ready to forgive you, Miss Denny, if only you will explain why you felt obliged to snub me."

Miss Denny shook her head despairingly, but the Duke observed that her eyes were bright with laughter. "I don't know that I *can* explain, your Grace. It was a foolish blunder on my part. You must know this is the first party I have ever attended in London, and I am far from being conversant with fashionable manners."

"But surely there must have been something that prompted so particular an insult," persisted the Duke. "Did you take one look at my face and contract an instantaneous dislike for me?"

"No, indeed! Quite the contrary, in fact. I could not help liking you when I saw how you behaved to Lady St. Stephen and her odious daughter. Oh, dear, I ought not to have said that either!'' Miss Denny clapped her hands to her mouth and threw the Duke another look of laughing dismay. He shook his head, a smile touching his own lips.

"You need not guard your tongue in my company, Miss Denny. In fact, I would counsel you to say just what you think. Only by pursuing a policy of complete and undeviating honesty can you hope to convince me of your goodwill. At the moment I am inclined to suspect that you class me in the same category as the DeVeres.''

"Oh, no,'' said Miss Denny, laughing and looking horrified at the same time. "I would not want you to think that, your Grace. Very well, if you will have the whole story—the fact is that when my sister introduced me to Lady Emily and her mother earlier this evening, they both treated me as though I were quite beneath their notice. And that irked me, as you might suppose. Indeed, I would think it would irk anyone, though Fanny did not seem to mind their rudeness. But the sad fact is that I disliked it very much, your Grace. And so when I saw them hurry over to you and ask you for whatever it was they were asking—''

"I believe the gist of their petition was that I should lead off the next set with Lady Emily as my partner,'' said the Duke with a self-deprecating cough.

"Was that it? Gracious, how forward of them! Well, anyway, when I saw them ask you to dance with Lady Emily, and then saw you refuse so coolly—well, it was very satisfying. Of course it was very wrong of me: I ought not to have rejoiced over someone else's downfall, even if they were very rude to me beforehand. But I am afraid that I did rejoice to see Lady St. Stephen and Lady Emily discomfited.'' Miss Denny gave the Duke a guilty smile. "Your Grace must think me very low and ill-bred to be saying these things.''

"Not at all, Miss Denny,'' said the Duke, smiling back at her. "It would be rank hypocrisy if I did, for my opinion of the DeVeres is no better than yours. I avoid them when I can, and when I cannot avoid them, as on the present occasion, I do my best to—ahem—depress their pretensions. They do not depress easily, however. I shall be surprised if I do not sustain a second attack from the Marchioness before the evening is over."

"No doubt she is hoping you will make Lady Emily an offer," said Miss Denny sagely. "I expect you have any number of ladies wishing you to marry them, if it comes to that. It must be a great bore for you."

The Duke tried to remain sober, failed, and laughed aloud. "Now how can I answer that, Miss Denny?" he said. "If I agree, I must sound like the greatest coxcomb in nature."

"Oh, no," Miss Denny assured him with great seriousness. "If you said that there were hundreds of ladies dying of love for you, *that* would certainly be a coxcombish statement. But there is nothing conceited in saying that a great many ladies want to marry you. Because you are a duke, you know," she explained helpfully. "I have no doubt that makes you tremendously eligible."

"Since you say so, I must agree," said the Duke in an unsteady voice. "After all, I cannot help having been born a duke." He surveyed Miss Denny with interest and appreciation. "Tell me, Miss Denny, would it make any difference to you if I were not a duke?"

"No, why should it?" said Miss Denny, looking surprised. But a reminiscent smile appeared on her face a moment later. "Still, I suppose I can hardly expect your Grace to accept my word as regards to that. I have already admitted that I did not know you were a duke when I snubbed you. And now that I do know, here I am behaving toward you in a perfectly friendly fashion! I suppose the only way I can convince you of my impartiality is to snub you again."

The Duke laughed. "No, don't do that! I don't consider myself a conceited man in general, but receiving such an unmerited set-down was a great blow to my *amour-propre*. Ormand, of course, would have it that it was high time somebody did give me a set-down. He claims I stalk through society like a god on Olympus, giving myself airs." Still smiling, but with a searching expression, he looked down at Miss Denny. "Am I wrong to guess that it was some such reason that inspired you to snub me in the first place?"

"Some such reason, perhaps," owned Miss Denny, looking down with a blush. But an instant later she raised her eyes to smile at the Duke. "Still, if I was so wrong as to suppose you conceited, I have been punished by finding you instead so thoroughly amiable. I hope your Grace will forgive me for my rudeness."

The Duke was pleased by this speech. It would not have been too much to have said that he was pleased by everything about Miss Denny. He liked her frank way of speaking and the complete absence of affectation in her manner. He liked the laughter that seemed to bubble out of her like an ever-flowing spring. And when he scrutinized her face a second time, he discovered that she was by no means so plain as he had first thought her. There was an unsuspected charm in the smile that lit up her small face, and charm as well in her slender figure and in the riot of golden-brown curls that crowned her head. Schooling his features to an expression of sternness, the Duke shook his head.

"That is a handsome apology, Miss Denny, but I think something more is due me and my injured pride by way of restitution. Only if you will consent to dance this next dance with me will I know you have revised your first, unfavorable opinion of my character."

Miss Denny laughed. "But of course, your Grace! I will dance with you with the greatest pleasure. So long as the next dance is not a waltz, of course," she added prudently. "Much as I would like to oblige you, I dare not risk disobliging my sister and the patronesses of Almack's. I hope you understand, your Grace?" She looked up at him earnestly.

The Duke smiled. He thought he had never seen anything so delightful as the mixture of merriment and mischief, prudence and plain-speaking that seemed to make up Miss Denny's character. "If the next dance should be a waltz, I will engage to use my influence with the patronesses of Almack's to grant you the indulgence of dancing it with me,'' he said, tucking her arm within his. ''I am happy to say that with all the disadvantages of being a duke, there are a few advantages as well! So let us get our punch, Miss Denny, and then you may begin making your reparations on the dance floor.''

Chapter V

It must not be supposed that while Miss Denny was making the Duke's acquaintance, her sister was in ignorance of her activities.

Lady Spicer had, it is true, missed seeing the initial encounter between the Duke and Miss Denny as well as their subsequent formal introduction. But as she was chatting gaily with Countess Lieven (and thinking complacently how much handsomer her own toilette was than that lady's gaudy robe of beetroot gauze and yellow satin), she saw the Countess's thin arched brows rise in an expression of surprise.

"Upon my word, Fanny, you seem to be doing pretty well for your sister," she said in her charmingly accented voice. "To fête her so lavishly would be enough—but however did you manage to convince Ashland to take her up? I would not have thought her quite his type."

Lady Spicer, with some surprise, followed the Countess's gaze just in time to see her sister coming out of the refreshment parlor on the Duke's arm. The sight nearly struck her dumb. More striking still were the expressions on both their faces. Miss Denny was saying something to the Duke, smiling up at him and looking as much at her ease as though he had been some childhood acquaintance. But it was the Duke's expression that chiefly struck Lady Spicer. He was looking down at Miss Denny, and in his eyes was an expression far removed from his usual cool and ironic gaze. If he had been any other gentleman than the Duke of Ashland, Lady Spicer would have been tempted to say he looked smitten.

"Ashland looks quite *bouleversé*," said Countess Lieven, also surveying the Duke with interest.

"Yes," said Lady Spicer faintly.

To say that she was shocked by this development would have been putting it mildly. As a member of the *ton,* she knew the number of the Duke of Ashland's titles, the extent of his wealth, and his celebrated taste in matters as diverse as art, fashion, and literature. As a hostess, she knew him for a reserved and slightly eccentric gentleman who seldom accepted any of the countless invitations which came his way and who, when he did accept one, generally confounded his fellow guests by saying things nobody knew how to take and who could never be depended on to behave as his long-suffering hostess would wish.

In sending him an invitation to her sister's coming-out ball, Lady Spicer had indulged no hopes that he would attend. Far less had she dared hope that he would distinguish Miss Denny in any way. It was not his habit to devote himself to young ladies just out of the schoolroom. In fact, he generally had little to do with ladies of any age, preferring to keep to men's society when he went into company. There had been a few women his name had been linked to, of course—what man of fashion had not his flirts? But previous to now these had all been women of a recognized type, whom no one could suppose he was seriously courting. Watching him now, bending over her sister with that look of tender amusement, Lady Spicer felt a strange presentiment stir within her heart.

She immediately repressed it, however. Since the Duke had been good enough to distinguish Miss Denny, it clearly behooved her, Lady Spicer, to take advantage of the fact and to make as much hay as she could while this noble and erratic sun was still shining upon her sister. So she responded to the

Countess's question with an indulgent laugh and a shake of her head.

"Oh, Ashland! I hoped he would attend, of course, but he is such an unaccountable creature. One never knows whether he will oblige one or not. He does seem quite taken with Judith, doesn't he? I am sure it is not to be wondered at. Perhaps I am prejudiced, but I always thought her a very charming girl. Queen Charlotte paid her a very pretty compliment this afternoon, did you hear?"

As Lady Spicer recounted to Countess Lieven the story of Miss Denny's conversation with the Queen, she kept an eye upon the Duke and her sister. They had come into the ballroom just as the third dance was drawing to an end, and as the waltzing couples were coming off the floor, they stood near the refreshment parlor door, talking in a confidential manner. Lady Spicer longed to know what they were talking about. She was tempted to excuse herself to Countess Lieven and go see for herself, but she felt it better not to betray too much concern over the matter. Far better to pretend that it was the most natural thing in the world that the Duke of Ashland should be taking an interest in her sister!

If the Duke had been a dangerous seducer of maidens, of course, it would have been a different matter. In that case, Lady Spicer would have known her duty and done it, however exalted the Duke's rank or distinguishing his notice. But there had never been allegations of that nature leveled against Ashland. Probably this was merely one of his freaks, like the time he had attended a party at Carlton House and spent the whole evening talking to one of the Regent's footmen. She could only be grateful that on this occasion the Duke's freakishness had brought such distinguishing attention upon her and her sister.

So Lady Spicer remained where she was, chatting to Countess Lieven, until presently the Countess excused herself to go and speak to another acquaintance. Lady Spicer, left temporarily to her own devices, stole another look in the direction of the Duke and Miss Denny. They still appeared to be deep in conversation. Once again Lady Spicer longed to know what they were talking about. It seemed to her that she might now make some inquiry on the subject without appearing unduly anxious on her sister's behalf. Looking about, she spied her husband standing not far off, idly rattling the fobs on his watchchain and looking as though he would rather have been at his club. Lady Spicer summoned him to her side with a minatory wave of her hand.

"What is it, Fan?" he asked, strolling over to join her. "Anything wrong?"

"No, nothing is wrong, Geoffrey. I merely wish you would give me your arm for a moment, so I may go and speak to Judith."

"Judy's over yonder talking to Ashland," said Sir Geoffrey, inclining his head in the direction of the refreshment parlor. "Saw them talking together a minute ago when I went to get a glass of champagne."

He spoke as though it were a commonplace for his sister-in-law to be *tête-à-tête* with an eligible duke. At any other time, Lady Spicer would have been exasperated by this display of masculine insensibility, but on the present occasion she thought it best not merely to tolerate it but to emulate it. "Ah, yes, so she is," said Lady Spicer lightly. "Take me to her, if you please, Geoffrey."

Sir Geoffrey obediently gave her his arm, and together they crossed the ballroom floor. The Duke observed their approach and broke off his conversation with Miss Denny to bow to them both. Sir Geoffrey bowed politely in return, while Lady Spicer dropped a deep curtsy and prepared to take the offensive.

"Why, good evening, Ashland! I did not see you come in, or I would have greeted you sooner. So glad your Grace could attend our party this evening. I hope you are enjoying yourself?"

"Very much, Lady Spicer," he said, bowing politely once more. "A most delightful party. You and Sir Geoffrey are to be congratulated."

"Thank you, your Grace." With a smile, Lady Spicer looked at Miss Denny. "I see you have already made the acquaintance of my sister."

"Oh, yes, Mr. Ormand introduced us," said Miss Denny

blithely. Smiling up at the Duke, she added, "It looks as though the next dance is beginning, your Grace. If you are still insistent on my dancing with you, we had better be taking our places."

There was a hint of mischief in her eyes as she made this speech. An answering spark of mischief was in the Duke's eyes as he replied, "Nothing less will satisfy me, Miss Denny. Let us take our places, by all means."

Lady Spicer ached to know the meaning of this exchange, but thought it better not to inquire. As the Duke and Miss Denny moved toward the floor, she heard her sister remark in a dulcet voice, "You will not be obliged to use your influence on this occasion, your Grace. You observe it is to be boulanger, not a waltz."

"How disappointing," said the Duke, with a shake of his head. "And here I was looking forward to impressing you with my ducal consequence."

Lady Spicer could not hear what Miss Denny said in reply to that, but her words made the Duke throw back his head and laugh. Several people standing nearby turned to look curiously, first at him and then at his companion.

Ashland laughing out loud! Such a thing was never heard of in all the years he had been on the Town. Lady Spicer uttered a silent prayer of thanksgiving that this miracle had taken place at her party. Taking her husband's arm once more, she began to make a circuit of the room, intent on making sure all her friends had all taken full note of her triumph.

The triumph, such as it was, was not limited to this one circumstance alone. Before the evening was over, Lady Spicer had the additional gratification of seeing the Duke lead her sister out for a second dance and then stand talking to her for the space of one dance more. When he finally took leave of her a little later in the evening, Lady Spicer lingered near enough to overhear a portion of his parting address.

"It has been a pleasure making your acquaintance, Miss Denny. I have greatly enjoyed talking to you this evening and hope I shall have the pleasure of seeing you again soon. Did you say you were going to Almack's Wednesday evening?''

Miss Denny nodded cheerfully, as though it were nothing out of the ordinary for one of the highest peers in the realm to be making such an inquiry of her. "Yes, it will be my first time there. I hope I shall not disgrace myself. Fanny has been lecturing me so earnestly on the importance of behaving myself properly at Almack's that I am practically certain of doing something wrong, out of sheer nervousness."

The Duke smiled. "I am unlikely to be much help to you there, Miss Denny. It's been more than three years since I've attended an Almack's assembly myself. But I shall stick close by you, and perhaps with the two of us to prompt each other, we shall manage not to disgrace ourselves. And if we are very lucky, we may even get that waltz together."

That would be delightful,'' said Miss Denny, and gave him her hand with unaffected pleasure. The Duke saluted it, then took leave of her, saying that he was looking forward to seeing her Wednesday night.

"Oh, my love, was there ever anything so fortunate?'' The words burst from Lady Spicer's lips several hours later, as the two sisters were seated together in Lady Spicer's boudoir. Waving away her dressing woman, who was hovering nearby waiting to undress her, Lady Spicer went on exultantly. "I am in raptures, Judy, positively in raptures. Who would have thought Ashland could have been so complaisant, so obliging?''

Miss Denny turned a look of astonishment upon her sister. "Whatever do you mean, Fanny?'' she asked. "Are you talking about the Duke?''

"To be sure I am talking about the Duke, you foolish child! That he should have distinguished you in such a way! I never would have dared hope for anything half as good. He must have spent quite an hour with you—and then to dance with you twice, when everyone knows he scarcely dances at all! You are made, Judy—absolutely made, upon my word. To keep Ashland at your side for over an hour! And then for him to make a positive engagement to meet you at Almack's! I cannot imagine how you contrived it. Tell me everything he said to you, Judy—every word, as nearly as you can remember.''

Miss Denny found herself curiously reluctant to comply with this demand. ''We talked a great deal, but I don't know that we spoke of anything in particular,'' she said slowly. ''He seemed a very polite, sensible gentleman. I was rude to him at first, as you told me to be, but later on, when we had been formally introduced—''

Here she was interrupted by an exclamation of horror from Lady Spicer. ''Rude to him! Oh, no, how is this? I never told you to be rude to Ashland!''

Miss Denny regarded her with honest surprise. ''You told me that I might take it as general rule that the more eligible a gentleman was, the worse I ought to treat him,'' she said. ''He appeared to me very eligible, so I snubbed him. And I am obliged to say that it answered very well, but I was quite ashamed of the way I had behaved when I found out how nice he was.''

''As well you might be! To snub Ashland, as though he were a pushing mushroom! You might as well have snubbed the Prince Regent himself!''

Miss Denny gave a gurgle of laughter. ''Yes, that's what I said when I found out who he was, but he assured me he did not regard it.''

''Judith, you do not mean to say you addressed him in that style? As though he were one of the Smith boys back home?''

Miss Denny looked a trifle guilty, but nodded defiantly. ''Yes, I did, Fanny. And what's more, I don't think he minded in the least. He is quite as nice as the Smith boys, though he *is* a duke. I liked him extremely.''

Lady Spicer was by this time pacing up and down the boudoir wringing her hands. ''Oh, but this is dreadful! What must he have thought of you! I only hope you may not have given him a disgust by your rude behavior.''

''I only treated him rudely in the beginning, and that was because you told me to,'' said Miss Denny, rather hurt by these strictures. ''And I am quite sure he was not offended, Fanny.

He spoke of seeing me again at Almack's, you know, and he need not have done that if he had taken me in disgust."

"Yes, that's true," said Lady Spicer, brightening a little. "I heard him talking to you just before he left, and it did sound as though he means to see you again. However, I don't suppose we ought to depend on it," she added, with a return to her former dejection. "Ashland is a freakish creature, liable to take flight at the slightest excuse. And he hasn't set foot in Almack's in years."

"Yes, that's what he said," agreed Miss Denny, happy to be able to confirm this one point at least. "But I am sure he means to go to Almack's Wednesday, Fanny. When I told him I was afraid I might do something wrong there and be disgraced, he said he was afraid he might, too, and that he would stick by me so that we might support each other."

Lady Spicer shuddered. "My love you must not—indeed, you must not say such things," she said earnestly. "And to Ashland, too, of all people! If he does indeed come to Almack's Wednesday evening, you must be sure to treat him with a proper respect. Perhaps he was amused by your naiveté tonight, but I assure you that in the ordinary way he is accustomed to hold himself on a very high form indeed."

"I saw no sign of it," said Miss Denny stoutly. "He seemed to me perfectly easy and pleasant."

"You must not rely on his remaining so," snapped Lady Spicer. "I tell you that Ashland is one of the great men in the land, Judy. He is probably the richest peer in England—rich enough to buy Geoffrey a dozen times over. He holds I know not how many acres of property in every corner of England, and he is used to being treated with the greatest deference by men and women of a thousand times more consequence than you. You do not realize the extent of his influence, Judy. For him to have paid you as much notice as he did tonight is quite enough to bring you into fashion—but he could equally well turn and crush you if you were to offend him."

"Oh, surely not," protested Miss Denny, looking amused but also a little uncertain. "You make him sound like an Olympian god, Fanny,'' she added, smiling as she remembered the duke's own words on this subject.

"He might as well be an Olympian god, as far as you are concerned," retorted Lady Spicer. "It puts me out of patience to hear you prattle on about his being 'easy' and 'pleasant!' My dear girl, do not imagine the Duke of Ashland has any personal interest in you. If you were able to engage his attention for an hour, you may rejoice in your good fortune, but it will not do for you to depend on being so fortunate another time."

"I don't depend on it," said Miss Denny with spirit. "All I said was that I found the Duke very pleasant company. I do not imagine his having a personal interest in me, any more than Mr. Manville or Mr. Blessington or any of the other gentlemen I danced with."

This speech happily served to give Lady Spicer's thoughts a new direction. "Yes, I noticed Mr. Manville seemed quite taken with you," she said. "He danced with you twice and invited you to go out driving with him, didn't he? Now that is a relationship that might bear fruit, Judy. I spoke to his mother, and though she makes no secret of her hopes to marry him off to an heiress, she has admitted there is no positive need for him to hang out for a rich wife. I think she could be brought to countenance his marrying you, if he were really set on it. And that is where Ashland could prove useful."

"Useful!" exclaimed Miss Denny, in a voice that expressed equal parts of disbelief and disgust. Lady Spicer gave her a quelling look.

"Yes, useful, Judith. If Ashland is good enough to notice you in the future, it would be a vast boost to your consequence and bring you to the notice of other gentlemen. And that, in turn, will greatly improve your chances of making a good match. You must know that gentlemen are curious creatures, my love. They are much more likely to want a thing if they think other men want it, too. We will have to consider how best to turn Ashland's friendship to account—assuming, of course, that you did not completely disgust him with your behavior this evening."

Miss Denny said nothing. Although she still felt that she had been correct in her own reading of the Duke's character, Lady Spicer's words had shaken her so that she was now much less certain on the subject. There could be no doubt that her sister was in a better position to know the Duke's true character than she was. She had never exchanged a word with a nobleman in her life before coming to St. James's Square, whereas her sister was in almost daily contact with the exalted creatures. Perhaps she had been wrong to treat the Duke as though he were merely any other personable man.

In novels, certainly, dukes tended to be imperious, capricious, awe-inspiring personages who routinely fought duels, kidnaped innocent maidens, and took a terrible vengeance on anyone who thwarted their will. Miss Denny had never taken such characterizations seriously, however, any more than she had believed that deranged monks, romantic brigands, and sinister crones were true representatives of their types. But when she thought of all her sister had said about the Duke's wealth and consequence, she could not help seeing that a man who occupied such a lofty position might naturally adopt a demeanor to match.

Frowning, Miss Denny sought to summon an image of the Duke to her mind. Her memory instantly responded with a picture of him smiling down at her, a light of amusement in his clear blue eyes. He was undeniably a handsome gentleman, and there was certainly a high-bred look about his features, but no corresponding height of manner that she could recall. Yet it was possible that she had seen only one side of his personality. Another evening might show him a good deal quicker to take offense and a good deal less willing to overlook any lapses in her behavior.

Looking back over her conduct that evening, Miss Denny supposed she might have been wrong in treating him so informally. She already felt she had been wrong to snub his friendly apology at their first meeting. The Duke had been good enough to overlook her lapse this time, but perhaps next time it would be as well to err on the side of safety.

So Miss Denny listened meekly as her sister outlined the strategy she was to follow at Almack's Wednesday night. "Of course Ashland may not be there, but if he is, mind you let him recognize you first and don't be going out of your way to speak to him. If he does address you, you must take care not to let your tongue run away with you. A simple 'Good evening, your Grace' will do. If he chooses to prolong the conversation beyond that, of course you will not discourage him, but take care how you address him when you speak and do not be putting yourself forward in any way. For your dress, I think the white spotted silk would be best. You look younger in that, and the younger you look, the more likely Ashland will be to attribute any errors you make to youth and ignorance.''

By the time Lady Spicer had finished addressing every separate point of her sister's conduct, Miss Denny was feeling as though her first visit to Almack's were an ordeal to be endured rather than a treat to look forward to. As she left her sister's boudoir and trudged up the stairs to her bedchamber, she reflected that taken as a whole, the life of a young lady of fashion was nothing to envy.

Chapter VI

The Duke left the Spicers' ball with the sensation of having discovered a blooming oasis amid the bleak desert of London society.

Contrary to Lady Spicer's suppositions, he had found Miss Denny's behavior neither forward nor naive, but merely delightful. Never before had a young lady addressed him in just that style—a style candid, lively, and completely unself-conscious. She seemed refreshingly lacking in the airs and affectations with which most society misses abounded.

Nor was it merely Miss Denny's lack of affectations that he had found attractive. Himself an intelligent man, he had been quick to appreciate the wit that underlay her most prosaic observations. It did not hurt that she was also a very pretty girl, though the Duke was inclined to discount this aspect of her attractions. At thirty, he considered himself past the age of being influenced by a girl's face, no matter how pretty it might be.

But there was no denying that he had found Miss Denny enjoyable company that evening. As he entered his carriage and gave the order to his coachman, he found himself anticipating

Wednesday evening with an eagerness which Almack's staid assemblies had never yet inspired in him on their own account.

He reached home just as the clock in the square was striking the hour of midnight. This was an early hour for a gentleman of fashion to retire: most of his contemporaries would only now be going on to their second or third party that evening and might well choose to round off the night with a visit to White's or Watier's that would last until the early hours of the morning.

But the Duke was no ordinary gentleman of fashion. Gambling and heavy drinking had long ago ceased to hold any attraction for him. And since he invariably found himself bored in the company of those who were singlemindedly devoting themselves to these pursuits, he preferred to come away from parties early unless some special attraction was offered. It was a lamentable fact that of late, special attractions had been very rare. He was quite sure that nothing so attractive as Miss Denny would appear at any of the score of other routs, balls, assemblies, and ridottos for which he had received cards that evening.

Early though it was, his arrival caused no surprise or consternation among those appointed to wait on him.

"Good evening, your Grace," said the porter who opened the door to him. As a longtime retainer of the duke's, he ventured to add in a familiar voice, "Chilly night to be abroad, ain't it? I don't wonder your Grace decided to come home early. We'll have rain before morning if I'm not mistook."

"I shouldn't be surprised, Peters," said the Duke pleasantly. Passing into the house, he encountered next his butler, Norbury, who greeted him with a fatherly air while efficiently relieving him of his hat and coat.

"Good evening, your Grace," said Norbury, handing the Duke's habiliments to one of the attendant footmen hovering nearby. In a confidential voice, he added, "Miss Montfort and Miss Louisa returned home only a short time ago, your Grace. I believe they are sitting in the Rose Saloon. If you would like to join them, I'll order James to bring you some fresh tea."

"No, thank you," said the Duke hastily. "No need to trouble

my cousins, Norbury. I shall retire early tonight. Please send Prentiss up to me as soon as he comes in.''

''I believe your Grace will already find him in your Grace's chambers. He had an idea you would not care to keep late hours tonight and so returned early himself.''

''Oh, he did, did he? Very well, Norbury. Good night to you, and I'll see you in the morning.''

With a sensation half of amusement and half of irritation, the Duke crossed a vast expanse of echoing hall chilly with marble and dimly lit with flickering lamps. At the far end of the hall stood a massive double flight of stairs that wound their way to the house's upper stories. The Duke climbed the stairs to their topmost flight, paying no heed to the ornately carved banisters or the graceful bronze figures bearing lamps that ornamented the newel posts.

When he reached the top of the stairs, he crossed another hall only a degree less vast and chilly than the one below. Reaching at last the double doors that led to his own private apartments, he found the portal guarded by a pair of footmen resplendent in scarlet and gold livery. These worthies bowed low on perceiving his approach, then flung open the doors for him to pass through.

''Thank you. Now go to bed,'' he told them as he entered the room. ''This is your doing, Prentiss,'' he said, as soon as the doors had closed behind him. He fixed an accusing look on the melancholy, middle-aged individual dressed in black who had come hurrying into the room from the adjacent closet. ''I have told you before that it is completely unnecessary to keep the footmen up till all hours just to open the door for me. I am quite capable of opening my own doors—and indeed, prefer to do so.''

The melancholy individual's expression became a degree more melancholy. ''Your Grace forgets what is due your Grace's consequence,'' he said, in a voice as doleful as his countenance. ''If your Grace wishes to dispense with the footmen's attendance, of course it shall be done, but—''

''I do wish it. In fact, you may take it as a direct order, Prentiss. You and Norbury and Peters may immolate yourselves on the altar of duty if you like, but I'm damned if I'll have half the servants in the house kept out of their beds for such a whim.''

Prentiss bowed his head in a gesture of melancholy resignation. ''I don't know what your Grace's grandfather would have said,'' he observed with a gusty sigh. ''He was a great one for keeping up the old ways, was the Fourth duke. No footman in his day would have dared sit down for a minute while he was on duty, as the young hedgebirds we hire nowadays think nothing of doing. And as for opening his own doors—why, he'd have sacked every servant in the house if he'd ever found himself obliged to do such a thing.''

''As I never knew my grandfather, I can't say what acts of folly he was capable of. From all I have heard of him, however, I have no doubt he would have been quite as jealous of my consequence as you are, Prentiss. That must be your consolation, for I still intend to have my own way in this matter.''

Prentiss nodded, but looked somewhat cheered by these words. ''Just like the fourth Duke in that, you are,'' he said with melancholy satisfaction. ''Is your Grace wishful to retire now, or will you be going to your study to work?''

''I shall retire now, I think. Please see that I am called early tomorrow, Prentiss. I have a deal of business to get through with Adams in the morning.''

''It shall be just as you say, your Grace,'' said Prentiss, with the fervor that never failed to irritate the Duke. For all his faults of manner, however, he was an efficient valet, and in an amazingly short time had relieved the Duke of his evening raiment and seen him disposed in the vast curtained four-poster that dominated that even vaster ducal bedchamber.

The Duke's last thought, before he drifted off to sleep, was that there was something he was looking forward to. Something pleasant, it was—ah, yes, he recalled it now. He was to meet Miss Denny on Wednesday night at Almack's.

''Almack's,'' he said aloud, with drowsy satisfaction. ''I am pledged to go to Almack's this Wednesday evening, Prentiss. Mind you don't let me forget.''

''Just so, your Grace,'' came Prentiss's voice from outside

the bedcurtains. "I will see that the proper evening dress is laid out for your Grace on that occasion."

"Thank you, Prentiss," murmured the Duke with gratitude, and promptly fell asleep.

He was awakened early the next morning in accordance with his instructions. After dressing and swallowing a hasty breakfast, he sent for his steward, shut himself in his study, and devoted himself to discharging the accumulated business which that gentleman presented for his attention. This absorbed the entirety of the morning and a good part of the afternoon. As soon as the steward had bowed himself away with expressions of gratitude and satisfaction, the Duke called for his curricle and drove to Jackson's Boxing Saloon in Bond Street, where he was greeted with pleasure by the great ex-champion.

"Ah, I thought we'd see you yet today, your Grace. You're near as regular as clockwork. I've just been telling Mr. Lacey here that he'll never shape into a fighter unless he comes to me more often than once a week."

Having disposed of Mr. Lacey with a few well-placed blows and kindly pointed out to him the error of dropping his off-hand while attempting a punch with the other, Jackson strolled over to supervise the Duke's warm-up. Having respectfully corrected his technique with the heavy bag, he then condescended to partner him in a few rounds. The Duke distinguished himself at this exercise, actually managing to land a hit over Jackson's guard and earning a round of applause from the other gentlemen present, who had gathered around to watch. Flushed with his triumph, he thanked Jackson and retired to the changing room to be rubbed down by the attendants there. Here he encountered Mr. Ormand, who was likewise being rubbed down after a session at singlestick with one of Jackson's men.

"Hallo, Ashland," said Mr. Ormand, greeting his friend with his usual air of insouciance. "Didn't know you meant to come to Jackson's this afternoon. Why, we might have gone a round together if you'd told me ahead of time."

"You might have known I'd be here," said the Duke, wincing a little at the attendant's energetic ministrations. "I generally manage to visit Jackson for an hour or two in the afternoon."

"Aye, but you told me last night you'd a deal of business to get through today. Not that I believed a word of it." Mr. Ormand threw his friend a look of sparkling mischief. "I mean to say, what business could a fellow like you possibly have? You're rich as Croesus, and you've any number of people to handle your affairs for you. I don't suppose you have to lift a finger, other than tell 'em how much money you want from day to day."

The Duke turned to regard him with sardonic amusement. "Indeed," he said. "Call me overly punctilious if you will, Charles, but I have a strong notion I would be a good deal less rich if I left my affairs solely in the hands of other people. I spent six hours with my steward today, and only got away when I did because I got an early start this morning. I expect you were just staggering home from Watier's about the time I began," he added in a malicious voice.

"Aye, I expect so," said Mr. Ormand cheerfully. "We made a pretty batch of it at the Great-Go last night, I can tell you that. Ramsey got foxed and tried to box the Watch on the way home."

"He always does, doesn't he?" said the Duke in a bored voice. "I don't imagine I would have found much to entertain me in that."

"That's because you're above being pleased," said Mr. Ormand with a touch of asperity. "I tell you, I wish I had your advantages, Ashland. I'd find something better to do with myself than sit with my steward all morning."

"You were telling me last night you were glad you didn't have my advantages," said the Duke with a smile.

"Did I? Oh, aye, when you were fighting off the Haviland chit. She did everything short of turning cartwheels to get you to dance with her, didn't she? Bet she felt blue when she saw you leading out Fanny Spicer's sister instead. By the by, I notice you seemed devilishly taken with that gel. Danced with her twice, didn't you?"

"Yes," said the Duke shortly. Aware that Mr. Ormand was looking at him speculatively, he summoned a short laugh. "Indiscreet of me, wasn't it? I suppose the gossips are already publishing the banns."

"Well, it did look queer, y'know, old man. Mean to say, if you was a regular fellow like me who danced with all the girls, nobody would have thought twice about it. But I can't remember the last time you stood up with anybody. Not since you and Maria Medford were—well, you know."

"Yes," said the Duke, more shortly still.

"And the Denny girl's not an Incomparable like Maria— not by a long chalk. A pretty enough girl, mind you, but not a beauty."

"No, certainly not," agreed the Duke. Yet when he summoned an image of Miss Denny's face to his mind's eye, he felt a certain doubt about this statement. She was not a classic beauty, to be sure; nor had she the kind of striking good looks that must dazzle the beholder at first sight. But there was a subtle harmony about her features, a grace to her slender form, and an inner glow that seemed to radiate from her smiling brown eyes which gave her an appeal equal to—perhaps even greater than—the more obvious kind of beauty.

As the Duke reflected on this anomaly, he became aware that Mr. Ormand was once again regarding him with interest. He shook himself mentally, fighting back a ridiculous urge to blush.

"Certainly not a beauty," he said again, in his most decisive voice. "But a taking little thing, considered altogether. Fanny Spicer ought not to have any difficulty finding a husband for her."

"No, I shouldn't think so," agreed Mr. Ormand. "Look at the way young Manville was hanging at her heels. Daresay she'll be married before the Season's out."

The Duke found this idea oddly disturbing. Although he was not personally acquainted with Lord O'Henry's heir, Mr. Manville had struck him as a clumsy youth, devoid alike of grace or wit. He was certainly not an appropriate husband for a charming young lady like Miss Denny. As the Duke frowned over this idea, he became aware once more that Mr. Ormand's eyes were on him. There was a knowing light in those eyes that made the Duke hasten to change the subject.

"I am sure Miss Denny will do very well for herself," he said with finality. "Trust Fanny Spicer for that. Do you go to Tatt's this afternoon, Ormand? I've a mind to buy a new pair for my curricle."

Mr. Ormand at once declared his willingness to accompany his friend on this errand. As soon as the two were dressed, they took their leave of Jackson, drove to Hyde Park Corner, and spent the rest of the afternoon surveying the various prime bits of horseflesh to be offered over the block on Tattersall's next sale day.

The Duke continued to think about Miss Denny, however, long after he had ceased to speak of her. Even as he discussed the points of a pair of chestnuts with Mr. Ormand and a knowledgeable groom, he found himself anticipating Wednesday more as the date of the next assembly at Almack's than as the date which would enable him to make these prime-goers officially his. There was something almost boyish about the way he looked forward to seeing Miss Denny again. He felt as he had felt twenty years ago, when he was a schoolboy anticipating some long-awaited holiday.

Becoming aware of this state of mind, the Duke laughed at himself. It was ridiculous for a man of his years to pin so much importance on the prospect of a few minutes' conversation with a chit of a girl.

"But it isn't as though I'm developing a *tendre* for her, or anything of that sort," he assured himself. "It's merely that I found her interesting, an intriguing personality. She speaks well, and isn't afraid to speak her mind, and she has a sense of humor, too. After all these years of doing the social round and meeting nothing but the same old types, of course it's refreshing to meet someone new and different. But I don't have any intention of letting matters go beyond, at most, a light flirtation. And depend on it, she doesn't expect anything more from me herself. She isn't Fanny Spicer's sister if she does."

These arguments were eminently logical and served to a great extent to quiet the Duke's conscience. Nevertheless, he still found himself looking forward to Wednesday evening with great eagerness. And when that evening finally arrived, and he was properly attired in the long-tailed coat and knee-breeches that were *de rigueur* at Almack's, he found himself in a state of nerves unusual to a man of his years and experience.

Miss Denny was feeling nervous, too. Over the past two days, her sister had so incessantly dinned into her ears the necessity of comporting herself properly in the Duke's company that she almost hoped he would not come to Almack's that evening. Almost she hoped it—but at the same time she owned to herself that she would be disappointed if he did not come.

Lady Spicer's descriptions had given her no desire to see Almack's on its own account. It sounded a pretentious place, full of pitfalls for inexperienced country girls and offering no attractions beyond what were available back home at the monthly Winfield Assemblies.

The only advantage Miss Denny could see was that it gave her the opportunity to wear one of the new and elegant evening dresses which Lady Spicer had ordered for her. And even this pleasure proved to be tainted. For on trying on the ornately flounced and beribboned robe of white spotted silk which her sister had decreed the proper wear for Almack's, she could not feel it became her as well as the simpler rose-colored dress she had worn at her coming-out ball. Lady Spicer tacitly admitted as much, but told her it did not signify.

"White is the most suitable color for a girl just out. I daresay half the young ladies at Almack's will be wearing white, and it might well displease the Patronesses if you make yourself too conspicuous. Then, too, as I mentioned before, I think it as well that we should emphasize your youth tonight. That's why I had Françoise put your hair up in curl papers. You can wear your hair down in clusters of ringlets with a few flowers tucked here and there, and it will look very pretty and *ingénue.*"

So Miss Denny had her hair dressed in ringlets as her sister dictated, but when she surveyed the finished result in the glass she could not wholly approve it. The heavy clusters of curls over her ears seemed to her fussy and artificial, as unsuited to her face as her dress was to her figure. This made her feel uncomfortable, and since Lady Spicer could not resist the opportunity to give her a great deal of last-minute advice on what to say and do at Almack's, she was feeling harassed as well. Something of her state of mind must have shown in her face, for as she and Lady Spicer stood in the hall waiting for the carriage to be brought around, Sir Geoffrey paused on his way out the door to address some words of reassurance to her.

"On your way to Almack's, eh? You look dashed pretty, Judy. Just you keep your chin up, and you'll hold your own with anybody, never fear."

"Thank you, Geoffrey," said Miss Denny, smiling rather wanly. In a wistful voice, she added, "Are you going to your club? I wish you were coming with us to Almack's instead. I feel sure I would be better able to keep my chin up if you were there to lend your support."

Sir Geoffrey hesitated, shooting an indecisive look at his wife. Lady Spicer returned the look impassively. "Oh, you won't need me," he said. "Doubt I could get near you with all the beaux that'll be clustering around."

"I anticipate no clusters of beaux. Indeed, I would be glad to have at least one partner I might depend on."

Sir Geoffrey appeared to waver. "I'm not dressed for Almack's," he said, looking dubiously down at his pantaloons.

"It wouldn't take you a minute to change," urged Miss Denny. "Fanny and I don't mind waiting, do we, Fanny?"

"No, to be sure," said Lady Spicer in an unenthusiastic voice.

Sir Geoffrey looked again at his pantaloons, then at Miss Denny. She gave him a hopeful smile, which seemed to bring him to a sudden decision. "I'll do it, by Jove," he said. "Tell Rivers I won't need my phaeton after all, Fanny. I'm going to Almack's with you and Judy." Not waiting for an answer, he set off up the stairs two at a time.

Lady Spicer sighed. "Now we will be late," she said, looking fretfully at the longcase clock on the landing. "Why did you ask him to come with us, Judy? I am sure he would have been happier at his club.''

Miss Denny gave her a look of surprise. ''Don't you want him to come with us, Fanny?'' she asked.

Lady Spicer colored a little under her sister's gaze. ''To be sure, if I thought Geoffrey meant to dance and behave like a reasonable being, I would be happy to have him accompany us. But you'll see, Judy. He'll go off to the cardroom the minute we get there, and we'll be lucky if we get another glimpse of him all evening.'' Despite these predictions, however, she greeted Sir Geoffrey with a pleasant smile when he came downstairs a few minutes later and complimented him on the speed with which he had accomplished his change of raiment. Sir Geoffrey responded gallantly by complimenting her on her dress, then turned his attention to assisting her and Miss Denny into the waiting carriage.

Miss Denny, eager to foster this newfound amity, insisted on occupying the forward seat, while Sir Geoffrey took the front-facing one beside her sister. She had fancied that since the night of the ball, they had been on better terms with each other, and she hoped that with careful management this positive trend might continue.

It continued during the drive to Almack's and during their subsequent admission into the rooms. Miss Denny, who had so taken her sister's words to heart as to fear she might be turned away from the door, was quite overwhelmed by the civil reception accorded her by Almack's patronesses. She received a polite greeting from Lady Sefton and a voluble one from Lady Jersey, and though Mrs. Drummond Burrell vouchsafed her only a nod, still it was a gracious nod, accompanied by a small but perceptible smile.

''Depend on it, she has heard about you and the Duke,'' whispered Lady Spicer. ''I do hope he means to put in another appearance this evening. It would be such a triumph for you, Judy! And if he danced with you again, it would make your position quite unassailable. But I fear that is too much to hope for.''

Miss Denny nodded gloomily. She had seen at a glance that

the Duke was not among the guests already assembled in the ballroom. She told herself stoutly that it was early yet, and that he would undoubtedly appear before the evening was over, but still she could not help feeling a little disturbed. She was even more disturbed a moment later when Lord Henry Nathorp detached himself from the crowd and strolled over to greet her sister.

"Good evening, Fanny," he said, taking lady Spicer's hand familiarly in his and bowing over it. "I rejoice to see you here tonight. I had begun to think the evening a dead loss—but now it is an undoubted gain. You look beautiful as always."

"And you flatter me as always," said Lady Spicer. "But I thank you for the compliment, Henry."

"You are welcome to it, I assure you," said Lord Henry, smiling in a manner that Miss Denny thought unpleasantly wolfish. "Have you a partner for this next dance?"

"Oh, I have no intention of dancing," said Lady Spicer with a coquettish laugh. "You must know I consider myself to be relegated amongst the chaperones, Henry, now that I have my sister to think of."

"I am sure your sister would not wish you to abjure all your pleasures, my dear Fanny. It would be criminal to refrain from dancing for such a trivial reason. As well declare you have no intention of dancing merely because you are married." Lord Henry let his eyes slide to Sir Geoffrey in a manner that held a distinct challenge.

Miss Denny also looked at Sir Geoffrey, expecting he would answer Lord Henry's unspoken challenge and perhaps declare his intention of dancing with his wife himself. Instead, however, he turned away from Lady Spicer with a brusque movement. "Fanny, Judy, I beg the two of you'll excuse me. I'll be in the cardroom if you want me."

Lady Spicer gave Miss Denny an eloquent look. "You see, my dear? What did I tell you?" she said in a whisper. Aloud to Lord Henry, she added, "Perhaps I will dance with you later, Henry, but first I must see Judy settled. Come to me later in the evening, after the first set of dances, perhaps."

"You may be sure I shall. Your most devoted servant, ma'am," said Lord Henry, bowing and smiling more wolfishly than ever as he took leave of Lady Spicer.

Miss Denny was much vexed by this episode, but she had no time to dwell on it. Her old acquaintance Mr. Manville had just caught sight of her from where he stood beside his mother's chair. As soon as Lord Henry had gone, he came hurrying over to her, a beaming smile on his freckled face.

"How d'ye do, Miss Denny? Glad to see you again. I hope you took no ill from our drive yesterday?"

"No, none," said Miss Denny. Putting aside her vexed reflections on Lord Henry's conduct, she smiled back at Mr. Manville. "It is as I told you yesterday, Mr. Manville. I never take ill, and certainly not from a little thing like a carriage ride on a chilly day. I enjoyed our outing very much, east wind or no east wind."

"And so did I," said Mr. Manville, bowing with awkward gallantry. "Perhaps you'll do me the honor of standing up with me for this next dance? I'll do my best not to step on your feet!" He grinned at her shyly.

"Certainly I will dance with you, Mr. Manville," said Miss Denny, smiling back at him. "But I'm afraid I cannot engage to make the same promise in return. This next dance is a quadrille, you know, and I find the figures are danced somewhat differently here than they were back home. I shall have to mind my feet carefully if I am not to disgrace us." Mr. Manville earnestly promised to make all possible allowance for her feet, and together they went out on the floor.

During the quadrille that followed, he was able to congratulate Miss Denny on her successful execution of that complex dance. She experienced no difficulty in remembering the proper sequence of figures. Indeed, she had anticipated none, for in expressing her fears on the subject, she had been motivated more by a desire to set Mr. Manville at his ease than by any real anxiety about her dancing. Her subterfuge achieved its object, however. Mr. Manville danced better than he had at any time during their acquaintance, and several people on the sidelines were heard to remark what a well-matched pair they were.

The Duke arrived on the scene just in time to see Miss Denny execute a last graceful *pas de basque* as she looked laughingly into her partner's face.

Chapter VII

The Duke smiled to himself at having discovered Miss Denny in such a characteristic attitude.

It seemed to him only right that she should be laughing and enjoying herself. For such a lively mind as hers, even a dull place like Almack's could provide entertainment. One of the things that had pleased him most about her during their initial interview was the enjoyment she seemed to take in everything she did. And though he was slightly less pleased when he observed that on this occasion she was finding enjoyment in the company of young Mr. Manville, he charitably made allowance even for this circumstance. Mr. Manville was certainly unworthy of being more to Miss Denny than a mere dance partner, but in that role he must be considered unexceptionable. So, having rationalized away his momentary twinge of jealousy, the Duke stationed himself near the edge of the dance floor, where he might intercept Miss Denny as soon as she came off the floor.

He stood with his arms folded across his chest, watching Miss Denny with an indulgent smile. So absorbed was he in this occupation that he completely missed seeing the sensation his appearance was causing.

The news that the Duke of Ashland had deigned to come to Almack's after several years of pointed absence had spread through the room like wildfire. Hundreds of eyes watched curiously to see what he would do. There was a persistent rumor, spread by nobody knew whom, which had it that his object in coming had been to dance once more with Fanny Spicer's little sister, whom he had distinguished in such a marked manner at the Spicers' ball. This rumor was received with derision by a number of ladies of lofty lineage, most of whom were themselves marriageable or had marriageable daughters to dispose of.

"Mere wishful thinking on Fanny Spicer's part," sniffed Lady St. Stephen, who was in attendance that evening with Lady Emily. Having carefully adjusted the pearl tiara that adorned her daughter's dark curls and adjured her to keep her shoulders well back, the Marchioness boldly approached the Duke where he stood, a welcoming smile on her thin painted lips. But the Duke brushed her aside with absent good humor.

"I beg your pardon, ma'am, but there is someone I must speak to," he told her, and walked away without even paying the tribute of one glance at Lady Emily. Lady St. Stephen stood incredulous, her breast swelling with indignation, as the Duke went forward to greet that little upstart Miss Denny, who was sprung from no one knew where and who could not boast one-tenth of her daughter's beauty.

A stir of excitement ran round the room as the Duke took Miss Denny's hand in his. This was meat and drink to the gossips, who watched with straining eyes to catch every shade of expression on the Duke's face. Miss Denny was aware of their scrutiny and felt highly uncomfortable. She had felt uncomfortable for several minutes now, ever since she had first espied the Duke standing at the edge of the dance floor.

He had looked even handsomer than she remembered, and that was handsome enough, heaven knew. The satin knee-breeches that so pitilessly exposed the gawkiness of Mr. Manville's figure admirable became the Duke's lean hips and well-turned legs. His black evening coat fitted without a wrinkle across his shoulders, and his silver-blond hair gleamed in the light of the chandeliers.

As the Duke bowed over her hand, Miss Denny was seized by a sudden sense of panic. It was impossible that this elegant gentleman could be the same pleasant companion she had joked with two nights ago. He looked more like the Olympian being her sister had described. "Apollo in knee-breeches," she said aloud, with a nervous gasp of laughter.

"I beg your pardon?" said the Duke, straightening up to regard her with a surprised look.

"Nothing," said Miss Denny, swallowing hard. She was appalled at having made such a slip. Her sister had spent hours lecturing her upon the importance of minding her tongue this evening, and now here she was making a fool of herself with her very first words! It was vital that she somehow recover the ground she had lost. Recalling her sister's instructions, she dropped a stiff curtsy. "Good evening, your Grace. I hope I find you well."

His face relaxed into the smile she remembered so well. "Good evening, Miss Denny. I hope I find you the same," he returned, pressing the hand which he held in his.

Mr. Manville, who had stood mute while this exchange was going on, now bowed and stammered out something unintelligible. The Duke accorded him a formal, unsmiling bow in return, which made him blush, stammer out a farewell, and scuttle off with great celerity. The Duke looked after him with raised eyebrows.

"Your friend seems a bit lacking in the social graces," he observed to Miss Denny. "I wonder what he was about, rushing off like that? He ought to have seen you safely back to your sister, or at least made sure you were in good hands before he abandoned you. Not that my hands are *not* good, but he had no means of knowing that before he left."

"Yes," admitted Miss Denny. Feeling that this speech was not quite fair to Mr. Manville, she felt obliged to excuse him as far as she could. "But I daresay he knew who you were, your Grace, and thought I would be safe in your company. Mr.

Manville is not at all unmannerly in the usual way, I assure you. It is only that he is rather shy.''

"Obviously," said the Duke in a dry voice. Although he would hardly have admitted it to himself, he was annoyed by Miss Denny's defense of Mr. Manville. But since it was ridiculous that he should be jealous of such a thing—and of a gauche youth like Mr. Manville—he pushed his annoyance aside and smiled down at Miss Denny once more. "In truth, I am glad we are rid of Mr. Manville, Miss Denny. I have need of your undivided attention."

"Oh, yes?" said Miss Denny. She hardly knew what she was saying. Her mind seemed incapable of functioning, divided between a fear of saying something inappropriate to the Duke and the unnerving sense of being scrutinized by several hundred pairs of curious, critical, and hostile eyes.

"Yes, for I depend on you to see me safely through the evening. I arrived in good time, as you see, and was admitted readily enough in spite of my former apostasy. But I have a feeling that I am only here on sufferance, and that the slightest gaffe will see me ignominiously ejected. It will take all your efforts to prevent such a mishap."

A weak smile was the only answer he received to this sally. Rather surprised by his companion's reticence, the Duke went on, dropping his voice to a confidential murmur. "I think it would be particularly well if we stayed away from Mrs. Drummond Burrell. She gave me a most scathing look when I came in a few minutes ago. Even now I can feel her looking in our direction."

It was on the tip of Miss Denny's tongue to reply, *"Everyone* is looking in our direction." This was the kind of remark Lady Spicer had earnestly cautioned her against making, however, and so she only curtsied again and said in a subdued voice, "I am sure your Grace need have no fear of Mrs. Drummond Burrell."

The Duke looked at Miss Denny in surprise. It did not seem to him that she was behaving like the girl he remembered. Looking at her closely, he observed that her appearance, too, was different than he remembered. Her dress was frillier and more conventional than the one she had been wearing the other night, and her hair seemed also to have been changed. It was not a change for the better in the Duke's opinion, but though he did not realize it, he was already past the stage where this would have made any difference in his feelings. Miss Denny might have draped herself in sackcloth and twisted her hair in elflocks atop her head, and he would have thought her charming, if only she would have smiled and spoken to him as she had before.

This she seemed curiously reluctant to do, however. The Duke could only suppose she was ill-at-ease. This was perhaps natural enough under the circumstances; looking around him, he perceived quite a number of people who seemed very interested in his and Miss Denny's conversation. It was clearly incumbent on him to remove her to a situation of greater privacy if he wanted to enjoy a return to their former easy converse.

"Do you care to dance, Miss Denny?" he asked. Among half-a-hundred other couples on the dance floor, it seemed probable that he and Miss Denny might enjoy at least a measure of privacy.

"Yes, thank you, your Grace," she said. She looked and sounded more at her ease in making this speech, and there was even a hint of a shy smile in the look that accompanied her words. Much relieved, the Duke smiled back at her.

"I am honored to have your company. Let's see, shall we have to brave the patronesses to obtain permission to waltz?"

Miss Denny looked toward the dance floor, where couples were beginning to form in a line down the center. "No, it looks as though this will be a country dance, your Grace."

"Ah, then no permission will be necessary," said the Duke. He spoke cheerfully but was conscious of a feeling of disappointment. The lively give and take of a country dance would give him scant opportunity to converse with his partner, and that had been his chief reason for inviting Miss Denny to stand up with him in the first place. He consoled himself with the reflection that he might ask her to dance with him a second time without offending even the strict propriety of Almack's. And perhaps that second dance might be a waltz if he exercised a little management. Resolving to throw his all into this endeavor, he took his place opposite Miss Denny in the set and prepared to extract what enjoyment he could out of the next half-hour.

As he had feared, this was not very much. It was impossible to do more than exchange a few commonplaces while he and Miss Denny advanced and retreated, bowed and promenaded opposite each other. "Do you find your first visit to Almack's all you hoped?" he asked, taking advantage of a moment when the steps of the dance brought them together.

Since Miss Denny was called on that moment to beat a hasty retreat, she had time to do no more than smile and nod in reply. On their next encounter she enlarged on her reply a little. "The rooms seem very handsome, your Grace. I confess, I had envisioned something grander from Fanny's descriptions, but that is nothing. It is the company that matters more than the rooms, and I am obliged to say everyone has been very kind to me tonight."

"I am very glad to hear it," was all the Duke had time to say. He tried again on their next encounter. "You must not be expecting anything grand in the way of food and drink, either. Almack's is famous for the paucity of their refreshments. They don't even serve champagne—nothing but tea, lemonade, and orgeat."

Miss Denny smiled, but once again had no time to reply. As she retreated to the opposite side of the room with the other ladies, she meditated what her response should be. Her first and natural impulse would have been to laugh and assure the Duke that she liked lemonade better than champagne anyway. A moment's reflection assured her this would be a *faux pas,* however. Lady Spicer had cautioned her against saying anything that might brand her as a provincial, and it was undoubtedly provincial to prefer lemonade to champagne.

Then, too, such a remark might be construed as a hint that she wished the Duke to procure her refreshments when the dance was over. Miss Denny would have liked very well to drink lemonade with the Duke, but she preferred that the invitation to do so be his and completely unsolicited. She might disgrace herself by appearing a tongue-tied fool, but at least she would avoid the opprobrium of appearing to pursue him.

So she merely smiled and said, "Indeed," a remark which she felt to be miserably inadequate but better than nothing. The Duke received it with outward composure, but inwardly he felt surprised and disappointed once more. He had enjoyed talking to Miss Denny Monday evening, and though he was not coxcomb enough to suppose he had swept her off her feet, still he had felt that she had enjoyed his company, too. Why then was she treating him with such reserve tonight?

Of course it was difficult to converse during a country dance. The Duke reminded himself of this fact, but still he felt Miss Denny might have made more of an effort than she was doing. It almost seemed as though she were trying to discourage him. That was ridiculous, of course, for she need not have accepted his invitation to dance if she had wanted to discourage him. But he had to own that she did not seem to be in spirits tonight. He kept up his flow of conversational remarks throughout the dance, all the while watching Miss Denny closely. By the dance's end he had satisfied himself that something was disturbing her.

In this he was quite correct. Although Miss Denny had gotten over the first crisis of nerves which the Duke's appearance had inspired in her, she was still laboring under a sense of oppression. Every time she looked at him, she could hear her sister's voice telling her that the Duke of Ashland was one of the wealthiest and most powerful men in the land, capable of blighting her career at the outset should she say or do anything amiss.

Nor was this all. She had been disturbed earlier when Lady Spicer had openly flirted with Lord Henry in front of her husband. As the evening wore on, she found a fresh source of disturbance in her sister's conduct. While attempting to respond to one of the Duke's conversational overtures, Miss Denny had caught sight of Lady Spicer and Lord Henry seated together on a bench at the back of the ballroom. She could not see Lord Henry very well, for he was sitting with his back towards her, but she could see her sister's face quite clearly, and the expression on it had given her a shock. Lady Spicer was smiling the same soft, intimate smile she had used to give Sir Geoffrey when the two had first been engaged.

This sight had shaken Miss Denny so badly that she had been quite incapable of responding to the Duke's question. Throughout the rest of the dance, she answered his remarks quite at random, her mind filled with uncomfortable speculations.

The Duke sensed her abstraction but continued his flow of polite remarks, content to bide his time until he could question her more closely. At the dance's end, he addressed her with a bow. "A most enjoyable dance, Miss Denny. I hope you will do me the honor of dancing the next set with me as well?"

To the Duke's surprise, Miss Denny hesitated visibly before answering his question. He saw her eyes flicker across to where her sister sat. "You needn't worry," he said, misinterpreting her hesitation. "Even at Almack's, it is quite permissible to dance twice with the same partner. Three times, of course, would put one beyond the pale—but we will not venture so much as that. I would not dare to flout convention while I am still on probation, as it were."

Miss Denny smiled, but the Duke saw she was still looking at her sister. "I don't know," she said in an uncertain voice. "Perhaps I ought to sit this next dance out, your Grace."

"If that is your wish, then of course I must accede to it. I am bound to own myself disappointed, however. This next dance will be a waltz if I mistake not, and I had looked forward to the pleasure of waltzing with you. You remember we spoke of it Monday night."

Miss Denny looked at him then—the first time she had really looked at him that evening, the Duke thought. A tremulous smile touched her lips. "Of course," she said. "You were going to dazzle me by demonstrating your influence with the patronesses, were you not? You must not think I do not *wish* to waltz with you, your Grace. I should like to very much, only—"

"Only what?" prompted the Duke, as she hesitated.

"Only I don't know if I should," she said, with another look at Lady Spicer. "It seems to me that perhaps I ought to sit with my sister awhile and keep her company."

"But your sister already has company," said the Duke. "I see her over there talking to Lord Henry Nathorp. Of course, if you have any doubt on the subject, we can always go over and ask her."

Miss Denny looked at her sister again, then at the Duke, trying to make up her mind. It seemed to her that sisterly duty called her to sit the dance out, but the Duke's offer represented a definite temptation. Moreover, she knew that if asked, Lady Spicer would certainly urge her to dance with the Duke.

"I suppose that is not necessary," she said at last. "But if you truly wish to waltz with me, your Grace, you shall have to use a little of that influence you were boasting of. I dare not do it without permission from one of the patronesses."

"That is easily obtained," the Duke assured her with a smile. Yet he was beginning to wonder if the results would repay the effort. Miss Denny's manner was so odd and withdrawn that he could not look forward to waltzing with her with the same enjoyment he had anticipated earlier.

He had already committed himself, however, and so he sought out the good-natured Lady Sefton, whom he liked better than any of the other patronesses. That lady acceded to his request with a readiness that ought to have increased his standing in the eyes of Miss Denny, if she had been at all susceptible to such an influence.

"To be sure, Ashland. It is a pleasure to see you at Almack's once more. And Miss Denny, if it is you who have brought him here, then I must congratulate you on having exercised such a beneficial influence on his Grace. We do not see him at our assemblies nearly so often as we should like."

This speech made Miss Denny color and murmur a confused reply that was part thanks, part disclaimer. The Duke looked down at her quizzically as he led her away from Lady Sefton.

"I do not know whether to accuse you of modesty or hypocrisy, Miss Denny. You must know it was your influence and no other which brought me here this evening."

This brought Miss Denny's eyes to his face once more. There

was a ghost of a smile on her lips as she replied, "No, how can your Grace say so? I am persuaded you only put in an appearance this evening in order to show everyone that even the haughty patronesses of Almack's must bow to your will!"

"Just so," said the Duke, pleased beyond measure to have won this response. It was the first thing she had said that evening that was at all typical of the Miss Denny he remembered from Monday night. As they joined the other couples on the dance floor, he smiled down at her. "Once again you have discerned my true motives, Miss Denny. I beg you will not betray me, for you must know my reputation hinges on not seeming to care what anyone thinks of me."

Miss Denny opened her mouth to make a laughing retort, then shut it again. Her sister's instructions on that head had been very clear. She was to address the Duke respectfully, and not disgust him with her chattering tongue and impertinent attempts at humor. Her joke about his influence over the patronesses had clearly been out of order, and though the Duke had not seemed to mind it, it would be better not to push matters by attempting any further pleasantry. So she merely smiled guardedly and replied, "Your Grace is pleased to joke with me."

"Very pleased, but at the same time I am also pleased to be speaking the truth, Miss Denny. You must know that among the denizens of high society, it is counted a great weakness to betray any interest in the opinions of one's fellow men."

Miss Denny considered this. "Yes," she said finally. "Fanny has told me much the same thing. It struck me as quite humorous when I first came to London. One spends every waking hour trying to dress and talk and behave so as to impress people, yet one must not seem to care in the slightest if they *are* impressed."

"Yes, it is rather humorous, isn't it? Speaking from experience, however, I can say that the pose is a very effective one—particularly when it happens not to be a pose. I have never cared very much for society's good opinion, and the result is that I find myself avidly courted by people whom I actively despise."

He spoke in a tone half deprecating, half cynical. Miss Denny gave him a look of surprise. "I daresay being a duke has something to do with it, too," she pointed out. "If you were plain Mr. Smith or Brown, I doubt you would be so much courted as you are." In a diffident voice, she added, "Do you really despise them? All these people?"

"No, not all of them. There are many who amuse me, some few whom I like, and even a handful whose opinion I value." The Duke looked down at Miss Denny. "You, for instance."

"Me?" Miss Denny spoke in genuine surprise. "But you have known me only a few days, your Grace."

"True, but I pride myself on being something of a judge of character. You struck me on first acquaintance as a remarkable young woman, and nothing I have seen tonight has caused me to revise that judgment. There have been one or two things that have puzzled me, however." The Duke looked down at Miss Denny once more. "I would give a good deal to know what has been disturbing you this evening."

Looking into the Duke's clear blue eyes, Miss Denny knew a sudden impulse to confide in him. Such a thing was plainly impossible, however. She could not possibly tell him that she was laboring under a sense of inferiority brought on by his own ducal status. Still less could she confide to him her concerns about Lady Spicer. She gave a little laugh, which sounded unconvincing even to her own ears.

"I am very stupid this evening, I know," she said. "I think perhaps I have a touch of the headache, your Grace."

As she spoke, her eyes strayed to her sister, still deep in conversation with Lord Henry. The sight of them *tête-à-tête* made her wince and look away. In doing so, she encountered the Duke's eye and was shocked by the look of sympathy and comprehension she read there.

"I am sorry to hear you have the headache, Miss Denny," he said. In a softer voice, he added, "If it is your sister's relationship with Lord Henry that gives you concern, I think you worry needlessly. Lady Spicer has always conducted herself in a manner that does honor to herself and her high position."

Miss Denny was grateful for this speech, yet she could not

think it right to be discussing her sister's private affairs with a gentleman who was, in point of fact, a virtual stranger. "Yes, of course," she said repressively. In a lighter voice, she added, "Is not this music delightful? What a fine orchestra Almack's has, to be sure."

The Duke agreed that the orchestra was very fine, and for the remainder of the dance he and Miss Denny talked of music, books, and similar impersonal subjects. The Duke observed that she had lapsed once more into what he would call her mode of repression. She spoke little, said nothing which was not perfectly trite and proper, and liberally interlarded her speech with the words "your Grace." When at last the waltz was over, the Duke felt actually relieved—but at the same time remarkably frustrated.

"Thank you for a delightful dance, Miss Denny," he lied, as he led her back to her sister. She shot him a quick sideways look, as though she suspected the words were mere courtesy. When she spoke, however, her voice was as colorlessly polite as his own.

"You are quite welcome, your Grace. Thank you for inviting me."

They had reached Lady Spicer by this time. That lady broke off her conversation with Lord Henry to greet the Duke and Miss Denny with a broad smile.

"Ah, here is Judith! And Ashland, too. So good to see you again, your Grace. I was just telling Henry how much Judith enjoyed talking with you Monday night."

" 'Evening, Ashland," said Lord Henry, surveying the Duke with some curiosity. "Didn't look to see you at Almack's tonight."

"No, I am not a frequent visitor here," said the Duke, according him a polite bow. He bestowed another on Lady Spicer, then turned to Miss Denny. "I must take leave of you now, ma'am. I hope I shall have the pleasure of seeing you again soon."

The words were mere civility, but Lady Spicer seized upon them eagerly. "Yes, and I am sure Judith would enjoy seeing you again, too, your Grace. Do you go to the Winchcombs'

Venetian Breakfast next week? Perhaps the four of us might go as a party—you, me, Henry, and Judith.''

It was the kind of scheme frequently propounded to the Duke by the relatives of marriageable young ladies. A cold refusal would have been his usual response to such an invitation, and indeed, an appropriate set-down was already trembling on his lips. But when he happened to glance in Miss Denny's direction, he found his tongue suddenly arrested. She regarded him with a timid, troubled expression, almost as if she knew the thoughts that were passing in his head. The Duke found himself incapable of making the brusque reply he had intended. Instead, he merely bowed again and said, ''I fear I shall be unable to make one of your party, Lady Spicer. I think—I rather believe—I have another engagement for that afternoon.''

To his annoyance, Lady Spicer took the civility of his refusal as encouragement to press the issue. ''But surely you are not engaged for the *whole* of the afternoon, your Grace,'' she persisted. ''Even if it were only for an hour or two, I know Judith would enjoy seeing you again. Wouldn't you, Judith?''

''Yes,'' said Miss Denny softly. She raised her eyes to the Duke's face. ''But if his Grace has other plans, Fanny, then we must not importune him.''

In her eyes was a look so eloquent of apology and unhappiness that the Duke was completely disarmed. He spoke out impulsively. ''I cannot promise, Miss Denny, but I will try to attend. It might be possible for me to come to the Winchcombs' for an hour perhaps, later in the afternoon.'' Bowing again, he wished her a good evening, then hurried off before Lady Spicer could say anything more.

Chapter VIII

After the Duke's departure, Miss Denny found the remainder of her evening at Almack's singularly flat.

His departure ought to have been a relief to her, for she had been feeling oppressed and ill-at-ease all the while she was in his company. Certainly she had no cause to feel neglected in his absence. The circumstance of the Duke of Ashland's twice dancing with her had been fully noted and appreciated by her fellow guests, and throughout the rest of the evening she was mobbed by gentlemen eager to sit with her, dance with her, and fetch her refreshment.

Her own sex was scarcely less backward in their attentions. Several young ladies who had heretofore ignored her were now unexpectedly friendly, and several very great ladies who had merely stared at her before now condescended to smile and nod. Even the haughty Mrs. Drummond Burrell unbent far enough to wish her a good evening as she, Lady Spicer, and Sir Geoffrey were leaving the assembly rooms at the close of the evening. In spite of these triumphs, however, Miss Denny left Almack's in a mood not far removed from dejection.

The evening had not gone at all as she had hoped. To begin with, she had witnessed a further deterioration in the relations between Sir Geoffrey and her sister. Although Sir Geoffrey had passed the entire evening in the cardroom, some word of Lord Henry's attentions to his wife seemed to have reached him even in that stronghold, or perhaps he had merely witnessed Lord Henry's protracted farewell to Lady Spicer as she was stepping into the carriage. In any case, Sir Geoffrey had entered the carriage looking like a storm cloud and had maintained a complete and discouraging silence all the way to St. James's Square.

"I'll be in the library. Bring me a bottle of brandy and see that I'm not disturbed," he ordered the butler as soon as they reached home. Having given these orders, he excused himself curtly to his wife and sister-in-law and shut himself in the library.

"And there he may stay, for all I care," said Lady Spicer, angrily regarding the library door. "You see what I must endure, Judith? It is infamous that Geoffrey should treat me this way— absolutely infamous."

"I think he is merely upset, Fanny," said Miss Denny, striving to be diplomatic. "I think perhaps he disliked seeing Lord Henry pay you such particular attentions. You know he did hold your hand a rather long time when he was helping you into the carriage."

Lady Spicer tossed her head. "Well, what of it? You notice Geoffrey didn't lift a finger to help me! Indeed, if I had not sent a servant to call him, he would still be in the cardroom."

"Yes, but I do not think he would have gone to the cardroom in the first place if you had not been so—well, I can only call it flirtatious, Fan. As soon as Lord Henry came up, you completely ignored Geoffrey to flirt with him."

Lady Spicer looked self-conscious, but shook her head stubbornly. "If Geoffrey does not like my flirting with Henry, why does he not flirt with me himself?" she demanded with a sniff. "The truth is that men are dogs in the manger, Judith. They never want anything unless they think someone else wants it." She gave another sniff, this one sounding more like a sob. "And if Geoffrey really minded my flirting with Henry, he would do something about it rather than go off to the card-room.''

Miss Denny recognized that with this statement, they had reached the crux of the issue. "Perhaps Sir Geoffrey thinks you prefer Lord Henry's company to his,'' she said, speaking carefully. "You know he is a rather proud man, Fanny. It might go against the grain with him to feel he had to compete for his wife's attention.''

Lady Spicer folded her lips stubbornly. "So too am I proud—too proud to beg for attention from my own husband. The truth is that Geoffrey no longer cares for me, Judith. If he did, he would not spend all his time at his club and shut himself away from me the few hours he does pass at home.''

"But perhaps that is only because he thinks you do not care for him, Fanny—not because he does not care for you.''

"It comes to the same thing, Judy. I have always found that if a man really cares for one, the idea of competition does not daunt him but merely puts him on his mettle.''

"Yes, perhaps that is true during courtship. But you and Sir Geoffrey are married,'' said Miss Denny, stumbling a little as she sought to express her feelings. "If I were a man, I think I would dislike it if I felt I had to continually compete for my own wife's attention.''

Lady Spicer laughed, a hollow sound that had little of real mirth about it. "But you are not a man, Judy. You are judging by your own feelings as a woman, and I assure you that men feel differently. Half of what made me desirable to Geoffrey in the first place was knowing I was desirable to other men. If I had behaved like a perfect Griselda from the time we were married and refused to dance or flirt with anyone else, do you think it would have made him like me better? No, I am sure he would have tired of me years earlier than he did.''

Although Miss Denny had no way of refuting these arguments, she felt strongly that her sister was mistaken. In fact, she was beginning to feel her sister might be mistaken about other matters than these. And in no matter had she been so mistaken as in her advice about the Duke.

There was no denying it. The evening at Almack's had been

a disaster from beginning to end, at least so far as the Duke was concerned. Miss Denny knew, as certainly as if she had been able to read the Duke's thoughts, that he had been disappointed in her. And it was Lady Spicer's advice that had caused all the trouble. Of course, there was no saying that the Duke might not have been disappointed in her anyway, even had she behaved like her normal self. Miss Denny recognized this, but still she thought she would have preferred to disappoint him honestly, rather than be faulted for a character that was not hers.

Over and over she reviewed her conduct that evening, wincing at the memory of every stiff phrase and trite expression. The Duke must have thought her unpardonably stupid—or worse yet, unpardonably hypocritical. He was, after all, an intelligent man, quite capable of guessing that she was playing a role that evening. If his reasoning had taken him this far, it could be only a matter of time before he guessed what the motive for her behavior must have been.

This idea struck Miss Denny with terrible force. Until now, it had never occurred to her how ignoble her conduct was. She had been deliberately exploiting the Duke's acquaintance for her own social gain. And if, as she feared, he was astute enough to guess what she had been doing, she could not doubt he would despise her for it. She well remembered the curl of his lip when he had spoken those fateful words earlier in the evening: "I find myself avidly courted by people whom I actively despise."

There could be no question that she, with her sister, was now firmly classed in that category. Miss Denny shuddered when she recalled that moment at the end of the evening when Lady Spicer had tried to coax him into attending the Winchcombs' breakfast. It proved how little her sister understood him, if she could suppose such methods would succeed with him.

Miss Denny, on the other hand, felt she understood him only too well.

She had been quite sure he had been going to answer her sister's importunings with a well-deserved snub. Miraculously

he had abstained, but that only proved he was too much a
gentleman to give Lady Spicer the set-down her impertinence
had merited. As for his half-promise to attend the Venetian
breakfast, Miss Denny disregarded it as mere politeness. After
this evening's events, of course he would want nothing more
to do with her or any other member of her family.

This idea tended to depress Miss Denny much more than
the loss of a mere twice-met acquaintance should have done.
She scolded herself roundly for her foolishness, however. It was
unfortunate that she should have alienated the most agreeable
gentleman she had met in London thus far, but what was now
done could not be undone, and there was no use crying over
spilt milk. The thing to do would be to make sure such a disaster
never happened again. Miss Denny resolved that from now on,
she would conduct her personal affairs in accordance with her
own judgment rather than her sister's advice.

She felt much better when she had made this resolution. A
good night's sleep made her feel better still, and during the
days that followed she was able to shake off her depression
and take a moderate interest in the plans which her sister had
devised for her entertainment. The Season was now in full
swing, with balls, assemblies, and theater parties every night.
Miss Denny threw herself whole-heartedly into these pleasures,
and by the time the date of the Winchcombs' Venetian Breakfast
rolled around, she was able to congratulate herself on having
put the incident of the Duke largely behind her.

The Duke was not so lucky. On the drive home from
Almack's, he had made up his mind to think of Miss Denny
no more. She had proven to be merely an ordinary girl with
insipid manners, no conversation, and a vulgar, pushing sister.
As such, it was clearly his duty to put all thought of her out
of his mind. Yet in the days that followed he found himself
thinking of her almost constantly, and the sum total of his
thoughts was a feeling of intense frustration.

How was it possible that a young lady who had been so
charming one night could prove so totally insipid two nights
later? The Duke thought back over that first evening at the
Spicers' ball and the conversation he had had with Miss Denny.

Surely it was beyond the power of any young lady to feign such wit and exuberance!

But if wit and exuberance were Miss Denny's natural state, then why had she been so stiff and conventional at Almack's? Because she had the headache? For a time, the Duke tried valiantly to believe in Miss Denny's headache. But it was of no use. His common sense soon pointed out that Miss Denny had shown no signs of headache when she had been dancing with Mr. Manville. It was only when he himself had approached her that she had seemed seized by a sudden indisposition.

This idea opened up a whole new train of disagreeable reflections to the Duke. He could think of only two reasons why Miss Denny would have purposely been so stiff with him. The first was simple shyness—and that was possible, though the Duke felt it would have been more natural for her to be shy on their first meeting than on their second. The only other reason he could think of for Miss Denny's reserve was that she was trying, for some unknown reason, to discourage him. And that was plainly ridiculous.

"Why would she discourage me?" he asked himself over and over, during the days that followed the Almack's Assembly. "Surely she cannot believe I have designs on her virtue or anything of that nature! It would be insufferable egoism if she did, for I know dozens of women much better looking than she is—women whom I might have for the snap of my fingers. But it's equally ridiculous to suppose she would discourage me for any other reason. Her sister must have told her of the position I occupy in London society."

Certainly Fanny Spicer would not have neglected to mention to her sister how much good might come of the Duke of Ashland's patronage. The Duke remembered with distaste Lady Spicer's gushing manner and the bold way she had tried to inveigle him into attending the Winchcombs' breakfast. *Her* motives were clear enough, at any rate. It was only her sister's that were shrouded with mystery.

Or were they?

The Duke's brows snapped together suddenly as a thought occurred to him. Was it not possible that Fanny Spicer hoped to promote a match between him and her sister? Many less likely candidates had been put forward for his inspection, after all. And if that were the case, then Miss Denny's behavior might spring from a ladylike desire to spare him pain—because she had no intention of accepting him.

Of no other woman could the Duke have believed such a thing. He did not rate his personal attractions high, but ten years spent dodging the snares of matchmaking mamas, avaricious demi-reps, and flirtatious demoiselles had taught him what a glittering prize his wealth and title made him in feminine eyes. He had often cynically reflected that if he were to propose to any single woman of his acquaintance—no matter whom, or on what short notice—she would almost certainly find the temptation of becoming the Duchess of Ashland too much to resist.

But if ever there had been a young woman capable of resisting such temptation, that young woman was Miss Denny. The Duke could not have said how he knew this, but he felt that he did know it, and the knowledge both amused and offended him.

"I wonder if that's it?" he said to himself. "Chivalrous of her to hint me away, if so—but her chivalry is wasted in this instance. I have no intention of proposing to a country-bred girl with neither name nor countenance to recommend her. However, she is new to London, and her sister doubtless misled her. I can believe any folly of Fanny Spicer. Miss Denny cannot know how unlikely it is that I should propose to a girl just out of the schoolroom!"

When the Duke really considered the matter, however, he had to admit that Miss Denny's apprehensions were not so foolish as they appeared at first sight. He himself might know that he had no intention of proposing to her, but she could not know his thoughts. She had only his actions to judge by, and his actions in this instance had been rather equivocal. He could not remember the last time he had danced with any unmarried girl, let alone paid her the compliment of attending an Almack's Assembly on her account. Looking back on his conduct throughout his acquaintance with Miss Denny, the Duke saw he had been indiscreet. It would not be wonderful if wiser and more experienced heads than hers had been misled by his seeming partiality for her company.

Of course the mistake was easily remedied. He had only to stay away from Miss Denny in the future, and any gossip to which his imprudent behavior had given rise would soon die down of its own accord. The Duke was quite aware of all this, and was thus at a loss to explain why, as the appointed date drew near, he kept experiencing such a strong urge to attend the Winchcombs' Venetian Breakfast.

He tried hard to reason himself out of this urge. "I hate al fresco parties," he reminded himself on the morning of the party. "Invariably it rains, and this early in the year it's certain to be cold as well. And breakfast parties are my especial detestation. One always eats and drinks too much because there's nothing else to do, and then one is spoiled for anything else the rest of the day. Why should I wish to stand around shivering and courting dyspepsia in the Winchcombs' garden all afternoon? It's a nonsensical idea, and I won't give in to it."

Vexed with himself and his irrational weakness, he went down to the breakfast parlor and found therein more to vex him. His two cousins, Louisa and Philippa Montfort, were seated at the table, languidly consuming toast and tea. Normally the Duke rose and breakfasted early solely to avoid these ladies, whose personalities reacted on him in the manner of a strong abrasive.

"Good morning, James," said Louisa, raising a pallid hand in greeting. She was a fragile-looking woman in her mid-twenties with a scraggy figure and high, meager shoulders. In features and coloring she bore a strong resemblance to the Duke, a resemblance so exaggerated as to verge upon caricature. Louisa's skin and hair were not merely fair but virtually colorless, and the aquiline nose that gave the Duke's face so much character was in her intensified by a receding chin and sloping forehead. Her manners were invariably languid. She moved slowly, never raised her voice above a murmur, and was rarely seen to show emotion over anything.

Her elder sister Philippa possessed these same characteristics to an even greater degree. Philippa was a shade paler, a touch

thinner, and even more languid in her manner than Louisa. So
languid was she, indeed, that she seldom troubled herself to
speak at all, and Louisa generally acted as mouthpiece for them
both. This occasion was no exception. Where Louisa had wished
the Duke good morning and raised her hand in greeting, Philippa
merely smiled and fluttered her fingers, as though the effort to
fully lift her hand were too much for her.

"Good morning, Lou. And good morning to you, my dear
Phil. I wonder if I might trouble you to pour me a cup of
coffee?" said the Duke, regarding his elder cousin with sardonic
amusement. Although he knew it to be a futile effort, he could
never resist trying to shake her out of her languor.

"I'll pour your coffee for you, James. You must know Philippa is feeling rather poorly this morning," said Louisa, answering for her sister as usual. When she had poured a cup of coffee
and set it in front of the Duke, she folded her hands in her lap
and addressed him in a voice even lower than her habitual
murmur. "You must wonder at our being downstairs so early,
James. The fact is, there is something Philippa and I particularly
wanted to ask you."

"Oh, yes?" said the Duke, taking a sip of his coffee. "What
was it you and Phil wanted to ask me, Lou?" He always made
a point of addressing his cousins as Phil and Lou, finding humor
in attaching these masculine eponyms to two such exaggeratedly feminine ladies.

"Why, we wondered if you were going to the Winchcombs'
Venetian Breakfast this afternoon."

The Duke took another sip of coffee, stalling for time as he
thought rapidly. He knew his cousins well enough to be sure
their question was no idle inquiry. "I have considered attending
the Winchcombs' party," he answered at last, in a guarded
voice. "Why do you ask, Lou?"

"Why, we wondered if you might escort us there, James.
We were wanting to go, but you know how easily Philippa tires.
And today she is feeling rather poorly anyway, as I mentioned
before. We would both feel better if you were of our party, so
you might assist us if one or the other of us should feel unwell."

The Duke shook his head gravely. Ever since his cousins

had taken up residence in his home a few years before, they had been finding one reason or another why he ought to accompany them to social functions. He would have had no objection to lending them his escort now and then, had he not suspected them of ulterior motives. Louisa and Philippa were among those members of his family most vocal in urging him to marry and settle down, and the kind of lady they described as most suitable for him to marry invariably bore a striking resemblance to themselves. Having no desire whatever to encourage them in this ambition, the Duke generally found reason to avoid their company whenever possible.

Accordingly, he set about excusing himself from their current proposal. "But why invite me, Lou?" he said. "I should think Dr. Biggs would be a more useful addition to your party. Surely his assistance would be much more to the point than mine, if you fear you or Phil will be unwell."

Louisa sighed deeply, and even Philippa threw him a look of languid reproach. "Don't be ridiculous, James. It is not illness but merely fatigue which we anticipate. If you were there to give us your arm, I am sure we would manage perfectly well. Upon my word, I shall think you very disobliging if you refuse us this favor, James. I am sure you can have nothing else to do this afternoon."

The Duke hesitated, then took a sudden decision. "As a matter of fact, I do have a previous engagement, Lou. I have already promised to attend the Winchcombs' breakfast as a member of someone else's party."

Both ladies looked politely skeptical. "Oh, really?" said Philippa, speaking for the first time in her die-away voice. "You surprise me extremely, James. Whose party have you promised to join?"

"Fanny Spicer's," said the Duke reluctantly. He was already regretting his momentary impulse. He went on, however, in a dogged voice. "It was arranged more than a week ago that I would meet Fanny and her sister at the Winchcombs' this afternoon."

His cousins' reaction to this speech was exactly what he had anticipated. Their pale, delicately arched brows rose simultaneously on their high, sloping foreheads.

"Fanny Spicer!" exclaimed Louisa. "It is a new turn-out for you to be making one of *her* party, James!"

"Yes," said the Duke shortly. He hoped against hope that no more need be said on the subject, but was not really surprised when Louisa went on in a thoughtful voice.

"Fanny Spicer and her sister, you say. Why, that would be the Miss Denny I have been hearing so much about, wouldn't it? Do you know, James, I heard the most astonishing story concerning you and Miss Denny the other day. Barbara Blalock told me that you danced with her not once but twice at the Spicers' party, and then arranged to meet her at Almack's the other night, so that you might dance with her again. Did you ever hear anything so ridiculous?"

The Duke, goaded, had no choice but to contest this statement. "The story is quite true, Lou, as it happens. Though I don't know what business it is of anyone's if it is," he added aggressively.

Louisa gave him a pitying smile. "Really, James, you must know that your smallest move is subject to the most intense scrutiny. People of our station commonly are a source of interest and speculation to those of the lower classes, I believe. I must say, however, that in paying such particular attentions to Miss Denny, you were leaving yourself open for just that kind of ill-bred speculation. Why, Barbara actually had the gall to hint you might have serious intentions regarding this Miss Denny. You, the Duke of Ashland! Of course, I lost no time scotching *that* rumor. But if you continue to see the girl, you will only add fuel to the fire, as it were."

"Indeed, yes, James," said Philippa, adding her languid mite. "I am afraid that in agreeing to be of her party today, you were not thinking of the possible consequences."

"Much better you should have made up a party with us, if you had a desire to go to the Winchcombs'," agreed Louisa.

"Well, I am already committed to go with Miss Denny," said the Duke, pushing back his chair. "So I fear I must decline to take charge of the two of you this afternoon. And perhaps it's just as well," he added maliciously. "With the poor health you habitually enjoy, it is probably better that you stay home anyway."

This speech was by no means agreeable to the two ladies to whom it was addressed. "Nonsense, James. Chronic ill-health is a great cross, to be sure, but neither Philippa nor I consider it excuses us from doing our social duty," said Louisa firmly.

"Certainly not," agreed her sister. "I, for one, have always endeavored to carry on, no matter how great my sufferings."

"And so I do not at all see why we must miss the Winch-combs' party. Nor do I see why you cannot escort us there, James. Even if you cannot form one of our party, you can at least give us a seat in your carriage."

"Very well," said the Duke, resigning himself to the inevitable. Still, he could not resist a final, mischievous thrust. "I'm afraid, however, that you two ladies may find yourself a trifle cramped if you insist on going with me. It's such a fine day, I had planned to drive myself to the Winchcombs' in my curricle."

"The town carriage will be much more comfortable," said Louisa firmly. "I will speak to Norbury about it. Be ready to leave at two o'clock, James. The party begins at one, I believe, but Philippa and I dare not venture out so close to mid-day. The sun's rays are very injurious at that hour, you must know."

"Two o'clock will do very well," said the Duke, and escaped from the breakfast room before his cousins could impose on him further.

Chapter IX

After leaving his cousins, the Duke spent the rest of the morning ruing the impulse that had committed him to attending the Winchcombs' Venetian Breakfast.

It had been purely an impulse, as he assured himself. He had been eager to escape making one of his cousins' party and had seized upon the first excuse that came to mind. He certainly had no desire to sacrifice the best part of an afternoon at an al fresco breakfast party (a type of entertainment he abhorred), eating and drinking an assortment of indigestible viands in the company of a young woman whom he had resolved to avoid.

Yet as the morning wore on, he found himself consulting his watch more and more frequently, impatient of time's slow progress. At one o'clock, he went upstairs to dress for the party, though he knew this business would not occupy more than half an hour. At one twenty he was ready, attired in a blue Bath cloth topcoat and fawn-colored pantaloons, his neckcloth exquisitely tied, his boots beautifully glossy, and every hair in place. At one twenty-five he was seated in the downstairs hall waiting for his cousins, though it was fully half an hour before he could reasonably expect them. The Duke sat, consulting his watch every now and then and absently watching the comings and goings of his servants as they went about their household duties.

At one fifty-five he began casting impatient looks toward the staircase, expecting that any moment would bring his cousins down to join him. By five minutes past two he was feeling decidedly restive and sent a maidservant up to the ladies' rooms with word he was waiting for them. By a quarter past two he was pacing the hall impatiently, and when Louisa and Philippa finally came downstairs at twenty past two, they found him just quitting the house, having left word with his butler that he had decided to go on to the Winchcombs' and that his cousins might follow or not as they pleased in one of the other carriages.

"Why, James, how rude," said Louisa reproachfully, when she and her sister had been seated in the Duke's carriage and they were on their belated way to the Winchcombs'. "Whatever caused you to behave in such a hasty way? I believe if we had been five minutes later, you would have left without us."

"You are quite justified in that belief, Lou. Having called for the carriage at two o'clock, I did not feel inclined to keep either my coachman or my horses waiting for more than twenty minutes."

"Are we that late? We would have been earlier, only Philippa had a spasm while she was dressing, and I had to give her a dose of salts."

Philippa, who had been reclining on the banquette with her eyes closed, corroborated this statement with a nod and feeble smile. "But you might have known we would be down as soon as we could, James," continued Louisa. "I cannot think why you were so impatient to be off. Surely your Miss Denny is not so exacting that she would begrudge you twenty minutes?"

"I am sure she would not, if it were genuine illness that delayed me. Whether she would have much sympathy with Phil's malingering is another matter."

"Really, James," said Louisa, throwing him a look of reproach. Philippa merely closed her eyes with a martyred air and said nothing. The Duke, under cover of looking out the window, once more took out his watch and surreptitiously consulted it. He could not have said why he was so impatient

to arrive at the Winchcombs'. He had not agreed to meet Miss
Denny there at any set time. Indeed, he had been at pains to
impress on her that he might not come at all.

Yet when he thought that he might arrive at the Winchcombs'
to find Miss Denny already gone, he was assailed by a feeling
of panic. He told himself it was merely because he wished to
speak to her one more time, just to find out if he had been
correct in his conclusions. But he had no clear idea how he
planned to do this. He could scarcely ask Miss Denny outright
if she had treated him coolly at Almack's because she feared
he might force on her an unwelcome proposal of marriage. All
he could really do was to talk to her, observe her manner, and
try to gauge from that what had prompted her inexplicable
behavior the other night.

The Winchcombs' home lay in Chiswick, some miles outside
the city limits. The Duke and his cousins did not reach its
environs until after three o'clock. As the Duke assisted Louisa
and Philippa from the carriage, he fretted that he might not be
in time to speak to Miss Denny. But he need not have worried.
Miss Denny and her sister had reached the Winchcombs' only
a short time before and had joined the party on the lawn less
than ten minutes before the Duke and his cousins arrived on
the scene.

Miss Denny had come to the party with only moderate expec-
tations of enjoyment. She had never attended a Venetian Breakfast before, so there was a measure of novelty in that, and she
was eager to see the Winchcombs' home and gardens, which
her sister had described to her in enthusiastic terms. There was
also enjoyment to be found in her dress for the occasion, a
delicate froth of peach-colored muslin worn with a velvet spen-
cer of slightly darker hue and a straw bonnet trimmed with
flowers and knots of ribbon. In her hand she carried an ivory
silk parasol which her sister had pressed upon her, fearing that
her bonnet should prove inadequate to shield her from the
sun's rays. But Miss Denny, surveying the overcast sky, felt
an umbrella would have been a more useful adjunct. She felt

sorry for the Winchcombs, who had obviously put a great deal of time and effort into planning their Venetian Breakfast.

The Winchcombs' home was a charming Palladian villa, built of stuccoed brick and standing in the midst of extensive gardens. A gaily-striped tent had been erected to house the refreshment tables, and another smaller tent sheltered the musicians who were doggedly working their way through a series of *scherzandi, divertimenti,* and *cassaziones.* To further the Venetian theme, Mrs. Winchcomb had gone so far as to place gondolas on the narrow, algae-laden canal that bisected the lawn. A pair of embarrassed-looking rustics in doublets and plumed hats stood ready at the oars, proclaiming their willingness to pilot anyone who wished to go upon the water.

Few of the guests chose to take advantage of this offer, however. With the sun making only spasmodic appearances, the temperature of the day was definitely chilly, and most of the guests huddled about the lawn in dispirited groups, flinching under the assault of the wind that came gusting across the lawn from the east, ruffling the ladies' skirts and sending an occasional gentleman chasing after his hat.

Miss Denny did not mind the wind or the chill. She was more warmly dressed than the majority of the female guests, many of whom had chosen to wear nothing more than a thin scarf or shawl draped over their muslin dresses. She was, moreover, accustomed to the harsher climate of Derbyshire, where it had been her habit to take outdoor exercise in all weathers. "Are we not going to look around the gardens?" she asked impatiently, as her sister paused beneath the entrance awning.

"Oh, Judith, it's too cold to walk around in this awful wind," said Lady Spicer, drawing her shawl around her shoulders with a shiver. "Let us get something to eat and drink first, and perhaps by then the wind will have died down a bit."

Miss Denny glanced toward the refreshment tent, where a pair of distracted-looking footmen were endeavoring to keep the cups, saucers, and napkins from blowing off the table. "I'm not hungry just now," she said. "Besides, it looks as though it will be raining before long, Fanny. I think we had better see the gardens while we can."

"I'm sorry, Judith, but it's simply too cold to go walking around. If I am to survive at all, I shall have to stay here by the house, where there's at least a little shelter from the wind."

"I told you you should have worn something warmer," said Miss Denny, casting a disapproving eye over her sister's primrose gauze dress and cobweb shawl. "But you know if you were walking about, you would probably feel the cold less, Fanny. Nothing makes you colder than just standing."

"Nevertheless, I prefer to remain here," returned Lady Spicer, huddling deeper into her shawl. "I don't care to become windburned and blowsy for the sake of feeling a little warmer."

"Then I hope you don't mind if I go and see the gardens by myself, Fanny. I shall think myself ill-used to be brought all the way to Chiswick only to stand around and shiver."

Lady Spicer raised only a feeble protest to this speech, being too much occupied in rearranging her shawl over her bare shoulders in a vain attempt to warm them. Miss Denny took leave of her therefore, and set off across the lawn at a brisk pace, rejoicing in her successful escape. She was not sorry to be spared the tedium of another social gathering. During the past week she and Lady Spicer had attended at least one party every night, and already Miss Denny was beginning to tire of smiling and making social chit-chat with people with whom she had nothing in common.

If she could have found someone like the Duke to talk to, of course, it would have been different. But the Duke had said he could not attend the Winchcombs' party that afternoon, and Miss Denny had no expectation of seeing him. Indeed, she had no expectation of seeing him again at any time during her London stay. He had so clearly been disgusted by her manners that evening at Almack's that he would doubtless take pains to avoid her in the future.

Miss Denny was determined not to repine over the Duke's defection, but still she could not help feeling rather blue when she thought of it. She had not found so many congenial companions in London that she could spare even one, especially when that one was as pleasant and amusing as the duke had been. Mr. Manville was very pleasant, too, of course, but it was tiresome to have to explain every joke she made two or three times before he could understand it. The Duke had known immediately when she was joking and had not hesitated to respond in kind.

Really, it was a pity he could no longer be counted a friend. Miss Denny walked slowly now, reflecting on this unfortunate state of affairs. She had almost reached the edge of the canal when she heard her name called from behind.

"Miss Denny?"

Miss Denny turned around and saw the Duke coming toward her. All of a sudden she felt as though the sun had come out, although the clouds overhead remained as dense and threatening as ever. She stood beside the canal, a slow smile dawning on her face, as the Duke came over to join her.

"Your Grace," she said, curtsying. "I had not expected to see you here today. Did your other engagement fall through?"

"Yes, in a manner of speaking. Perhaps it would be more accurate to say I thought better of it," said the Duke. He was delighted to see Miss Denny smiling and speaking to him in her old friendly manner, just as she had done at the Spicers' ball. It was curious what an effect her smile had on him. Only a moment ago he had been cursing the wind and the cold, but now he felt in a perfect glow of good spirits, quite impervious to the weather.

Miss Denny looked pleased by his words but also rather dubious. "You must be wondering now if it was a better thought after all, your Grace," she said, with a shake of her bonneted head. "I'm afraid it's not a very nice day for an outdoor party."

"No, but I intend to make the best of it now I am here," returned the Duke. "And I do not doubt it will be a very enjoyable afternoon—assuming, of course, that you will allow me the pleasure of your company."

He looked down at Miss Denny as he spoke. Something in his expression made her cheeks suffuse with color. "Why, certainly, your Grace," she said shyly. In an impulsive rush, she added, "As a matter of fact, I was just thinking about you and wishing you were here."

"Really?" said the Duke in surprise. "I wondered what you were thinking of, walking along so somberly all by yourself. But I had made up my mind it must be something quite serious and solemn—the state of the King's health, perhaps, or the proposed amendment in the Corn Tax."

Miss Denny could not help smiling, though her color had heightened further at this speech. "No, it was you, your Grace," she said. "I was thinking that I would probably never see you again, after the gooseish way I behaved at Almack's last Wednesday."

The candor of this speech took the Duke's breath away. This was the Miss Denny he remembered from her sister's ball: the Miss Denny who had frankly confessed to snubbing him and had managed to both charm and disarm him in the process. This was an admission still more disarming, and the Duke was forced to admit it was very charming, too. Indeed, for a moment he felt a mad impulse to grasp Miss Denny's hand and respond with a speech that was definitely imprudent. He stifled the impulse, however, and managed to return a light laugh.

"It would be unchivalrous for me to let such a statement pass," he said. "You were certainly a trifle subdued at Almack's, but not what I would call gooseish."

Miss Denny shook her head mournfully. "Gooseish," she repeated with a sigh. "Your Grace must have been quite disgusted with me."

"No, but I will confess to having been rather surprised." The Duke gave her a searching look. "May I ask what it was that prompted your want of spirits? I know you claimed to have a headache, but I wondered at the time if there might not be another explanation."

Miss Denny gave him a quick, shy smile. "Yes, there was. Fanny had been lecturing me, you see—about your being a duke, and about my having behaved with a want of proper respect toward you at my coming-out ball. And so I was feeling rather oppressed that evening. Whenever I looked at you, I seemed to see you surrounded by an aura of ermine and strawberry leaves. It made it very difficult to carry on a conversation!''

"I imagine that it might," said the Duke, smiling. "But you must know I save the ermine and strawberry leaves for state occasions, Miss Denny. They are hardly appropriate wear for balls, and you see I also eschew them for breakfast parties."

Miss Denny laughed. "Yes, of course. As I say, I was a goose that evening, your Grace. I don't intend to behave so ever again."

The Duke was entertained by this ingenuous speech. "I am glad to hear it," he said gravely. "I am really not such an awe-inspiring personage, you know."

Miss Denny gave him another shy smile. "Well, but you are, you know," she said candidly. "I don't feel it so much at the moment, but when I see people bowing and scraping to you and treating you like royalty, it is hard not to take the infection. However, I am determined not to let it affect me in the future." She gave him another smile, this one tinged with mischief. "From now on I am resolved to think of you as a quite ordinary gentleman—a superior shopkeeper's assistant, perhaps, whom I am not afraid to order about according to my whim."

The Duke laughed. "I will be delighted to take orders from you, Miss Denny. Have you any commissions for me at present?"

"Yes, you may give me your arm, so I can explore these lovely gardens. Let us go over and look at those gondolas, to begin with."

"To be sure, ma'am," responded the Duke, offering his arm with a servile air that made Miss Denny laugh. Together they strolled over to the head of the canal, where the gondola men stood leaning dispiritedly on their oars.

"Care for a ride, sir?" one of them offered, with a tentative bow. "Glad to take you and the lady aboard, if you'd like."

The Duke regarded Miss Denny with a smile. "The decision must be the lady's. She and she alone is ordering our movements at present. What do you say, Miss Denny? Shall we risk the canal?"

Miss Denny looked with interest at the exotic craft bobbing on the canal. "Yes, I think so," she said. "I have never ridden in a gondola before, and I don't suppose I shall ever have another chance. Besides, it must be very vexing to Mrs. Winchcomb, to have gone to all the trouble of providing gondolas for her guests and then have no one use them. It would make her feel much better if we went for a ride."

"I suppose so," said the Duke, surveying without enthusiasm the brackish water at his feet. "I only hope we may not be rewarded for our philanthropy by being dumped into this filthy canal."

Miss Denny said cheerfully that he was a great deal too nice. "The water is not filthy at all, only a trifle stagnant. I don't suppose it would hurt us a particle if we fell in. In any event, I consider it our duty to take the risk, your Grace. For I expect that if you are seen taking a ride, the other guests will come and do it, too."

"A case of *noblesse oblige,* in fact," said the Duke gravely. "Very well, Miss Denny, but with your permission I will fetch us some champagne before we venture on this risky enterprise. I would like to be fortified a trifle before I step aboard one of those singularly unseaworthy-looking craft."

Miss Denny graciously gave her permission and waited by the canal while the Duke went to fetch champagne from the refreshment tent. He returned a minute later carrying a glass in each hand and a bottle tucked under his arm.

"You must have qualms indeed about this business if you require as much fortification as all that," said Miss Denny, surveying the bottle beneath his arm with amusement. "I would not have supposed you the type to take refuge in Dutch courage, your Grace."

"Indeed, yes. I'm an awful craven at heart, Miss Denny," the Duke assured her meekly as he assisted her into the gondola and took his place beside her. The gondola man stepped ponderously aboard, pushed off from shore with his oar, and the gondola began to move down the canal.

Miss Denny smiled at the Duke. "There, you see, your Grace? Your fears were quite unjustified. We have neither of us been so much as splashed thus far."

"No, but it's early days yet," returned the Duke. Having deftly extracted the stopper from the champagne bottle, he filled the glasses and handed one to Miss Denny. "Is the experience of riding in a gondola all you had hoped for?" he inquired.

"Well, it would probably be more romantic if we were in Venice, on our way to a masked ball," said Miss Denny, cautiously sampling her champagne. "But since I'm never likely to get to Venice, this will have to do. It's rather nice, isn't it?"

"It would be nicer if it were about twenty degrees warmer," said the Duke. Yet his complaint was only half-hearted. Even with an east wind chilling the air, there was something very agreeable about sitting in a gondola beside Miss Denny. He took a drink of his own champagne, admiring the trim lines of her figure and the golden-brown curls framing her piquant little face. It struck him that she looked very pretty in her peach dress and flower-trimmed bonnet, and he said so. "You must allow me to compliment you on your toilette, Miss Denny. You look eminently suited to a garden party—quite like a flower yourself."

Miss Denny gave him a look of surprised pleasure. "Why, thank you, your Grace. That is a very pretty compliment. I have never been likened to a flower before." She took another sip of champagne and looked toward the refreshment tent, where the majority of the guests were still huddled. "Really, when you think of it, all of us look like flowers," she said reflectively. "All of us ladies, that is. Fanny is a primrose in her pale yellow, and Mrs. Fulbright a poppy in that gorgeous red. And Lady McKearney is a rather imposing heliotrope." She turned a smile upon the Duke. "It is only the gentlemen who spoil the prospect. You are more ornamental than most, your Grace, but even so I cannot say you look like a flower."

"No, I suppose not," said the Duke meekly. "I must atone for my want of aesthetic value by making myself useful. May

I give you some more champagne? It isn't very good champagne, I'm afraid, but after the first glass one's palate mercifully becomes inured.''

"I don't see that it's any nastier than any other champagne," said Miss Denny, holding out her glass to be refilled. "Call me a rustic if you like, but I've never been able to understand why people like the stuff. I much prefer lemonade."

"That's because you've never had good champagne," said the Duke with authority. "If you had, you would most certainly prefer it to lemonade, Miss Denny! I must make it a point to bring you a bottle from my own cellars sometime."

Miss Denny laughed. "I daresay I should still prefer lemonade, your Grace. But I thank you for the offer all the same. Shall we get out here? The canal doesn't seem to go any farther, and there's a fountain over there I'd like to have a look at."

"As you wish," said the Duke promptly. "You know it is my pleasure today to gratify your every whim." Having assisted Miss Denny from the gondola, he stepped out himself, bestowing a coin on the gondola man, who bowed and swept off his plumed hat.

"Now where shall we go?" he asked Miss Denny. "What was it you wanted to look at?"

"The fountain first," said Miss Denny, scrutinizing the landscape around her. "And there are some statues and things over there that look very interesting, too."

The Duke gave her his arm, and together they strolled over to survey the fountain, a lofty structure laden with dolphins and water nymphs. From there they descended a flight of steps into a sunken Italian garden ornamented with urns and classical statuary.

"Very pretty," said Miss Denny, looking around her with approval. "Imagine having all this on one's own grounds. At home we have only a rather dampish shrubbery to walk in and no gardens to speak of except kitchen ones."

"And where is home?" asked the Duke. "I don't think I ever heard where you came from, Miss Denny. Indeed, I have always assumed you were a gift sent directly from the gods."

Miss Denny laughed. "Hardly that," she said with a shake of her head. "My origins are much more prosaic, your Grace. And much more obscure—even if I were to tell you where I came from, I doubt you would be any the wiser." Pressed by the Duke, however, she obliged with a description of Winfield and its surroundings.

"My father is rector of the parish church there," she explained. "Winfield itself is very small, but it's a nice place, I think. Of course I may be prejudiced in having lived there all my life. This visit to London is the first time I have been out of Derbyshire."

"Is it indeed?" said the Duke, amused by her candor. "And what do you think of London so far, Miss Denny?"

Miss Denny considered. "I like it very well, for the most part. I think I would like it better if Fanny were not so determined to see me a social success. It is very exhausting trying to be a social success, I find. There are so many rules to remember." She gave the Duke a sidelong smile. "I'm afraid I have been breaking most of the rules today, your Grace. I must trust you not to betray me to Fanny."

"Certainly you may trust me not to do that, but what rules have you broken?" said the Duke. "It seems to me that your behavior has been exemplary."

"Oh, no," Miss Denny assured him. "I have made half-a-dozen blunders at the very least."

"Name them," said the Duke, with a disbelieving smile.

Miss Denny began to count upon her fingers. "Let's see . . . I ought not to have said I prefer lemonade to champagne. That made me sound a perfect provincial, which I am, of course, but I ought to be trying to conceal it. Then I ought not to have told you about my coming from Winfield, or about my father being rector there, or about our family being in such modest circumstances that we can afford only a shrubbery to walk in. I certainly ought not to have teased you about being afraid of the gondolas, and I put myself beyond reproach by telling you I intended to treat you like a shopkeeper's assistant. Fanny would lift up her hands in horror if she knew how I have been speaking to you."

The Duke hesitated before replying, not wishing to offend Miss Denny by seeming to criticize her sister. "Lady Spicer is no doubt erring on the side of caution," he said. "I am sure there are noblemen who insist on being treated with the utmost ceremony and who would be mortally offended if one were to omit the smallest observance due their rank. I am not one of that number, however. Pomp and patronage are commodities I can very well do without—indeed, there are times when I find the constraints of my position very tiresome. It is quite refreshing to be treated like a shopkeeper's assistant for a change, Miss Denny. I have been enjoying your company very much, I assure you."

"I'm glad," said Miss Denny, sounding unwontedly shy. She soon recovered herself, however, and went on in a thoughtful voice. "I suppose it must be rather tiresome to be a duke sometimes. I had never really considered the matter before, but now I have been around you a bit, I can see how you might tire of having people grovel in front of you only because of your title."

The Duke laughed. "Yes, but I do not mean to complain, Miss Denny. It is as I told you before: there are advantages to being a duke as well as disadvantages. Whenever my position grows tiresome, for instance, I can console myself by reflecting that I am spared the cost of postage by being able to frank all my letters."

"That's an advantage, certainly," agreed Miss Denny with affected solemnity. "Why, it is full twopence merely to send a note across Town! But I am sure there must be more material advantages to being a duke than that, your Grace."

"It depends what you term advantages. If I had any taste for politics, for instance, I might find consolation in the fact that I can sit in Parliament without taking the trouble to win a seat."

"And that is no small perquisite, your Grace, as I am in a position to tell you. My elder brother has parliamentary ambitions, and when our borough came open last year it cost him near three hundred pounds to stand for election."

"Have you a brother in parliament? I did not know it," said the Duke, regarding Miss Denny with interest.

Miss Denny shook her head sadly. "No, he ended up losing in spite of the three hundred pounds. Just between you and me, we are convinced there was foul play on the part of his opponent, though we have no means of proving it. But that ought to show you how fortunate you are to have a seat without the trouble and expense of campaigning for it, your Grace. And as a Lord, you have also the privilege of attending royal levees, and of having an excellent seat for such events as coronations and royal weddings."

"Yes, if you count that as a privilege," said the Duke without enthusiasm. "Had you ever attended a royal levee, you might rather term it an infernal bore."

"Well, I do count it as a privilege. You are merely spoiled, your Grace, and have come to see only the disadvantages pertaining to your position rather than the advantages. Why, only think: if your Grace meets an earl or marquess coming through the door, by rights he must stand aside and give you the precedence!"

"If I cared for such things, that would be a very gratifying reflection, certainly," agreed the Duke gravely. "What other advantages do I take for granted, Miss Denny?"

Miss Denny solemnly began to enumerate all the advantages pertaining to the ducal state as they appeared to her. The Duke listened with an appreciative grin and was frequently betrayed into a chuckle as the list grew ever more inventive. "Last but not least, you may ornament all your possessions with coronets and be perfectly proper," said Miss Denny, producing this final point with the air of one clinching an argument. "I am sure that if I were a duke, I would have coronets emblazoned on every object I owned."

The Duke laughed. "Then you would be delighted with Ashland Palace, Miss Denny. My ancestor, the First Duke, followed that policy wholesale in building and decorating the Palace. There are ducal coronets everywhere, even on the— er—bedroom vessels. Truth to tell, I have always questioned whether their presence on such objects might be construed as something less than a compliment to my rank!''

Miss Denny laughed. "I should think you might," she agreed. "But I expect your ancestor saw nothing to object to. People seem not to have had much sense of humor in the old days. Do you really live in a palace?''

"Yes—part of the time, at least. I have several homes, but Ashland Palace is my principal one.''

A dim memory stirred in Miss Denny's mind: an image of a vast battlemented building depicted in some long-ago book of famous residences. "I've heard of it, I think," she said. "Is it not a very grand and historic house?''

"Yes, and a very uncomfortable one. Everything in it was designed for appearances, you see. As a monument to the glory of the Dukes of Ashland it is very effective, but as a mere human residence it falls a long way short of the ideal. I am sure my own cottagers live more comfortably.''

Miss Denny shook her head reprovingly. "And I am sure you are exaggerating, your Grace. It is only that you are spoiled, as I said before. If you want to experience discomfort, you ought to try growing up in a drafty old rectory with five brothers and sisters! Not that I mean to complain," she added conscientiously. "I'm sure I was always very happy living at home, but now I have seen Fanny's house I can see why Mama used to sigh about ours now and then. The rectory really is the most rackety, old-fashioned place, quite lacking in modern conveniences.''

"If so, it's cut from the same piece of cloth as Ashland Palace," said the Duke firmly. "You would find yourself quite at home there, Miss Denny—except I daresay your rectory is much more comfortable.''

"And I am sure it is no such thing," returned Miss Denny. She and the Duke argued this matter amicably for some minutes, drinking champagne as they strolled arm in arm through the gardens. At last, having finished all the champagne and seen everything Miss Denny wished to see, they began to retrace their steps toward the house.

"Why, look at that, your Grace. It looks as though the sun's trying to come out," said Miss Denny, pointing to a patch of blue that had appeared among the clouds. "I believe this day may not turn out so badly after all."

"I'm quite sure of it," said the Duke, drawing her arm more firmly within his own.

Chapter X

When the Duke and Miss Denny reached the lawn surrounding the house, they found it occupied by a more animated party than the one they had left an hour before.

With the sun's reappearance, the temperature of the day had grown measurably warmer, and the guests who had been huddled around the tents were now strolling through the gardens or scattered in merry groups across the lawn. A party of ladies and gentlemen was just disembarking from the gondolas, while a group of others stood at the edge of the canal ready to take their places. A stiff breeze was still blowing, but its direction had changed around to the south, and when it snatched the hat from the head of some male guest or swept away the shawl or scarf of some female one, the circumstance provoked only laughter.

A young gentleman in pursuit of his wind-borne headgear almost barreled into the Duke and Miss Denny as they approached the refreshment tent. "Here you are," said the Duke, deftly capturing the runaway hat. He accepted the young gentleman's breathless thanks with a smile and a nod, then turned to Miss Denny. "After all that walking, you must be in need of refreshment, Miss Denny. May I get you something from the refreshment tent?"

"I *am* getting hungry," admitted Miss Denny. "That would be very kind of your Grace. And perhaps after we have eaten, we might look around a bit more. Fanny says the Winchcombs have a trellis garden that is very pretty, and we haven't seen that yet."

"I will be happy to accompany you to the trellis garden or anywhere else you like," the Duke assured her with a smile, as they went together toward the refreshment tent. "You know I am yours to command this day, Miss Denny, just as you choose."

The refreshment tent proved to contain an elegant light repast: oyster patties, lobster salad, sandwiches, cakes, creams, ices, and jellies, together with champagne, punch, tea, and lemonade to drink. "I will have some of the ratafia cream, please, and a couple of those cakes," said Miss Denny, casting a knowledgeable eye over the table. "Oh, yes, and a bit of the flummery—and a few of those little strawberry tartlets."

"I perceive that you are fond of sweets, Miss Denny," said the Duke gravely, as he filled a plate in obedience to these instructions. "Don't you want a sandwich or two to round things off?"

"No, thank you. I would rather have the sweet things. I *like* sweet things." Miss Denny gave him a defiant look. "And don't tell me I shouldn't, because I already know it."

"I wouldn't dream of telling you anything of the kind," said the Duke, regarding her with amusement. "You ought to know your own taste best, after all. Why shouldn't you have sweets if you want them?"

"Well, Fanny says I eat too many," said Miss Denny, mollified by this speech. "She eats hardly any sweet things herself because she is afraid of putting on flesh. But I am too thin anyway, so I don't see what it matters even if I were to put on flesh—which I never do, alas. It is a great trial, being so thin."

"I don't think you're too thin," said the Duke, looking down at her. "I think you're the perfect size—for you." Becoming conscious that this was a rather particular speech for a gentleman to address to a lady acquaintance, he hurried on. "In any case, my concern was more that you should make yourself sick than that you should make yourself fat."

"Oh, I am never sick," Miss Denny assured him. "Even Fanny's chef's cooking doesn't make me sick, although the way he drenches everything in sauces and cream and odd spices is enough to put me off my appetite now and then. I don't wonder Sir Geoffrey prefers to dine at his club."

The Duke observed a pensive look on Miss Denny's face as she spoke these words. He said nothing, but helped her establish herself on a nearby bench with her plate of cakes and creams and a glass of lemonade. Having returned to the refreshment tent to fetch a few cakes and sandwiches for himself, he joined her on the bench. "Now tell me why you look so thoughtful all at once," he said. "Is something troubling you? I hope you will tell me honestly and not put me off as you did the other night."

Miss Denny gave him a fleeting smile. "Oh, the other night! I do apologize for that, your Grace. That was merely because Fanny had been scolding me, as I told you before. It is possible I took her criticisms too much to heart."

"Much too much to heart," agreed the Duke in a dry voice. "Your sister would do well not to be so busy on your behalf, Miss Denny. In my opinion, you might better give her lessons in conduct than receive them of her."

"No, indeed! I am sure my conduct is far from perfect," protested Miss Denny. She threw the Duke a worried look. "May I ask why you say that about Fanny's conduct, your Grace? Is it—have you heard something about her? Something to her discredit?"

"No," said the Duke, surprised by this question. "I have heard nothing of Lady Spicer beyond the things one might expect to hear of any lady of her position. I know that she dresses well, and gives extravagant parties, and is rumored to have a flock of admirers. But none of those things is to her discredit in any way. Why do you ask?" He looked searchingly at Miss Denny.

Miss Denny hesitated, then shook her head. "It's nothing,"

she said. "I only wondered." Resolutely she took up a cake and bit into it.

The Duke watched her eat the cake, a slight frown on his face. "Of course I do not mean to force your confidence," he said, after a moment or two had gone by. "But if you have something you want to talk about, I would be glad to listen. That is what friends are for, you know, and I trust we may qualify as friends by now, Miss Denny. I hope so, at any rate." In a more jocular tone, he added, "If risking my life in that gondola was not an act of disinterested friendship, I don't know what would be! But it will all be in vain if you don't trust me."

Miss Denny looked distressed. "Oh, but I do trust you, your Grace," she protested. "It's only that I do not wish to bore you with my personal difficulties."

"I think I can answer for not being bored, Miss Denny. That is an emotion I have never yet felt in your company."

Miss Denny gave him a glowing smile. "And I can return the compliment, your Grace. I have greatly enjoyed your company, I assure you. But this is a very delicate matter which concerns other people than myself. Much as I would like to confide in you, I am not sure that it would be right to do so."

"That must be for your own conscience to decide," said the Duke. "I can only say that if you did choose to make me your confidant, you might rely on my absolute discretion."

Miss Denny contemplated the Duke for a moment or two with a look of indecision. "I think perhaps I *will* tell you," she said at last. "I would like very much to get someone else's opinion about this business. The truth is that I am rather worried about Fanny—about Fanny and her husband. Or perhaps it would be more accurate to say I am worried about Fanny and Lord Henry Nathorp."

"Ah," said the Duke with comprehension. "And that is why you asked if I had heard talk about her conduct."

"Yes," assented Miss Denny. She raised searching eyes to the duke's face. "Has there been gossip about her and Lord Henry?"

The Duke took his time responding to this question. "I do

not know that I am the best person to answer that, Miss Denny. I have certainly heard talk about Lord Henry's interest in your sister, but whether or not she is held to reciprocate that interest, I could not say. I do not often frequent the same society as your sister, you see, and so I am not in a position to hear what the gossips say about her.''

"I see," said Miss Denny, looking dejected.

The Duke regarded her with sympathy, wishing he had some word of comfort to give her. "I should be inclined myself to doubt that your sister favors Lord Henry above her other admirers. Have you reason to believe that she does?''

Miss Denny shook her head despondently. "I don't know. I don't think she favors him, exactly—indeed, I am quite sure that in her heart of hearts she doesn't care a fig for him. But I cannot deny that she encourages him. It is that which makes the situation so frustrating.''

"Oh, yes?" said the Duke. "But if she does not care for Lord Henry—''

"Yes, but Sir Geoffrey thinks she does," explained Miss Denny. "You must know that he dislikes seeing Lord Henry flirt with Fanny. And Fanny knows he dislikes it—but she holds that jealousy is good for Sir Geoffrey and will make him a more attentive husband. But instead, it makes Sir Geoffrey think she doesn't care for him at all. And so he spends all his time at his club—and Fanny flirts with Lord Henry all the harder, trying to make him pay attention! It is all an awful muddle.''

"It sounds it," said the Duke, smiling a little. "Rather like the plot of a Shakespearean comedy.''

"Yes, it does, doesn't it?" said Miss Denny, smiling a little in her turn. In a thoughtful voice, she added, "I believe the main problem is that Fanny has such a tortuous mind. If she would just speak out and tell Geoffrey what she wants him to do, I am convinced he would do it, for he loves her, I know. But instead she tries to manipulate him into doing what she wants through all this plotting and counterplotting. Of course I have never been in her situation, but if it were me, I think I would prefer to have everything open and honest and aboveboard. Intriguing takes such a lot of time and effort. It just seems to me there are more enjoyable ways to spend one's time.''

The Duke regarded her silently for a moment. Then he reached over, took her hand, and raised it to his lips. ''I could not agree with you more, Miss Denny,'' he said. ''You are a woman in a thousand.''

Miss Denny was surprised by this display, but did not allow herself to show it. ''What, because I have no taste for intrigue?'' she said with a gurgle of laughter. ''It's probably a sign of laziness or of an inferior intellect, your Grace.''

''That is unkind, Miss Denny, considering I just claimed to share your taste!''

Miss Denny laughed again and shook her head. ''Ah, but you men are generally held to be simple, straightforward creatures anyway,'' she explained with a sparkling smile. ''A want of scheming instinct cannot be held to be as degrading in you as in us.''

The Duke, looking into her smiling face, felt an odd sensation in his breast. He opened his mouth to speak, then shut it again. Miss Denny, meanwhile, had been distracted by the sight of her sister moving through the crowd.

''Oh, here is Fanny now,'' she told the Duke in a low voice. ''It doesn't look as though Lord Henry is with her today at any rate, for which I must be grateful.'' In a still lower voice, she added, ''I know you will not let what I have been saying go any further, your Grace. Perhaps I ought not to have spoken of it at all, but I must confess it has been a great comfort to talk it over with someone as sensible as you.''

''I'm glad,'' said the Duke. He had no time to say more, for Lady Spicer was already sweeping down upon them with a cry of triumph.

''Judith! Here you are, you wretched girl. You have been gone an age—a positive age, I vow and declare. I was growing quite worried about you. But I see I need not have worried. It's clear you have been in good company.'' Her eyes flashed from Miss Denny to the Duke, avidly taking in their proximity on the bench and the mute evidences of the empty plates and cups beside them.

The Duke was annoyed, but concealed it beneath a matter-of-fact manner. "Yes, your sister and I met while she was exploring the gardens," he said, rising to execute a brief but civil bow. "I hope I see you well, Lade Spicer?"

"Very well, your Grace," said Lady Spicer, smiling broadly and dropping him a curtsy. Turning to Miss Denny, she went on in an arch voice. "I need not ask Judith if she was pleased with the gardens. With such a companion, I should imagine her enjoyment was secure."

"I thought the gardens very beautiful," said Miss Denny politely.

As she was speaking, their party received another, still more unwelcome addition. The duke's cousins, all pale muslins and fluttering veils, came drifting up to where he and Miss Denny were sitting. Pointedly ignoring Miss Denny and her sister, Louisa addressed herself to the Duke.

"James, Philippa is feeling unwell again. I am afraid she never really recovered from that spasm she had earlier. Or perhaps it is only this vicious wind that has brought on another attack. Such an inclement day for an outdoor party! I never can understand why al fresco entertainments enjoy such popularity. If you would be good enough to order the carriage, I think we should get her home as soon as possible."

Philippa, leaning heavily on her sister's arm, smiled wanly and hung her head as though embarrassed to be such a bother. Miss Denny, who had never seen the Duke's cousins before, regarded the two of them with open amazement. The Duke scowled. He was annoyed that his cousins should interrupt him at such a moment for what he suspected was a trumped-up excuse, and he was even more annoyed by their pointed rudeness to Miss Denny. He spoke in clear, deliberate tones.

"Of course I will order the carriage if you feel it necessary, Lou. But before you and Phil go, I should like to make someone known to you. Phil, Lou, this is Miss Denny. You will remember my speaking of her only this morning. Lady Spicer you already know, I'm sure." He smiled briefly at Lady Spicer, then turned again to Miss Denny. "Miss Denny, these are my cousins Miss Montfort and Miss Louisa Montfort. They have been eager to make your acquaintance."

"I am pleased to make *your* acquaintance, Miss Montfort, Miss Louisa," said Miss Denny, smiling and rising from the bench to curtsy to the two ladies.

Louisa acknowledged Miss Denny's greeting with a cold smile and the words, "Charmed, I'm sure, Miss Denny." She did not acknowledge Lady Spicer's presence at all beyond a contemptuous flicker of her eyes. Philippa's response was still more feeble. She made the tiniest possible inclination of her head toward Miss Denny, then shut her eyes and sagged heavily on her sister's arm, as though the effort had been too much for her.

"I am afraid Philippa is growing worse every minute, James," said Louisa, regarding her sister with a concern the Duke suspected to be largely spurious. "We must not waste any more time in getting her to the carriage. If you would be so kind as to take her other arm—"

"Certainly I will be happy to assist her to the carriage, Lou. Unfortunately I cannot accompany the two of you home, as I have promised to show Miss Denny the Winchcombs' trellis garden later this afternoon. Perhaps when you and Phil reach home, you would be so kind as to send the carriage back for me."

Louisa looked shocked, and even Philippa re-opened her eyes to regard him with injured surprise. "But of course you must accompany us, James," said Louisa. "I cannot take care of poor Philippa by myself. Only think what would happen if she should have a spasm on the way home!"

"I fail to see what use I would be in such a contingency," said the Duke in an acid voice. "If you will remember what I said on the subject earlier today—"

He was interrupted, not by Louisa, but by Miss Denny. "Oh, your Grace, you must not think of staying on my account," she said earnestly. "If your cousins need you, then of course you must go. I can see the trellis garden on my own, you know. Or perhaps Fanny will be kind enough to accompany me there."

"Certainly," said Lady Spicer, though without enthusiasm. Turning to the Duke, she addressed him with a dazzling smile. "If you must go, your Grace, of course Judith and I will release you from your obligation, but I hope we will see you again soon. It would be delightful if you called upon us some morning. We will be at home Wednesday, I believe—or no, I think we are promised to the Bradleys that day. Another day, perhaps—"

"I doubt our cousin will be able to wait on you anytime this week, ma'am," said Louisa, regarding Lady Spicer with distaste. "You must know his affairs keep him very busy."

"But not so busy as to preclude my calling upon my friends," said the Duke smoothly. He looked down at Miss Denny, addressing her as though the other ladies were not present. "I have greatly enjoyed renewing our acquaintance this afternoon, Miss Denny. It is a pity we must cut our visit short, but I thank you for giving me as much of your company as you did."

"And I thank you for giving me yours," said Miss Denny. She looked almost shy as she spoke these words, but the next moment she smiled and extended her hand with the simple friendliness that was characteristic of her. "Good afternoon, your Grace. I hope I shall see you again soon."

"You may depend on it," said the Duke, and for the second time that afternoon raised her hand to his lips.

"Gracious," said Lady Spicer faintly. Philippa blinked, and Louisa gave a smothered gasp, but the Duke ignored them all. Releasing Miss Denny's hand, he turned to Philippa and Louisa.

"If we must go, then let us go. Ladies, your servant." Addressing a last warm smile to Miss Denny and a formal bow to Lady Spicer, he took Philippa by the arm and began to haul her briskly across the lawn.

Chapter XI

The Duke was rather silent on the drive home from the Winchcombs'. His cousins noticed his preoccupation and, in their languid way, tried to divert him.

"A most insipid party," observed Louisa, pushing aside her veil with a weary hand. "Did you not think so, James? I know everyone talks about the Winchcombs' parties, but for my part I have never seen where the attraction lay. The refreshments are invariably poor, the surroundings paltry, and when one considers that one must drive all the way to Chiswick to partake of all this mediocrity, it's a wonder to me anyone chooses to make the exertion. And Amelia Winchcomb is such an insufferably pretentious creature. I have no patience with these women who give themselves airs over nothing."

The Duke threw his cousin an amused glance, but said nothing. Louisa went on, sublimely unconscious of her own hypocrisy.

"Yes, a most wearisome party. There was scarcely anyone of consequence there besides ourselves. The general run of the guests was very low—very low indeed. Did you see that odious Mrs. Fulbright? Flaunting herself about in that glaring bright dress as though she were an actress or an opera dancer. And at her age, too—why, she must be thirty if she's a day."

"I have always thought Mrs. Fulbright an extremely handsome woman," said the Duke provocatively.

"Nonsense, how can you say so, James? She is quite an antidote, and the most pushing creature besides. You cannot really admire her, I am sure. And though I do not wish to offend you, I must say also that I could see nothing to admire in this Miss Denny you seem so taken with. She seemed to me a very commonplace kind of girl, with neither beauty nor countenance to recommend her."

"Miss Denny is not a conventional beauty, perhaps," said the Duke, choosing his words carefully. "But I should say myself she has a great deal of countenance."

"Nonsense, James," said Louisa with energy. "She is a little brown squab of a girl without any countenance at all. And I found her manners very pert—most disagreeably pert, indeed. I cannot see how you failed to remark it."

"And I fail to see how you *could* have remarked it, Lou. As I recall, you exchanged hardly a dozen words with her."

Philippa, who had been sitting mutely with her eyes closed, now roused herself to speak. "For my part, I found nothing to dislike in Miss Denny's manners," she told the Duke. "It is rather the manners of her connections that I must deplore. I daresay it escaped your notice, James, but Fanny Spicer spent most of the afternoon boasting to her acquaintance about your predilection for her sister's company."

The Duke frowned. This was hitting him in a weak spot. He disliked being the object of gossip, especially gossip that tried to link him with marriageable young ladies. But much as he longed to damn Lady Spicer's effrontery, he could not do so without seeming to criticize Miss Denny. So he replied quite mildly, "I am sorry to hear it, Phil. But I suppose Miss Denny cannot help what her relatives do, any more than I can help mine."

This speech effectually silenced his cousins for the duration of the drive home. The Duke hardly noticed their reproachful faces. As soon as they arrived in the square outside the Duke's stately town house, he handed them out of the carriage, saw them into the house, and then retired to the fastness of his study to reflect upon the momentous truth which had been revealed to him that afternoon.

He was in love.

There could be no other explanation for the strange euphoria in his heart, or the strange disorder of his usually carefully ordered senses when he thought of Miss Denny. It was ridiculous that he, James Edmund Augustus Montfort, Duke of Ashland, should be smitten at the age of thirty by a country girl of merely genteel birth and no more than passable good looks. But the same intelligence that recognized this fact made it impossible for him to deny it. Love was a notorious promoter of the ridiculous, as everyone knew. One had only to glance through the engagement announcements in the *Morning Post* to see pairings far more disproportionate than his and Miss Denny's could ever be.

"Good lord, I must have it badly if I'm thinking about engagement announcements," he told himself, with a feeling of shock. He explored the idea carefully, but though he felt a twinge or two when he imagined Lady Spicer's jubilant reaction or his friends' incredulous one, these considerations were of purely secondary importance and quite insufficient to dissuade him.

He had always known it was his duty to marry. The necessity of producing an heir who would eventually inherit his title and dignities had been drilled into him since he was a boy. In the same way, he had long held fixed ideas about the kind of woman he wanted for his duchess. She must be beautiful, of course—surpassingly beautiful in form, features, and coloring. No less could be expected of one who was to occupy the high position of Duchess of Ashland. Then, too, her birth must be impeccable, and her breeding such that she could meet the demands of her station with unfailing dignity and grace.

So had the Duke always envisioned his future bride. Yet now, when he took out his long-cherished image of beauty, grace, and dignity, he found her a dead bore. The truth was that though he had demanded his future wife should possess the most sterling qualities of body and soul, he had never dared hope meet a woman who would be a true and sensible companion to him—a woman whose wit delighted his mind even while her smile enchanted his heart. And though Miss Denny might not be the perfect beauty he had originally determined on, she was quite sufficiently pretty to make the Duke feel no qualms about dismissing his dream duchess in her favor.

Such qualms as he did have centered more around Miss Denny's lack of noble antecedents. And even this did not give him more than a moment's pause. He did not like the idea of Fanny Spicer as a sister-in-law, but for the pleasure of having Miss Denny as a life companion, he felt he was willing to endure even greater crosses than that.

"I really must be in love," he told himself, half smiling at his own ardor. Then he grew serious again, reflecting upon what his future conduct toward Miss Denny ought to be.

With any other woman in the world he would have known exactly how to proceed. Indeed, he would have commenced his suit quite confident as to its eventual success. But this was Miss Denny, and Miss Denny was different from other women. That was one reason why he loved her, of course, but it also meant he must proceed cautiously and not take her consent for granted. What he had told himself earlier he still felt instinctively to be true: if ever there was a woman capable of resisting the worldly temptation which his suit represented, that woman was Miss Denny.

"I must set myself to win her just as if I were plain Mr. Smith or Brown," he told himself with a smile. "In fact, I'm not sure plain Mr. Smith or Brown might not have an edge with her. There's something so odiously dull and stodgy about being a duke. Still, I think she likes me, and that ought to count for something. I shall call on her tomorrow and take her some flowers, perhaps." And he fell into a pleasant reverie in which all difficulties melted away, and he was left to enjoy the successful outcome of his courtship.

* * *

Miss Denny was enjoying a pleasant reverie, too. She scarcely heard her sister's chatter on the drive home, being occupied instead in reviewing all the Duke had said and done that afternoon. On consideration, she decided it had been quite the most enjoyable afternoon of her life. The Duke had been such a pleasant companion, so amusing to talk to and at the same time so attentive to her wishes. Really, it was remarkable to reflect that she, Judith Denny, had had a duke of the realm waiting on her hand and foot!

And then there had been the attentive way the Duke had listened to her every word—and the way he had looked at her, too. Miss Denny was glad she was a sensible girl, not prone to let her imagination run away with her. If she had not been a sensible girl, she might have fancied the Duke's looks meant something more than they really did. Even as it was, she could not help feeling a little fluttered when she recalled that moment when the Duke had taken her hand in his and kissed it.

With a feeling of bemusement, Miss Denny looked down at her gloved hand. Not once but twice had the Duke kissed it, the second time in full view of her sister and his cousins! Almost Miss Denny was inclined to censure him for this conduct. It had been very kind of him to bestow such a distinguishing attention on her, of course, but he ought to have considered what might be the effect of such attentions on a country girl unaccustomed to the manners of fashionable London.

Doubtless he was unaware of how attractive he appeared when he was smiling down at one with that ardent light in his clear blue eyes. Miss Denny, recalling that light and that smile, thanked heaven once again that she was a sensible girl. As such, she would never imagine the Duke's attentions had their root in anything more than simple friendly interest, no matter how particular they might appear.

Miss Denny's certainty on this issue was rather shaken the following day, however. Returning from a shopping expedition with her sister, she was greeted by the sight of an enormous sheaf of red roses lying atop the hall table.

"They are for you, Miss," said the butler, addressing Miss Denny in a manner rather more respectful than was usual with him. "His Grace the Duke of Ashland called and left them for you a short while ago."

"Ashland?" exclaimed Lady Spicer.

"The Duke left those for me?" said Miss Denny, regarding the roses in a stupefied fashion. "For *me?*"

"Yes, Miss," said the butler, looking pleased by the sensation he was causing. "He left them for you most particularly." In a fatherly tone, he added, "A pity his Grace did not stop a little longer. He sat in the drawing room quite an hour, hoping you might return, but at last he was obliged to take his leave. He asked me to give you his compliments, however, along with his regrets that he was so unfortunate as to find you out."

Lady Spicer looked at Miss Denny. Miss Denny looked back at her wordlessly. "Well, I never," said Lady Spicer, drawing a deep breath. "To be sure, I did invite him to call, but I never dreamed he would really do so. This changes things, Judith. Come into the drawing room where we can talk."

The butler, looking faintly regretful at being excluded from this discussion, saw them both into the drawing room and carefully shut the doors behind them. When Lady Spicer had removed her bonnet and pelisse and disposed herself comfortably on the sofa, she looked at her sister. "Judy, I hate to say this—at least, I don't hate it, precisely, but I never supposed I *should* say it. But it looks now as though I were wrong in what I told you before. I don't think, after all, that Ashland *can* be merely amusing himself with you."

"No, it is gone well beyond that. As of today he can fairly be said to be trifling with my feelings," agreed Miss Denny faintly.

Lady Spicer regarded her with exasperation. "Judy, this is serious! The thing is that Ashland has never trifled with anyone's feelings before—anyone that I know of, at least, and I think I should have heard of it if he had. It really begins to look as though he must have serious intentions."

"I think you go too fast, Fanny. It is possible you are merely uninformed as to the depths of his iniquities."

"I do wish you would be serious," said Lady Spicer, but in no very acrimonious spirit. "I must have heard if Ashland had been paying serious court to anyone else. No woman would keep such a thing secret when it would be such a feather in her cap. No, Judy: I think we may conclude Ashland's intentions toward you are serious. And what that means I need not tell you, I am sure!"

"No, you need not," agreed Miss Denny. "And really I would much rather you didn't, Fanny. If the Duke means anything particular by sending me these roses, you may depend on it he will say what it is in his own good time. Until then I would rather not talk about it at all."

"That's all very well, my dear, but you know sometimes gentlemen need a bit of nudging to bring them to the point. We ought to have a plan, a strategy—"

"No, we ought not, Fanny. I do not care for plans and strategies, and neither does the Duke. You will have to trust us to handle this our own way."

Miss Denny made this statement in a voice of great finality. Even so, Lady Spicer looked as though she were going to dispute it. Then suddenly she laughed and flung up her hands in a gesture of resignation. "Very well, Judy. I suppose you know best how to manage Ashland. Whatever you have been doing up till now has obviously been successful enough, if one may judge by the results! I know of no other girl whom he has so distinguished in all the time I have been in London."

Miss Denny left the drawing room soon after this interview and went upstairs. She was glad to get away to the privacy of her bedchamber where she could reflect upon the Duke's behavior in private. Although she had made light of the matter in front of Lady Spicer, in her heart of hearts she agreed with much of what her sister had been saying. The Duke's intentions did appear to be serious, and that being the case, it was clearly her duty to decide what she was going to do about it.

A very little reflection was sufficient to show her her own inclinations. She like the Duke better than any other man she had met in her life, and the mere thought of being his wife made her heart soar. But was it the thought of being his wife or the thought of being Duchess of Ashland that accounted for the sensation of euphoria?

Carefully Miss Denny examined her feelings. She could not detect any mercenary spirit within her heart; quite the contrary, in fact. Toward the Duke himself she felt no ambivalence at all, but toward his position she felt a great deal. When she reflected that marriage to him would make her a duchess, she knew not whether to laugh or cry.

She, Judith Denny, a duchess! It seemed an impossible idea—a ludicrous idea. For the rest of the day she alternately embraced and rejected the picture of herself as the Duke's bride, feeling at one moment a strong desire to weep and the next to laugh out loud.

This unsettled state of mind continued to plague Miss Denny on into the following day. All morning she varied between the extremes of happiness and despondency, with occasional forays into simple panic. As she sat in the drawing room that afternoon, trying to interest herself in a novel, she found herself looking up eagerly every time she heard the sound of wheels in the street outside.

"I wish he would call again today," she told herself wistfully. "If I could see and talk to him, perhaps I wouldn't feel so queer and uncomfortable about it all. I don't have any difficulty behaving sensibly when I am with him, thank heaven—at least, not when I am allowed to be myself. And I don't think I should have any difficulty behaving like myself now, even if he does mean to propose to me. But it's the uncertainty of not knowing whether he will or not that makes me uncomfortable. That, and the way Fanny has been behaving. She nearly curtsied to me this morning when she offered me jelly for my toast. And then the way the butler asked me how I liked my eggs, as humbly as though I were the lady of the house! I shall go distracted if this keeps up much longer."

As Miss Denny was reflecting on the difficulties of her position, she heard the sound of carriage wheels outside in the square. This time the wheels did not continue past the house, but came to a stop in front of it. Miss Denny laid down her book and listened. She heard the knocker being sounded on the front door, and then the sound of voices in the hall below. Presently the butler came hurrying up the stairs to the drawing room, bearing a few cards on a silver salver.

"There are two ladies below who wish to see you, Miss," he said, presenting the cards to her. "Miss Montfort and Miss Louisa Montfort." In a confidential voice, he added, "I believe they are relations of his Grace, the Duke of Ashland."

"Yes, they are his cousins," said Miss Denny, regarding the squares of pasteboard with surprise. She had exchanged only a few words with the Montfort ladies, but even those few words had been enough to convince her that they regarded her with antagonism. It was a surprise to be receiving a visit from them now. But supposing vaguely that they must be here at the Duke's behest and that their visit was intended as a friendly overture, Miss Denny smiled and nodded. "Certainly I will see them, Rivers. Show them up, if you please."

"Very good, Miss," he said, bowing in the deferential manner he had been using toward her since the previous afternoon. With a mixture of amusement and annoyance, Miss Denny sat twirling the cards between her fingers until presently the Montfort ladies were ushered into the drawing room.

As on the previous afternoon they were dressed alike in pale muslins, gauzy scarves, and heavily veiled hats. Miss Denny, politely urging them to seat themselves, thought with inward amusement that she had never seen ladies so inhumanly pale and thin, or so exaggeratedly genteel in appearance. "Will you take some refreshment, ma'am?" she said, addressing the paler and thinner of the two ladies, whom she recalled to be the senior Miss Montfort.

It was the junior Miss Montfort who answered her, however. "No, I thank you, Miss Denny. Philippa and I called merely to see if we might induce you to accompany us on our daily airing. You must know we always take a little drive in the early afternoon, after the sun is past its peak."

"Bright sunlight is so injurious to the constitution," murmured her sister with a wan smile. "And I am unfortunate in possessing an extremely delicate constitution, Miss Denny. But at this hour, in a closed carriage, protected by a veil and perhaps a sunshade, I think there can be no danger.''

"That's very kind of you, ma'am," said Miss Denny, surprised and no little amused by this invitation. "But you see I am not dressed to go out." With a smile, she indicated her simple frilled lavender morning dress.

"Oh, but that is no difficulty, Miss Denny. Philippa and I would be glad to wait while you changed. Indeed, I daresay Philippa would be the better for a little rest. Climbing your stairs a minute ago was nearly too much for her."

"I am sorry to hear it, Miss Montfort," said Miss Denny, choking back a laugh. She found herself quite eager to accept the Montfort ladies' invitation, if only to see what fresh absurdities they would utter during the drive. It was true that the idea of a ride in a stuffy closed carriage on a warm day was less than inviting, but on the other hand, the entertainment value of the outing would probably make up for its discomfort. Besides, she reasoned that the Duke had probably had something to do with his cousins' sudden, pressing desire for her company. This possibility alone would have made her unwilling to refuse Louisa and Philippa's invitation.

So, having reasoned the situation out in this manner, Miss Denny smiled and nodded. "Very well, Miss Montfort, Miss Louisa. If you indeed don't mind waiting while I change, I should be happy to join you on your drive."

"Certainly we do not mind, Miss Denny. Take all the time you like."

Not choosing to avail herself of this generous permission, Miss Denny hurried to her bedchamber, hastily changed her attire, and presented herself back in the drawing room less than fifteen minutes later. She had chosen to wear a very smart buff and blue-striped carriage dress with a standing collar and pelerine. On her head was a toque of matching blue and buff plush trimmed with tassels and ostrich plumes.

Neither of the Montfort ladies remarked on this toilette, but Miss Denny observed that their eyes flickered over her with an expression of surprise. "Did they think I would show myself a dowd?'' she wondered with amusement as she accompanied them out to the carriage.

Once in the carriage, Louisa gave instructions to the coachman, then settled back against the upholstered squabs with the air of one about to undertake a disagreeable duty. "I am glad you were able to accompany Philippa and me today, Miss Denny," she said. "I daresay you may have wondered at our distinguishing you this way?"

"Yes, I did just wonder," said Miss Denny gravely.

Louisa nodded, quite unconscious of her guest's ironic tone. "It is not to be wondered at, Miss Denny. The fact is, we wished to have a few minutes' private conversation with you."

"Oh, yes?" said Miss Denny. She was careful to keep her voice conversational, but inwardly she was on the alert. Something about the way Louisa was looking at her made her suspect this was more than a mere friendly visit.

Her suspicions were soon confirmed. "Yes, Philippa and I wished to speak to you about a matter of great importance," said Louisa, sinking her voice to a whisper. "It concerns, as you may perhaps have guessed, our noble relative the Duke of Ashland."

Miss Denny nodded warily, her eyes fixed on Louisa's face. "Philippa and I are aware that his Grace has distinguished you during the past few weeks with what must seem a quite overpowering condescension," continued Louisa. "Perhaps you wonder at our speaking of the matter, but we believe it vital that you should not misunderstand his Grace's motives."

"If his Grace's motives require explanation, then I should think it was for him to do the explaining," said Miss Denny in a carefully controlled voice. "For my part, I am aware of no misunderstanding between his Grace and myself. I do not think it too much to say that we have always understood each other very well."

Louisa frowned, obviously taken aback by this bold statement. Philippa opened her eyes, glanced from her sister to Miss Denny, then spoke in a weary drawl. "If that is so, Miss Denny, then we concern ourselves needlessly. But where such an important matter is concerned, you must see that we prefer to take no risk.''

"Yes, and it is for your sake we speak, Miss Denny," said Louisa, speaking with more emphasis than before. "His Grace is a good man, but like all men his behavior can be rather thoughtless. It is quite possible he is unaware what impression his actions may be making on you."

"I think that most unlikely," said Miss Denny calmly.

Louisa and Philippa exchanged glances. After a little pause, Louisa went on, with a forced smile. "I do not mean to disparage your understanding, Miss Denny. I am sure that you are an intelligent girl, and I have no doubt that if left to yourself, you would appraise his Grace's actions at their true value. But it is possible that those around you might be less accurate in their appraisals. Speaking frankly, I cannot help fearing you may be led astray by the ill-founded ambitions of your near relations."

Louisa paused to let this statement sink in. Receiving no response from Miss Denny, she continued with the air of one delivering a scholarly disquisition. "His Grace's position puts him in a peculiarly delicate position. His every move, his every word, are all subject to the most public scrutiny. Behavior which in another gentleman would pass without notice is in his case widely remarked and commented on. You must see how it is, Miss Denny. Under such circumstances, it would not be wonderful if you allowed yourself to place undue emphasis on his Grace's friendly attentions."

Still Miss Denny was silent. Rousing herself from her half-recumbent posture, Philippa took up the refrain. "You must realize, Miss Denny, that the position of Duke of Ashland places certain obligations on our noble relative."

Louisa nodded. "Perhaps you have not reflected on this, Miss Denny. Indeed, considering what is your own position in society, I suppose it is hardly to be wondered at that you should not. As Duke of Ashland, our cousin is not only one of the highest ranking noblemen in the land, but the titular head of a great family—a family whose line has descended in unbroken succession from our common ancestor, Gascoigne de Montfort. It is his Grace's responsibility to see that the name of Montfort suffers no diminishment, but continues to blaze forth in all the glory of its ancient and honorable tradition.''

Louisa pronounced these words with the solemnity of a clergyman delivering a benediction. Miss Denny gave her an incredulous look, but said nothing. Louisa went on, warming to her theme. "Our cousin will of course marry one day. For all the reasons I have given, it is essential that he marry a lady who will continue the tradition set by the great ladies who have preceded her as Duchess of Ashland. His Grace's own mother, as you may perhaps know, was Lady Dorothy Trevelyan of Trevelyan, youngest daughter of Lord Trevelyan—''

"A lady of surpassing beauty, unimpeachable character, and exalted birth,'' murmured Philippa in a plaintive counterpoint.

"When his Grace takes a bride, you may be sure it will be a lady who possesses these same qualities. Surely you can see why this must be, Miss Denny.'' Louisa paused and looked at Miss Denny expectantly.

"Oh, yes, certainly,'' said Miss Denny in a quiet voice. There were a dozen caustic responses she might have made, but conscience kept her silent. Even if Louisa and Philippa considered her breeding inadequate, she was lady enough to resist the temptation of being drawn into a fruitless quarrel. Nothing she could say could possibly influence the Montfort ladies' way of thinking. And indeed, setting aside their assumption that she was a vulgar adventuress, there was a kernel of truth in much of what they said.

The Duke *was* the head of a noble family, obligated by tradition if not by law to seek a bride among those who were his social equals. He undoubtedly knew and felt this obligation even more strongly than his cousins. If ever he were mad enough to shirk his responsibilities by marrying someone like herself, nothing could be more certain than that he would eventually regret it.

All this was suddenly clear to Miss Denny—so clear that she wondered she had not seen it before. And it was this as much as anything that kept her from responding to Louisa's taunts. Why should she be offended because Louisa thought her unfit to be a duchess? She had found the idea ridiculous, too—so ridiculous that she had been laughing at it all the previous afternoon. Just because the Montfort ladies had presented their facts in an offensive manner did not negate their essential factuality. Facts were facts, and the fact was that she was completely unfit to be a ducal consort.

Louisa, meanwhile, was looking mollified by Miss Denny's docile answer. "I knew you would be sensible about it, Miss Denny. As I said, Philippa and I hesitated to speak, but we thought it our duty, and I am sure you will excuse us if we spoke out of turn. Now that you have been put on your guard, you will know how to take our cousin's friendship in the proper spirit and will not allow yourself to expect what can never be."

"Certainly not," said Miss Denny in a colorless voice.

Both Louisa and Philippa smiled at her approvingly. Philippa reached out to pat Miss Denny's hand with her own frail one. "Dear Miss Denny," she said in her soft voice. "I knew we might depend on your good sense."

Chapter XII

Having achieved the object of their interview, Louisa and Philippa wasted no time in idle chatter but returned Miss Denny forthwith to St. James's Square. Miss Denny, wearily entering the house, found her sister awaiting her at the top of the stairs in a state of goggling anticipation.

"Rivers said Philippa and Louisa Montfort came to call on you, Judith! And though I could hardly believe it, he assured me that they took you out driving with them as well! Oh, Judy, this is flying high indeed. I never would have believed it. Ashland must needs be serious if he could prevail on those two to visit you. In general they hold themselves ridiculously high, you must know. Were they very gracious to you?"

"Not very, no," said Miss Denny, smiling a little at this understatement. "But I suppose they were civil enough, considering the circumstances."

"Well, that is more than I would have bargained for. It's common knowledge that they had hopes of marrying Ashland themselves."

"Really?" This was a new idea to Miss Denny, and a disturbing one, too. But endeavoring to conceal her perturbation, she went on in a would-be cheerful voice. "They ought to have known *that* plan could come to nothing, Fanny. Even such a great man as the Duke can only marry one lady at a time, after all.''

Lady Spicer laughed. "Oh, Judy, you must know what I mean. Louisa and Philippa hoped he would marry one or the other of them, not both at once.''

"Ah, that is more likely, I suppose.'' Inwardly, Miss Denny was considering the information her sister had just given her. It went a long way toward explaining the antagonism she had sensed in the Montfort ladies' attitude, but she could not find it made any real difference where her own situation was concerned. Even if selfishness or spite was behind Louisa and Philippa's "friendly'' counsel, it did not follow that their counsel was automatically bad.

Aloud, she said, "I am a little tired after my outing, Fanny. I think I shall go up to my room and lie down until dinner.''

"Oh, yes, certainly,'' said Lady Spicer, all solicitude at once. "I'll send one of the maids up to help you undress. And perhaps you would like some tea and something to eat, too. A few sandwiches, perhaps—''

"No, thank you,'' said Miss Denny, speaking with unusual firmness. "I want nothing, Fanny, except to be left alone.''

Once in her bedchamber, Miss Denny took steps against any further unwanted interference by locking her bedchamber door. Having removed her dress, hat, and shoes and put them away, she lay down on her bed in her chemise. She had no expectation of sleeping, but it was necessary that she think and reflect and—if possible—come to some conclusion about her situation in regard to the Duke.

For the first hour or so she could not think, but only feel. She felt by turns intolerably hurt, then achingly sad, then blazingly angry. While anger held her in its grip, she found herself regretting that she had not given Louisa and Philippa the set-down they deserved. There would have been some satisfaction in telling them exactly what she thought of them and their behavior.

But when her anger cooled, she was able to recognize once more the validity of the Montfort ladies' viewpoint. Nothing in her ancestry or upbringing had made her a fit bride for a man like the Duke, and if he was unable to recognize this obvious fact on his own, it would be for her to make him see it.

"So that's that, then," said Miss Denny aloud.

The hopes and dreams she had been cherishing since the previous afternoon had now to be put aside, barely twenty-four hours after their inception. Miss Denny looked ruefully at the bouquet of roses standing on her dressing table. They were still as fresh and lovely as when the Duke had brought them, but she could not look upon them now in the same happy spirit.

If Fanny was right, and they had been sent by the Duke as a token that his intentions were serious (a thing she was by no means so certain of now as previously), that meant she would presently have the unenviable task of refusing an offer of marriage from him. Miss Denny was not certain she would have the necessary strength of mind to perform such a superhuman act of self-denial. The idea of marrying the Duke had never seemed more appealing than now, when she knew it could never be.

"And it's not his title, or his fortune, or his position in society that I regret," she told herself unhappily. "I could do without all those easily—in fact, I should prefer to do so. If only he were plain Mr. Smith or Brown, how happy I might be with him! I never met a man I liked so well, or one who understood me so completely. But since it can't be, I had better make up my mind to hint him away if he shows any signs of proposing. Not that I really think he will. I daresay Fanny was mistaken about that, too, and he only sent the roses to be friendly."

This thought made Miss Denny sigh and look unhappily once again at the roses on the dressing table. She went on with her mental lecture, however, determined not to indulge this mood. "I'll show the Duke that I can be friendly, too, without expecting anything more," she told herself. "That ought to be easy enough, in all conscience. After all, nothing has really changed since the last time I saw him. If I can just set aside everything that's happened since yesterday afternoon, the Duke and I can go on as we did before, and soon I will likely forget I ever thought he might be more than a friend.''

This policy Miss Denny resolved to follow, though she feared it might be a long time before she would forget her short-lived hopes and dreams. But she was, she assured herself, a sensible girl, and she meant not to dwell on her disappointments. Rising from her bed, she dressed herself, tidied her hair, and went down to dinner, vowing to behave so no one would suspect she was not in her usual spirits.

In this she succeeded, and her success continued in the days that followed. Whenever Lady Spicer mentioned the Duke, Miss Denny merely smiled and said nothing. Whenever her sister went further and began to talk about the lofty position she would occupy as Duchess of Ashland, she turned the subject aside with a laugh or a joke. So completely typical was her behavior, in fact, that Lady Spicer had no suspicion that her sister had not only abandoned all expectation of receiving a proposal from the Duke, but had made up her mind to refuse one if it were offered.

The Duke, for his part, only gradually became aware that something was wrong. In the week following the Winchcombs' breakfast he called twice more in St. James's Square, but each time found Miss Denny absent. This he attributed to mere bad timing, for it never entered his head that she might be purposely avoiding him. When he did finally catch up with her, she seemed quite as usual, and so gay and full of spirits that he was charmed by her all over again.

"More roses? Your gift comes in good time, your Grace. The last ones are only now beginning to wilt," she told him, accepting the bouquet he offered her with a smile of what appeared to be genuine pleasure.

"I am glad you like the flowers, Miss Denny," said the Duke, clearing his throat. He felt absurdly shy all at once, now he was fairly embarked on his courtship. He watched Miss Denny ring for a servant and request an empty vase in which to place the roses. When this had been done, he ventured to speak again.

"I had hoped the roses might be acceptable. When I called

yesterday, your sister mentioned you were to attend the Beaucastles' ball tonight. I plan to attend, too, and I would consider
it a great honor if you would do me the honor of carrying my
poor offering.''

Miss Denny threw him an incredulous smile, then spoke as
if addressing the roses. ''There is no trait so irksome as false
modesty,'' she told them. ''He brings me what are undoubtedly
the finest flowers money can buy, yet has the gall to refer to
them as 'my poor offering!' ''

The Duke laughed, restored to his ease by her smiling
address. ''Well, yes, I suppose that was a rather pretentious
speech. But I hope you will not hold that against the flowers.
These particular roses are my head gardener's cherished darlings, and it nearly broke his heart when he was compelled to
part with them.''

''No wonder, they are so beautiful,'' said Miss Denny, touching the roses with admiring fingers.

''So you will carry them tonight?''

Miss Denny hesitated, looking down at the bouquet. ''I don't
know,'' she said. ''It seems a pity something so beautiful could
put me in such a dilemma, but the fact is I had planned to wear
my eau-de-nil taffeta tonight, your Grace. And you must see
that red roses and eau-de-nil taffeta will clash abominably. I
could wear my white silk or my rose sarcenet instead, of
course—but I have worn both of those within the last week or
so, and Fanny has told me that no lady with pretensions to
fashion wears the same dress twice in such short succession.''

''Your dilemma is easily resolved, Miss Denny. My gardener
grows white roses as well as red. I can have him send you
some white ones over later this afternoon, and you can keep
these for another occasion.''

To the Duke's surprise, this offer seemed to make Miss
Denny quite agitated. ''Oh, no! You must not think of doing
such a thing, your Grace,'' she said earnestly. ''I did not mean
to hint you should send me more roses on top of these. Upon
my word, I did not.''

''I know you did not, Miss Denny. The offer comes from

me quite freely, I assure you. Indeed, I would be delighted to
send you more roses."

"No, you must not think of it, your Grace." With a resumption of her previous light manner, Miss Denny went on in a
mock-serious voice. "I could not twice bereft your head gardener of his cherished darlings. It would haunt my conscience
forever."

"You need have no scruples on that score, Miss Denny. The
roses are mine, and if I choose to send them—"

"No, you must not send me anything else, your Grace,"
said Miss Denny with finality. "It would be shockingly extravagant, and I assure you it is not at all necessary. If you dare do
such a thing, I shall carry a bouquet of dandelions from the
park instead. I promise you, I shall!"

"That would be something original," said the Duke, laughing. "Upon my word, I have half a mind to send more roses,
just to see you do it!"

"But you will not?" said Miss Denny, smiling but looking
a touch anxious at the same time.

"No, since you make such a point of it, I will not," said
the Duke, smiling back at her. "But I warn you that next time
I shall inquire about your gown beforehand, so you will have
no excuse not to carry my bouquet."

A slight smile was Miss Denny's only reply to this speech.
"I was sorry to miss you when I called earlier this week,"
continued the Duke, thinking it best to change the subject.
"You seem to be keeping uncommonly busy."

"Yes, very busy," agreed Miss Denny. Her voice was perfectly easy and natural, but the Duke thought she looked a little
self-conscious. "I am sorry you put yourself to so much trouble
for nothing, your Grace."

"It was no trouble, Miss Denny." The Duke paused a
moment, then went on in a studiously casual voice. "Your
sister was in the last time I called, and I spoke to her for a few
minutes. I was surprised to hear that you had been out driving
with my cousins last week. I had not realized Lou and Phil had
called on you."

The Duke studied Miss Denny closely as he spoke these

words. He was sure he saw the color rise in her cheeks, but when she answered her voice was quite composed. "I daresay they forgot to mention it, your Grace. I felt very much honored to have them distinguish me in such a way, I assure you."

"I am glad you thought it an honor, Miss Denny. For myself, I would not consider it so, but then I do not get on with my cousins, as you may perhaps have gathered. They were civil to you, I hope?" Again the Duke looked at her keenly.

"Oh, yes, perfectly civil, your Grace. Why should they not be?"

There was more than a tinge of color in Miss Denny's cheeks now. The Duke wondered if she was embarrassed by the implications of a visit from his near relations, or if there were a deeper reason.

"There is no reason why Lou and Phil should not be civil to you," he said, watching her narrowly. "But I am obliged to admit that on occasion, they have attempted to meddle in my affairs in a very impertinent and unjustifiable manner. I should be sorry if I were to learn they had attempted anything of that nature where you were concerned."

Miss Denny hesitated, then shook her head firmly. "No, your cousins were very civil to me, as I said, your Grace. I had a very enjoyable drive with them."

The Duke bent an incredulous look on her. "Oh, yes?" he said. "You surprise me extremely, Miss Denny. Whatever did you find to talk about?"

Miss Denny, foreseeing this question, had ready an answer that was both truthful and reticent. "Oh, we spoke of the weather, and of your cousin Philippa's health," she said with a smile. "That latter subject alone would provide sufficient matter for any number of conversations, I gather."

The Duke was satisfied and returned her smile ruefully. "Yes, we hear a great deal on the subject of Phil's health at home," he said. "So much so, in fact, that I see no need for you and I to discuss it now. Especially when there are topics of much greater interest that we might be discussing."

"Such as?" said Miss Denny, looking interested but wary.

"Such as the Beaucastles' ball tonight. I have excused you

from carrying my bouquet, but in return for that concession I
hope you will grant me the privilege of dancing the first two
dances with you. If you are not already engaged to dance them
with someone else, of course," he added, seeing a slight frown
cross Miss Denny's brow.

"No," said Miss Denny slowly. "I am not engaged for those
dances, your Grace. But Fanny and I are attending a dinner
party before the Beaucastles' ball, and it is possible we may
not arrive until after the dancing has begun. Perhaps it would
be better if we did not make a definite engagement to dance
any specific dances, but rather left the matter to chance."

"On no account, Miss Denny. You shall not evade me so
easily. I shall present myself at the Beaucastles' on the stroke
of nine, and if you do not arrive in time for the first two dances,
I shall lead you out for whichever two follow on the moment
of your arrival."

"You have an answer for everything," said Miss Denny,
smiling reluctantly. "Very well, your Grace. The first two
dances shall be yours."

The Duke found her reluctance puzzling. He had almost
made up his mind to question her about it when Lady Spicer
came into the room.

"Ashland, how good to see you! If I had known you were
here, I would have come down sooner."

The Duke smiled politely, but inwardly he doubted this statement. He knew Lady Spicer and her kind well enough to be
sure she would never knowingly interrupt a *tête-à-tête* between
him and her sister. The Duke's suspicions on this score were
strengthened by Miss Denny's artless response. "But Fanny,
you must have known his Grace was here," she said, regarding
her sister with innocent surprise. "I sent Rivers to tell you as
soon as he arrived."

"Rivers must have misunderstood you. Never mind, my
love: I am sure you and Ashland were able to talk much more
comfortably without me." In an arch voice, Lady Spicer added,
"May I know of what you spoke, or is it a secret?"

Declared suitor or not, the Duke was not going to stand for
this sort of thing. "Not a secret at all, but of no great interest

to you, ma'am, I am afraid. Your sister will tell you of our conversation. I see by the clock that I have been here an unconscionable time already."

Brushing aside Lady Spicer's protestations, he then proceeded to take leave of her and Miss Denny. "Your servant, Miss Denny. I look forward to dancing with you tonight. Your servant, Lady Spicer. I shall look forward to seeing you tonight, too."

As he drove his curricle away from St. James's Square, the Duke brooded over the interview he had just had with Miss Denny. He was a little disappointed about the way it had gone, but not unduly so.

"She senses that my intentions are becoming serious, and so of course she is a little uncomfortable," he told himself. "One can hardly blame her for that. I am a little uncomfortable myself, if the truth be known. And it is particularly uncomfortable having that sister of hers about while we are trying to reach an understanding. If Lady Spicer can behave as she does to my face, I shudder to think how she goes on behind my back." And having satisfactorily explained to himself Miss Denny's somewhat reticent behavior, he fell to thinking with great eagerness of the evening ahead, and of his engagement to dance the first two dances with his inamorata.

When evening came, however, the Duke was destined to receive a second, more severe disappointment. Miss Denny arrived in time for the first dance, and the Duke's heart swelled when he saw how pretty she looked in her green taffeta ballgown with its trimmings of blond lace and seed pearls. She looked so well in this dress that he was quite able to forgive her for not wishing to carry his bouquet.

But he felt a good deal less forgiving and philosophical when he noticed that Miss Denny was carrying in one hand an elegant posy of ivory rosebuds and fern. It appeared she had some other source of flowers besides himself—someone who had been more successful in choosing a suitable offering to complement her toilette. Miss Denny observed the line between his brows when he came up to claim her for the first dance and instantly comprehended the reason for it.

"Your Grace is looking at my bouquet," she said, hoping her smile did not look as forced as it felt. "A pretty thing, isn't it? Mr. Manville sent it to me this afternoon, not long after you left. So you see it was quite unnecessary for you to send me white roses on top of the red ones, your Grace. I shall carry yours tomorrow night when we go to Almack's."

This speech somewhat soothed the Duke's feelings, but not entirely. Irrational though it might be, he resented having Mr. Manville's offering favored over his own. He managed to get the better of this mood while dancing with Miss Denny, for she was as enchanting a companion as ever, and if she was a little more reserved than usual he could attribute it to the fact he was now an avowed suitor instead of merely a friend. But his resentment flared up again when Mr. Manville presented himself at the end of the first dance and stammeringly requested the privilege of partnering Miss Denny in the next one.

"That privilege must be denied you, sir. Miss Denny is engaged to me for the next dance," said the Duke, fixing Mr. Manville with a hard stare.

"I beg your pardon, I'm sure, your Grace," said the unfortunate Mr. Manville, blushing and preparing to beat a hasty retreat. But he was stopped by Miss Denny, who extended her hand to him with a kindly smile.

"Never mind, Mr. Manville. It is true I am engaged to his Grace for the next dance, but I am quite free for the one after that, if you care to dance with me then."

"To be sure I should," said Mr. Manville, reviving like magic. With a flash of a surprisingly engaging smile and a quite creditable bow, he took himself off to await the third dance.

"What an unlicked cub that boy is," said the Duke, looking after Mr. Manville with disfavor. "His guardians ought to have seen that he acquired some small degree of polish before foisting him on society."

Miss Denny nodded absently. "It has been very difficult for him, I believe. He is naturally shy, and I do not think his mother has been very realistic in expecting him to make a splash in society. Neither has Lord O'Henry behaved as he ought. He has sponsored Mr. Manville to some degree, on account of his being his heir, but I cannot find that he has ever taken the least personal interest in him.''

"You seem to take a personal interest in him, at least," said the Duke, his tongue sharpened by jealousy. "He ought to be grateful he has found such an eloquent advocate in you, Miss Denny."

Miss Denny looked at the Duke in surprise. "I do not know that I am so very eloquent, your Grace, or that Mr. Manville has any reason to be grateful for my advocacy. He is a friend of mine, however, and I hope I shall always be true to my friends."

Although she spoke quietly, the Duke felt there was a reproach contained in her words. He was angry at himself for having provoked it, and throughout the remainder of the dance he exerted himself to be both polite and entertaining. Miss Denny responded suitably, and talked, laughed, and exchanged jokes with him as light-heartedly as ever, but the Duke felt she was keeping him mentally at arm's length. At the end of the dance, he handed her over to Mr. Manville with a most dissatisfied feeling in his breast.

Miss Denny's state of mind was not much easier, but it was quieter. She felt she was doing her duty—a disagreeable duty, to be sure, but one which could not be avoided. She had sensed the Duke's jealousy in regard to Mr. Manville and had instantly divined the reason for it, but the next instant she told herself she must be mistaken. It was presumption to suppose that the Duke of Ashland could be jealous on her account.

Even if he were jealous, there was no way she could set his mind at ease. She could hardly assure him that she enjoyed his company infinitely more than Mr. Manville's; that she treasured the bouquet he had given her more than any gift she had ever received and had only refrained from carrying it because she thought it better not to betray too much partiality for him.

This might be—probably was—unnecessary trouble on her part. The Duke had likely had no thought beyond friendship or flirtation. But even if he did not, she unfortunately now did, and for her own peace of mind it was better to take every precaution.

Miss Denny had all she could do to maintain this policy of caution in the weeks that followed. The Duke continued to single her out in a manner as striking as it was flattering. He sent her flowers and confections; he came to call; he asked her to dance with him whenever they attended a party or ball together. On all these occasions Miss Denny permitted herself to dance, laugh, and joke with the Duke as before, but if he made a remark that seemed too particular, she either pretended not to hear or turned it off with a laugh.

But though she clung resolutely to the role she had chosen, inwardly she was finding it more and more of a strain. And sometimes it seemed to her that the Duke was feeling the strain, too. She did her best to dismiss this idea as presumption, but there were times when they were together when he would merely look at her without speaking. On these occasions, there was something in his expression that made it difficult to keep up her pretense of cheerful insensibility.

By dint of tireless effort Miss Denny did manage to keep it up. She could not be said to be enjoying it, however. Now and then, in a fit of dejection, she told herself that she would have done better to have refused her sister's invitation and stayed in Derbyshire. Her sole consolation was that the end of the Season was now only a few weeks away. Miss Denny was too much of a realist to suppose all her sufferings would be instantly alleviated on that date, but she thought it not unreasonable to hope that once back in Winfield, with a hundred or so miles separating her from the Duke, she might be spared the pain of almost daily reminders of what might have been.

Chapter XIII

The Woodfords' masquerade, one of the last great events of the Season, took place on the thirty-first of May. Early that evening, in the privacy of his bedchamber, the Duke was grimly plotting out a plan of action.

He had watched with growing frustration as Miss Denny evaded all his efforts to express his feelings. A defense so perfect could hardly be accidental. The Duke told himself this; likewise he told himself that Miss Denny could hardly have failed to realize that he cared for her. The only possible explanation for her behavior was a humane and laudable desire to spare him the humiliation of needlessly declaring himself. Over and over the Duke assured himself of this fact, yet stubbornly, irrationally, his mind refused to accept it.

"Conceit, that's what it is," he told himself as he dressed for the party that evening. "I'm such a conceited fool I don't believe any woman could not want me. Upon my word, I begin to think it's no wonder Miss Denny doesn't." With a rueful expression, the Duke contemplated his reflection in the glass. "Funny how I never realized I was conceited before. This whole experience has been a very instructive one for me—at least it ought to have been. But somehow I can't bring myself to give up without making one last effort. That's conceit, too, no doubt. I'm so conceited that I can't believe she really means to refuse me until I hear her say so to my face."

This being the case, the Duke resolved to settle the matter once and for all that evening by proposing to Miss Denny in form. This, as he assured himself, was the highest form of conceit of all. Still, he was driven to make the attempt—driven by the strange, irrational conviction that Miss Denny was not so indifferent to him as she seemed.

"And what is that but conceit, too?" he muttered as he donned his mask and domino for the masquerade. Nevertheless, his irrational hope stayed with him as he left his room and went downstairs where his carriage was waiting.

He reached the Woodfords' shortly after the hour of ten o'clock. Early as it was, the party was already in full swing. The great house was ablaze with lights and packed with guests in fancy dress, while the steady stream of newcomers crowding into the already crowded rooms seemed to indicate that the party was sure to earn that most coveted encomium, "a dreadful squeeze."

The Duke threaded his way past brigands and Brahmans, shepherdesses and sailors, looking for Miss Denny's small figure. His ignored the seductive smiles of a voluptuous Delilah; he spared never a glance to a statuesque Rosamund scandalously clad in pantaloons. But as soon as he set eyes on a diminutive beggar-girl in a colorfully patched skirt, ragged shawl, and laced bodice, he was sure he had found his quarry.

Nor was he wrong. "I never heard anything so ridiculous in my life," she was saying to her partner, a gentleman garbed in the lavish costume of an eighteenth century court exquisite. In spite of his powdered wig and ruffles, the Duke recognized this gentleman immediately as his friend Mr. Ormand. "You cannot mean it, Mr. Ormand," continued Miss Denny, smiling up at him. "In fact, I am not sure I ought not to disbelieve every word you say."

"What's Ormand trying to put over on you, Miss Denny?"

asked the Duke, joining them. She turned to him with a smile that lit up her artfully begrimed face.

"Good evening, your Grace. I have just been dancing twice with Mr. Ormand, and he has been trying to tell me that at masquerades it is permissible to dance all evening long with the same partner. That is nonsense, is it not, your Grace?"

"Not entirely," said the Duke solemnly. "Ormand has neglected to mention one important detail, however. The permission you speak of applies only when you are dancing with gentlemen—and then only with gentlemen of a certain rank. My rank, in fact—and so I'll thank you to hand Miss Denny over to me, Charles. You mustn't be trying to trespass upon ducal privilege, you know."

"Ducal privilege, my foot," said Mr. Ormand, grinning reluctantly as he relinquished Miss Denny. "It's a dirty trick, that's what it is. You're lucky I don't call you out for this, Ashland."

"Go and rattle your saber at someone else," the Duke advised him. "I have things of importance to say to Miss Denny." He turned his back deliberately upon Mr. Ormand.

"You'll hear from my friends, sirrah," threatened Mr. Ormand, and flourished his sword dramatically in the air before stalking away. Miss Denny watched him go, then turned smilingly to the Duke.

"I must warn you, I don't believe in your talk of ducal privilege any more than I believed Mr. Ormand's foolishness, your Grace. You must not try to inveigle me into dancing more than twice."

"I don't wish to dance with you at all," said the Duke calmly. "What I told Mr. Ormand is quite true, Miss Denny. There are things of importance I wish to say to you, preferably in private. Will you come somewhere we can be alone? The Woodfords have a very fine conservatory, I believe."

Miss Denny, looking at him, felt her heart lurch within her breast. It might be presumption, but she felt instinctively that if the Duke got her alone in the conservatory, he would declare himself. This was something she had been working to avoid, and it was clearly her duty to avoid it now, but it was hard—

oh, so hard to deny herself a thing she longed for with all her heart.

"I don't think—I'm afraid it would be improper for me to go to the conservatory with you, your Grace," she said, casting down her eyes as she spoke. "My sister would dislike it, I'm sure."

The Duke smiled grimly. "And I am sure she would *not* dislike it, Miss Denny. But perhaps I am mistaken. If you think I should seek her permission first, I would be happy to do so."

"No, oh, no," said Miss Denny hastily. If she really were obliged to receive a proposal of marriage from the Duke, then she preferred that Lady Spicer should know nothing about it, at least not until after it had been irrevocably refused. Miss Denny had hoped in her heart that she might prevent his proposing in the first place, but a single glance at the Duke's set face was sufficient to convince her that this hope was vain. Whatever he had to say to her, he was clearly determined to say.

And perhaps it was better that she *should* hear him out, she reasoned, glancing up at him uncertainly. Once he had proposed and she had refused his proposal, then everything would be settled. She would probably never see him again, of course, but as she considered the matter dispassionately, she thought this might actually be a happier alternative than the strain of keeping up a pretense of disinterested friendship.

"I suppose there is no reason I cannot walk with you in the conservatory for a little while, your Grace," she said slowly. "But we must not stay too long, or my sister will worry."

"We shall not stay long enough to alarm your sister," promised the Duke. Miss Denny thought gloomily that he was quite safe in making this promise. So long as Lady Spicer knew her to be in the Duke's company, she was unlikely to express any emotion but delight in her absence—assuming she even noticed her absence. With a sensation of even greater gloom, Miss Denny observed that her sister was so busy flirting with Lord Henry Nathorp that she was unlikely to notice much of anything.

Others were most observant, however. As Miss Denny and the Duke were leaving the ballroom, they were assailed by a plump dame in a nun's dress who curtsied profoundly to the

Duke and stared at Miss Denny with a mixture of jealousy and avid interest.

"Your Grace! It is Ashland, isn't it? No, don't try to put me off, your Grace. I know you, you see, even in your disguise. 'The most distinguished gentleman in London' they call your Grace, and very rightly, too, I am sure. It is very good to see your Grace this evening. And who is the lady with your Grace?"

"Ah, I am not obliged to reveal *her* identity, even if you have been clever enough to guess mine," returned the Duke with a cool smile. "I wish you a good evening, ma'am." With a bow, he swept Miss Denny past the plump dame's frustrated gaze, through the ballroom doors and into the hall.

Although Miss Denny was suffering agonies of apprehension over the thought of the coming interview, she could not help laughing a little at this exchange. The Duke laughed, too, but his expression was irritated. "What an insufferable woman," he said. "I have no idea who she was, but she seemed to know who I was all right. However did she guess? There must be a hundred men here tonight in black dominoes."

"*I* knew who you were as soon as I saw you," offered Miss Denny diffidently. "I suppose it might be equally obvious to other people."

"How is it obvious?" asked the Duke, looking down at her.

Miss Denny was made uncomfortable by his intent gaze. "Oh, that's difficult to say, your Grace." Attempting to ease the situation with humor, she went on lightly. "How can I explain what gave you away? Your height—your bearing—a certain ducal *je ne sais quoi* in your manner, if you will."

"Oh, yes?" said the Duke. "Well, I'll take your word for it, Miss Denny. But I could wish I was without that particular *je ne sais quoi* on this occasion."

He spoke rather bitterly. Miss Denny, alarmed by his mood, had recourse to humor once more.

"Now do not be falling into a melancholy, your Grace," she said in a rallying tone. "We have already established on several previous occasions the numerous advantages you enjoy in being a duke. I believe you must be feeling a little liverish tonight. You must ask your physician to prescribe you a blue pill when next you see him.''

The Duke managed a smile, but inside he felt gloomier than ever. The implication of age and invalidism contained in Miss Denny's laughing suggestion was yet another thorn in his flesh. It seemed to him at that moment that more things set them apart than drew them together: age, background, position. ''I don't think there's any pill to ease my particular malady,'' he said bitterly.

Miss Denny gave him a quick, alarmed look. ''Oh, but that cannot be true, your Grace,'' she protested. ''Any good physician will tell you that there is a cure for every malady, even if it is only time. If all else fails, you may trust to time to work a cure in your condition.'' Hurrying on, she added, ''I am no physician, but it is my opinion that you are merely suffering this evening from a surfeit of servility. I did not keep exact count, but I am sure that woman back there called you 'your Grace' at least six times in as many sentences.''

''Yes, that sort of thing does grow tiresome,'' agreed the Duke. ''That is why I prefer my friends and family to call me by my Christian name.'' Looking down at Miss Denny, he continued in a sober voice. ''We are friends, I hope, and certainly we have been acquainted long enough to dispense with the formality of titles. Will you call me James?''

Miss Denny was made uncomfortable by this question, and even more uncomfortable by the look that accompanied it. But her common sense told her she would be wrong to deny the Duke such a reasonable request. Even if she meant to decline his offer of marriage, she could not rationally refuse to use his Christian name, considering the length of their acquaintance and the way he had qualified his request by using the word ''friends.'' Therefore she nodded. ''Of course I will call you James. And you must call me Judith—or Judy, if you prefer. That is what my friends generally call me.''

Again the Duke nodded. ''Judy,'' he said, pronouncing the name with an experimental air. ''Judy it is, then.''

The sound of her name on his lips struck Miss Denny as peculiarly intimate. Trying not to blush, she went on in what she hoped was a natural voice. "It's odd that your name should be James. I have a brother named James as it happens, only we generally call him Jim instead."

"Nobody calls me Jim," said the Duke morosely. It seemed to him that this one point symbolized all his difficulties. Miss Denny would naturally prefer a Jim: an easygoing, friendly, happy-go-lucky kind of fellow, unencumbered by the accumulated weight of generations of family tradition and dignity. He, on the other hand, was a James: a stiff, pompous, middle-aged individual whom she could never see as more than a friend.

Miss Denny wondered at the melancholy in the Duke's voice. "Well, I will call you Jim if you like," she said encouragingly. "Only you don't somehow seem like a Jim to me. James seems to suit you better."

"It would," said the Duke, more morosely still. "Never mind, Judy. James will do very well."

"All right, James," said Miss Denny, a trifle shyly.

Neither of them spoke again until they reached the conservatory. It was, as the Duke had said, impressive: a vast room of glass and iron tracery crammed with lush foliage and awash with the scent of flowers. The Duke led Miss Denny along a dimly lit gravel path, past rows of potted trees and flats of newly sown seed. "How lovely all this is," said Miss Denny, charmed out of her temporary shyness by the sight of the beauty around her. "It would never seem like winter if one had a place like this to come to. If I were rich, I am sure I would have one just like it."

The Duke cleared his throat. "I have a conservatory at Ashland Palace. Several conservatories, in fact, all larger than this one."

"They would be, of course. A duke would naturally be bound to have the biggest and best conservatories around. Except for the Prince Regent, perhaps." Miss Denny gave the Duke a saucy smile, which faded when she saw the way he was looking at her. Abruptly she turned away, pretending to inspect a tree laden with blossoms that overhung the pathway. "Now I wonder what kind of a tree this is? Don't the blossoms have a lovely smell? It's positively heavenly."

"They're orange blossoms," said the Duke. "They do smell divinely, don't they? I believe it is the custom to use them for bridals in France."

He spoke the word "bridal" with quiet significance. Miss Denny gave him an alarmed look, started to speak, then hesitated. "How interesting," she said at last, in a nervous voice.

"I wish I could believe you really thought so," said the Duke sadly. "But I am not a fool, Judy. I am perfectly aware that for the past month or so you've been doing your best to discourage me. I have no doubt—no doubt at all—that if I were to ask you to marry me this minute, as I came here on purpose to do, you would refuse me." He paused, looking down at her searchingly.

Miss Denny found her voice almost wholly suspended by a lump in her throat. She swallowed hard and nodded. "Yes, James," she said in a soft voice.

He nodded matter-of-factly, as though the words were of no moment. "Of course I knew you must say so. The question I would like to ask is—why?"

"Why?" repeated Miss Denny stupidly. She looked up at the Duke. There was puzzlement in the blue eyes that looked so frankly and directly into her own, and a touch of hurt that seemed to wring her already troubled heart.

"Yes, why, Judy? It's not that I'm such a coxcomb that I think you must care for me. I can think of a hundred reasons why you might not—but somehow, I can't believe in any of them. Right from the start it seemed to me there was something between us, and for me, at least, it's only strengthened as I've come to know you better. I love you, Judith Denny, with all my heart—and I wish with all my heart you loved me back. Do you truly not?"

Miss Denny felt as though her tongue were cloven to the roof of her mouth. She had prepared herself to reject the Duke's proposal of marriage, but not for a question of this sort. Clearly, it was necessary that she should lie—and equally clearly, the lie must be a convincing one if she were not to leave herself open to a round of inquiries as painful as they were futile. But the lie simply would not come. She stood looking up at the

Duke helplessly. His expression softened suddenly, and a half smile appeared on his lips.

"I always thought you were the most honest woman of my acquaintance, and now I know it," he said in a conversational voice. Putting his hands on her shoulders, he drew her toward him and kissed her deliberately on the lips.

Miss Denny's eyes widened with surprise. She remained standing where she was, looking up at the Duke. He contemplated her with an expectant and faintly apprehensive air, as though awaiting some further response. Receiving none, however, he boldly bent and kissed her again. Miss Denny knew it was her duty to protest or turn away, but instead she merely shut her eyes and surrendered to the Duke's kiss once more.

It was a longer and more intimate kiss than the first had been. The Duke's mouth possessed hers with an authority that seemed to awaken an instinctual response. Miss Denny moved closer, putting her arms around the Duke's neck and pressing herself close against him. He reciprocated by crushing her fiercely against his chest and showering her face with kisses.

"Judy, oh, Judy," he whispered between kisses. In some small, dispassionate corner of Miss Denny's mind, she was aware she ought not to permit this, but the Duke's arms around her felt so strong and comforting—and his lips on hers so overwhelmingly right and natural—that she had no thought of stopping him. Only when a soft peal of laughter suddenly shattered the quiet of the conservatory did she and the Duke draw hastily apart.

Miss Denny, in the first flush of a guilty conscience, assumed the laughter had been directed at her and the Duke. But when she looked anxiously around her, she saw nothing but the plants, trees, and flowers that had surrounded them in the first place. As she stood wondering if she could possibly have imagined the laughter, she heard it again. It seemed to be coming from the direction of the doorway. The laughter was followed by a whispered exchange that seemed to go on for a very long time.

Just as Miss Denny was beginning to wonder if she and the Duke might take advantage of the intruders' preoccupation to effect an escape from the conservatory through some alternate exit, the laughter came again, and there was the sound of rapid footsteps on gravel. A moment later Lady Spicer burst into view, followed closely by Lord Henry Nathorp. He was addressing her in a tone half querulous and half coaxing.

"Come on, Fanny, don't be so damned coy. If you didn't want me to kiss you in the first place, you shouldn't have—''

His voice broke off abruptly as he caught sight of the Duke and Miss Denny. Lady Spicer caught sight of them at the same moment and came to an abrupt halt on the pathway.

"Oh," she said, the color flooding her cheeks. After a minute she went on, still looking embarrassed but attempting a playful tone. "So this is where you went to, Judith! Henry suggested you might be in the conservatory with his Grace, but I did not believe him. I see he was right, however, and so I am glad he brought me here to look for you."

This speech was so palpably false that Miss Denny did not bother to respond to it. She was, indeed, beyond making any response at that moment. She merely looked at her sister, who colored deeper under her gaze.

"I hope I did not interrupt anything," said Lady Spicer, after a moment's awkward silence. "Your Grace, I trust you will forgive me if I chose a bad moment to intrude. A sister's concern—''

"No, you are not intruding in the least," said the Duke, cutting short Lady Spicer's expression of sisterly concern. "I was merely showing Miss Denny the conservatory. But we are done seeing it now, and there is no reason why she cannot accompany you back to the ballroom if you wish."

"No, certainly not," said Miss Denny, finding her tongue at last. "I am sorry I caused you concern, Fanny. Let us go now, if you please." Turning to the Duke, she spoke in a low, agitated voice. "Forgive me, James, I must go. You see how it is. I'm sorry . . . ." Looking at him pleadingly, she let her voice trail off.

"Yes, I see how it is," said the Duke. Reaching out, he took her hand in his and gently kissed it. She looked at him uncertainly, then turned away, withdrawing her hand as she spoke.

"Goodbye, James. As I said, I'm sorry."

"You need not be," said the Duke. *"Au revoir,* my dear."
Miss Denny gave him a last, doubtful glance as she left the
conservatory with her sister and Lord Henry.

Chapter XIV

Miss Denny left the conservatory feeling rather dazed. As she followed her sister and Lord Henry through the hallway that led back to the ballroom, she found she could still admire the Woodfords' stately house with its spacious rooms and tasteful furnishings, but its elegance suddenly seemed curiously unreal to her.

In the same way she was barely conscious of the stream of inconsequential chatter issuing from her sister's lips, or of the sullen silence emanating from Lord Henry. He made no response at all to any of Lady Spicer's determinedly cheerful observations, but strode beside her with a face like thunder. Only once did he speak, as they neared the ballroom. Taking Lady Spicer aside, he addressed her in a voice too low for Miss Denny to hear.

Miss Denny, disinterestedly surveying the two of them, saw her sister cast a nervous look in her direction. "Later, Henry," she murmured. These words he received with a curt bow, then turned and walked away, his face more like a thundercloud than ever.

Lady Spicer sighed, then arranged her face into a determinedly bright smile. "This has been an eventful evening, has it not?'' she remarked lightly to Miss Denny. ''Quite a fatiguing one, too. I am almost inclined to make my excuses to the Woodfords and call for the carriage. Should you mind very much if we went home now, Judith?''

''I would not mind at all,'' said Miss Denny, with heartfelt sincerity. She was too much fatigued in mind and spirit to welcome the idea of returning to the ballroom and trying to feign gaiety and good cheer for another three or four hours. All she wanted was to retreat to some secluded place where she might lick her wounds in private.

It would have been an unspeakable relief to have been instantly transported to the privacy of her bedchamber in St. James's Square. Unfortunately this relief could not be obtained without enduring first a long carriage ride *tête-à-tête* with her sister. Lady Spicer was not so talkative as usual, but she did speak once, partly to express her surprise at having found Miss Denny alone in the conservatory with the Duke and partly to apologize for having interrupted their interview together.

''I never even noticed you leaving the ballroom with Ashland, Judy. And if I had known you were in the conservatory with him, I certainly never would have interrupted you. Upon my word, I don't know how I came to do anything so *maladroite*.''

''It's all right, Fanny,'' said Miss Denny. ''I expect your attention was engaged with something else.''

She spoke in a weary voice. Lady Spicer looked at her suspiciously, but apparently concluded that she had had no ulterior motive in making this speech, for she smiled and shook her head.

''Yes, it was, but that is no excuse. As your sponsor, I ought to have had an eye out for your interests, even more than for my own. Tell me, Judy—'' She leaned forward with a look of eagerness. ''Did Ashland say anything of significance while you were together in the conservatory? Anything about marriage, I mean?''

Although Miss Denny could not lie to the Duke, she found she could dissemble to protect his interests. She paused as though thinking over the evening's events. ''He told me orange blossoms are much used for bridals in France,'' she offered at last, in an indifferent voice.

Lady Spicer considered this remark hopefully, but in the end was forced to dismiss it as inconclusive. ''Next time he says anything about marriage, you must use it as an opening to sound him out a little about his intentions,'' she instructed, reverting unconsciously to the manner she had used during the early days of Miss Denny's visit. ''You might, for instance, have asked him if he would like his own bride to wear orange blossoms, or something of that sort—''

''No, I couldn't,'' said Miss Denny with determination. ''Besides, it's entirely unnecessary, Fanny. I am quite sure— quite, quite sure—that his Grace and I will never be more than friends.''

Lady Spicer looked disappointed but not particularly surprised. ''Ah, well, I am sure we might be forgiven for hoping,'' she said with a sigh. ''Ashland has certainly been particular enough in his attentions these last few weeks. With anyone else, I would have said you were bound to receive an offer, but with Ashland one never knows. He does tend to be rather eccentric, no doubt about it.''

Miss Denny opened her mouth to protest this statement, then closed it again. Lady Spicer went on, not heeding her sister's expression. ''And Ashland *is* a duke, after all. I suppose it's a bit much to suppose a duke would take a bride out of a country rectory. However, we must be glad he has distinguished you as much as he has. His patronage has done you no end of good, and I'm sure if we apply ourselves, we can bring one of your other suitors up to scratch before the Season is over. Let's see, who would be the best choice? Mr. Manville has been very attentive, but Mr. Blessington is a good deal the richer, and I think he might be brought to the point with a little management. What do you think, Judy?''

''If you don't mind, I would rather not think about it at all right now, Fanny,'' said Miss Denny, more wearily still. Lady Spicer was inclined to take umbrage at this speech, but observing her sister's state of fatigue—and reflecting, perhaps, that Miss Denny might say something about her own conduct that evening if pressed too hard—she considerately suspended her conversation for the rest of the trip.

Once safely in her bedchamber, Miss Denny was able to give way to the emotion she had been holding in for most of that evening. She shed a few tears as she undressed and a few more when she caught sight of the bouquet standing on her dressing table. This bouquet had been the Duke's latest offering to her, and Miss Denny felt blue indeed when she reflected that in all probability it would be the last gift she would ever receive from him. The mere idea made her tears flow faster, until she could hardly see to unbutton her dress. She had subsided into sniffles by the time she was changed into her nightdress, but for several hours afterward she lay wretchedly in bed, looking unseeingly up at the fringed canopy of damask above her.

Her bridges were all burned behind her now. She had spurned the Duke of Ashland's addresses and told him that she would not marry him. Having done so, she must prepare herself never to see or speak to him again. Miss Denny made herself face this bitter truth, but reassured herself that she had only done what was best for both her and the Duke. It might feel like misery at the moment, but eventually they would both be glad she had acted bravely and denied her selfish inclinations.

So far Miss Denny was able to approve her conduct, but she felt less certain when she considered the way she and the Duke had parted. As long as she was in the business of self-denial, she ought really to have made an all-around job of it and refused to let him kiss her, too. By not doing so, she had permitted a certain ambivalence to creep into her refusal.

But surely the Duke had understood that she still meant to refuse him, in spite of that kiss? For a moment, Miss Denny felt rather doubtful, as she considered the Duke's parting address. *"Au revoir"* did not convey the same finality that a firm, English goodbye would have done. Then she recalled how well the Duke had always understood her—the way he seemed to know her thoughts and feelings even before she voiced them—and she was reassured.

Of course he had understood her, and it stood to reason that he had understood the kiss, too. It had been in the nature of a goodbye kiss, a last token of farewell before they parted ways forever. In any case, Miss Denny could not be really sorry she had permitted the Duke to kiss her. It had been a magical moment, one which she might treasure for years to come after the pain of the present moment was past.

"But for now, I must not think of it," Miss Denny told herself firmly. "I must think of the future instead and decide what I am going to do with myself."

More than ever she wished she were not obliged to stay in London until the end of the Season. She foresaw that the next two weeks were likely to prove a kind of purgatory in which she must try to act gay and insensible while the Duke (no doubt) favored some other lady with his attentions and her sister (no doubt) strove desperately to marry her off to some other, inferior suitor. If only there were some way she could go home to Derbyshire now instead of in mid-June.

"But perhaps there is a way," said Miss Denny, sitting up suddenly in bed. Lighting the candle on her nightstand, she reached for the letter that was lying beside it.

The letter was one of the weekly missives which Mrs. Denny had been faithfully dispatching to her daughter ever since Miss Denny had first come to London. This particular letter was entirely representative of its kind, containing a mixture of motherly advice, household news, and neighborhood gossip. It had reached Miss Denny the previous afternoon, but since she had been at that time preparing for the Woodfords' party, she had merely scanned its contents hastily and set it aside, intending to peruse it in a more leisurely fashion at a later time.

But though her first reading of the letter had been hasty, it seemed to Miss Denny now that it had contained a passage that might serve her purpose. Unfolding the letter, she scanned its single closely written page. It was not a mention of the Smiths' new carriage that she sought, nor laments about the housemaids' reckless consumption of tea and sugar, but rather a couple of small paragraphs near the close:

"I am happy to report that in general, we have all enjoyed very good health this spring. I myself have escaped having even so much as a cold; my sole complaint is a touch of hay fever, which as you know usually strikes me about this time of year. Your father, bless him, has had it that my sufferings have been more than usually severe this year—so much so that he actually took it upon himself to call in Dr. Knowles to examine me (not consulting me beforehand about the business, as you may be sure! I should certainly have refused to incur a two and sixpence fee for such a trifling malady).

I must own, however, that the regime the good doctor has prescribed for me does seem to have done something toward alleviating my symptoms. I am to adhere to a mainly vegetable diet; drink nothing but water; and be cupped low down on my chest once a week so long as I am troubled by fits of sneezing. Of course none of these measures is strictly enjoyable. I detest being cupped and find myself a good deal weakened by having to keep to such a low diet. But I am hopeful it may not be necessary for much longer. You know the worst of my hay fever usually subsides by the middle of June.

Regarding Mrs. Hibbert and her new baby—"

But Miss Denny had no interest in Mrs. Hibbert and her new baby. The paragraphs about her mother's illness were what she had been searching for, and she was satisfied that therein lay sufficient excuse for cutting short her stay in London. "I'll go home tomorrow, or the day after at the latest," she vowed to herself. She then extinguished the candle, lay down in bed again, and composed herself to get what sleep she could in the few short hours that remained before dawn.

"You cannot be serious, Judith!"

Lady Spicer, her teacup halfway to her lips, stared at her sister across the breakfast table. Miss Denny, attired for traveling in bonnet, pelisse, and plain muslin dress, looked back at her defiantly. "Indeed I am serious, Fanny," she said. "While Mama is ailing, I cannot think it right that I should stay here idling away my time with balls and assemblies. I am sure she could use my help about the house while she is feeling so low."

"But that is nonsense, Judy. I know Mama mentioned in her last letter to me how pleased she was with the way the new maids were working out. With two strong, willing girls to help her, she cannot want your assistance."

"You have been too long in London, Fanny. Sarah and Susan may be strong and willing, but they are also completely raw. One cannot simply tell them what to do and expect them to do it, as you do with your servants. They must be supervised every minute of the day."

"Let Tilda supervise them, then," said Lady Spicer impatiently. "She's almost fourteen, full of an age to start taking a hand with the housekeeping. Why, I was helping Mama take care of you and Cecil when I was half that age!"

"Yes, but you know Tilda has her own work to keep her busy, Fanny. It's unfair to make her put aside her studies to attend to the household work. I am the eldest daughter, and it's my duty to help Mama if she needs it."

"That is the greatest nonsense of all, Judy. You know perfectly well that *I* am the eldest daughter, not you. And I don't for a moment suppose Mama expects me to drop everything and run home to help her!"

"No," said Miss Denny quietly. "But you know our situations are rather different, Fanny. I am still living with Mama and Papa, while you are married and have a home of your own. I think most people would agree that your first duty must be to your husband, not your parents."

This speech made the color rise in Lady Spicer's cheeks. She glanced at Sir Geoffrey's empty place, then raised her teacup to her lips as if to screen her features from her sister's gaze. "It's out of the question, Judy," she said sharply. "I cannot permit you to go. Mama entrusted you to my care, and I know she would never want you to cut short your visit for such a trifling reason. It's not as though she's never had hay fever before, after all. She's had it more or less, every spring that I can remember.''

"Yes, but she says it is unusually severe this year. And the diet Dr. Knowles has her on makes her very weak. Under the circumstances, I think it only right that I should go to her.''

"I cannot allow it—'' began Lady Spicer.

"You cannot stop me, Fanny," said Miss Denny with determination. "I have made up my mind to go, and I *shall* go, if I have to travel on the stage.''

"And so you will throw away all your chances of making a good match? What will the Duke think, if he finds you have left Town without a word to him?''

"I doubt he will think twice about it, Fanny. As I told you last night, the Duke and I are merely friends. In any case, I hope the thought of him would not keep me from doing my duty by Mama.''

"Well, if you have no thought for the Duke, you should think of your other suitors. Mr. Manville and Mr. Blessington—''

Mr. Manville is a nice boy, but I have no thought of marrying him, Fanny. That is something you have set your heart on, not I. And I certainly would not dream of marrying Mr. Blessington. He is old enough to be my father.''

Lady Spicer sat silent a minute or two, biting her lip. "Very well," she said at last, in a mortified voice. "If you feel you must go, then I suppose I cannot stop you, Judith. Only I had thought you would have more consideration for me. To leave me like this, with no warning—''

Her voice broke as she was speaking. Miss Denny, regarding her with surprise, saw there were tears in her eyes. "I'm sorry, Fanny," she said in a softened voice. "I did not know you would mind my leaving so much. But you knew I must go home in a few weeks anyway, did you not? This is only anticipating matters a trifle.''

Lady Spicer merely shook her head and had recourse to her handkerchief. As she was dabbing at her eyes, Sir Geoffrey came into the room.

"Here, what's this?'' he said, looking in surprise from his wife's tear-stained face to Miss Denny's troubled one.

"I received a letter from Mama yesterday, saying she was feeling poorly," explained Miss Denny. "And I thought I ought to cut short my visit and go home to her. But Fanny seems to think I ought not to go."

"Does she?" said Sir Geoffrey. There was an indefinable expression on his face as he regarded his wife. "For my part, I think it's dashed fine of you to want to go to your mother, Judy. Of course Fanny and I will miss you, but we wouldn't be selfish enough to keep you here when you're needed at home, would we, Fanny?"

Lady Spicer blew her nose in an agitated manner. "Yes, go on and call me selfish," she said bitterly. "It's terribly selfish of me to want someone here to keep me company, instead of being left to myself all the time. I am nothing but a selfish beast and don't deserve anyone's consideration." With an angry sob, she rose from her chair and hurried out of the room.

"Perhaps I should go to her," said Miss Denny, looking after her with concern. "Do you think I ought to, Geoffrey? I would not like to leave her so upset."

Sir Geoffrey shook his head, a gloomy expression on his face. "No, better let her cool down by herself for a bit. She'll come around by the time you leave, I'm sure." He patted Miss Denny on the shoulder with an air of awkward kindness. "Don't suppose there's any need to say how sorry I am to see you leave us, Judy. I know Fanny's been glad to have you with her this Season. Well, that stands to reason: she wouldn't be taking on this way if she weren't sorry to see you go. And I've been glad to have you here, too. You've probably noticed things ain't what they should be between Fanny and me, but we seem to rub on a little better when you're around."

In spite of her own private misery, Miss Denny was touched by this avowal. Happiness might be forever beyond her own reach, but perhaps it was still within Sir Geoffrey's, if only he could be brought to accept a little much-needed advice on dealing with her sister.

"I *have* noticed that you and Fanny have been having difficulties, Geoffrey," she said, choosing her words with care. "Perhaps I am wrong, but I think Fanny feels rather neglected by your spending so much time at your club. Perhaps if you were to take her around more to parties and dinners in the evening, as you used to when you were first married—''

She stopped. Sir Geoffrey was shaking his head. "It's no use," he said. "God knows I'd be happy to take her about like I used to, but the plain fact is she don't want me to, Judy. She'd rather have that blackguard Nathorp fellow dancing attendance on her than her own husband.''

His voice was bitter as he spoke these last words. Miss Denny, conscious that she was treading on delicate ground, went on after a moment's pause, choosing her words even more carefully than before.

"It looks as though Fanny is fond of Lord Henry, I know," she told Sir Geoffrey. "But I am convinced she really does not care a penny for him. It is you she cares about, and if you would only pay her more attention, she would not think it necessary to flirt with him so much.''

"And it seems to me that if she cared about me as much as you say, she wouldn't encourage a scoundrel like that to flirt with her in the first place," said Sir Geoffrey obstinately. "No, it's no use, Judy. You mean well, I know, but the truth is that Fanny hasn't any use for me anymore. I'm better off spending my evenings at White's.''

And to this belief he clung stubbornly, despite Miss Denny's attempts to make him see things from her sister's point of view. It occurred to her more than once during the course of their conversation that he and her sister were well matched in obstinacy, if nothing else. But as neither was willing to be convinced that the other had any grievance, she was forced at last to abandon her efforts at reconciliation and finish making her preparations for leaving St. James's Square.

As Sir Geoffrey had predicted, Lady Spicer "came around" in time to see her sister off. "Oh, Judy, I wish you were not going," she said, watching unhappily as Miss Denny's belongings were loaded into the chaise. "I am convinced this is all quite unnecessary. And you must know it, too, if you only stopped to think. Mama would not want you to cut your visit short for such a reason. I know she would not.''

Miss Denny silenced her with a hearty embrace. "Perhaps not," she said. "But I am convinced I am doing the right thing, Fanny. In truth, it is not just for Mama's sake that I am going. I have other reasons, too."

She spoke the last words almost under her breath. Lady Spicer heard them, however, and gave her a look both surprised and wary.

"Other reasons?" she said. "What other reasons have you for leaving, Judy? It isn't what happened last night in the conservatory, is it? If you are concerned about Henry, and about the silly way he was talking—about kissing me, and so on, you know—then I beg you will put it out of your mind. You must know he was only teasing."

"Was he?" said Miss Denny. She looked full into her sister's face. Lady Spicer tried to meet her gaze, but her eyes kept dropping under Miss Denny's steady scrutiny.

After a moment or two, Miss Denny spoke again in a low voice. "I do not know Lord Henry as well as you do, Fan, and so I cannot say whether he was teasing or not. I can only say that he appeared to me to be in earnest." In a still lower voice, she added, "I would hate to see you involve yourself in difficulties, Fan. Perhaps—perhaps you ought to consider coming home with me to Winfield. I think it would do you good to get away from London for a while."

"I, go home to Winfield?" said Lady Spicer. It was obvious the idea was a new one to her. For a moment she looked irresolute; then her expression became shuttered. "No, I cannot possibly leave London right now, Judy. I have so many engagements at the moment that it is entirely out of the question. I could not possibly drop everything and leave on such short notice."

Despite the decided tone of these words, Miss Denny thought she detected a note of something rather less decided in her sister's manner. She went on in her most coaxing voice. "I do not mean that you should accompany me now, Fanny, though certainly I should be very glad of your company. But if you were to wait until the chaise returned and then follow me, perhaps in a week or so—"

"No—no, I cannot. But you must give Mama and Papa my love, and the children, too. I had intended to make them all presents, but I daresay money will be as welcome as anything. Here, Judy. There's a guinea apiece for Tilda, Cecil, and Kit, and some money for you, too, for the journey." Pressing a small purse into Miss Denny's hand, Lady Spicer embraced her one last time, then hurried up the steps of the house as though fearing she might be drawn into the chaise against her will.

Chapter XV

It seemed to Miss Denny that the journey home was far shorter than the one that had taken her to the metropolis in the first place. This phenomenon could not be accounted for by any difference in route, but rather by the difference in her own state of mind.

On her original trip, she had been so impatient to see London and her sister that every minute had seemed an hour in her impatient reckoning. Now, although she was glad to be leaving London, she had no particular impatience to reach home, where she knew she would be received with surprise if not with actual recriminations.

Even if her family were not upset with her for cutting her visit short, they would want to know her reasons for doing so. Miss Denny feared they would find the excuse about her mother's illness quite as inadequate as Lady Spicer had done. There would certainly be questions—questions which would tax her ingenuity to answer truthfully while at the same time preserving the discretion she felt was necessary.

Under the circumstances, then, Miss Denny was glad to postpone her homecoming as long as possible. But she soon found, like many a philosopher before her, that time was a relative concept, dependent on one's state of mind. Instead of dragging by, as on her previous journey, the miles now flew past with a celerity that was staggering. Barnet was reached before she would have believed possible; so was Stevenage; and though she broke her journey with an overnight stay at Stamford, it still seemed a matter of hours rather than days before the chaise was pulling up the familiar gravel drive in front of Winfield Rectory.

A small boy in nankeen breeches and a shirt that would have been the better for laundering was swinging by his heels from the branch of an elm tree near the rectory porch. He paused in his gyrations to stare first at the chaise, then at its occupant. A broad, gap-toothed grin suddenly dawned on his round freckled face; he let out a whoop and tumbled to the ground in a manner more precipitate than graceful. "Mama! Mama, Judy's here," he shouted, speeding toward the house. "Come quick, everybody. Judy's here, and she's dressed up fine as fivepence."

Within minutes, Miss Denny found herself gathered once more to the bosom of her family. "Judith! My dear, whatever are you doing here? We did not expect you for another two weeks," exclaimed Mrs. Denny, a handsome gray-haired woman who bore a distinct resemblance to Lady Spicer in figure and features. She embraced Miss Denny in a manner that lent little credibility to her claims of illness and debility. "Why did you not let us know you were coming, you harum-scarum girl? We might have driven into Derby for all you knew."

"What, all of you?" laughed Miss Denny, looking from her mother to her father, and then to the faces of the younger sister and brothers grouped around her. "Well, even if you had been gone, I doubt not that Susan or Sarah would have let me in. I trust I have not been gone so long that they have forgotten my face entirely."

This witticism produced a general laugh. Thirteen-year-old Matilda, who had been gazing meanwhile at Miss Denny's bonnet, now remarked in a respectful voice, "I say, Judy, you do look perfectly splendid! That's a ravishing bonnet. And your hair looks simply ravishing, too. I would not have thought you could look so dashing.''

"She does look well," said Mrs. Denny, inspecting her daughter's person with maternal pride. "Quite elegant and lady-like.''

"She will be an ornament to Winfield society, I have no doubt," agreed the Reverend Thomas Denny with a twinkle in his eye. "But I am more interested in learning why she is here when by all accounts she was so successfully ornamenting the society of London. From Fanny's letters, I would have judged she was the reigning toast of the town and liable to come home a duchess at the very least.''

Miss Denny's brothers hooted loudly at the idea of their sister coming home a duchess. Miss Denny flushed and gave her father a constrained smile. "Indeed, you must not take Fanny's letters too literally, sir," she told him. "Everyone was very kind to me in London, and I enjoyed myself very much, but after so many weeks I found I was growing tired of idling about every day and going to parties every night. And when I read Mama's letter and learned her hay fever was so bad, I could not feel it right to stay in London when I might be helping her about the house.''

"Oh, Judith, I never meant you should cut short your visit on my account," said Mrs. Denny, with a look of distress. "If I had known you would take it that way, I would never have said a word about my foolish hay fever.''

"Well, it's too late now. Here I am, and here I must stay, for I have no money to go back to London. Unless, of course, I use the guineas Fanny sent Tilda and Cecil and Kit.''

This artful speech brought about an immediate change of subject. There was at once an outcry from Matilda and Cecil and Christopher, followed by loud demands that Miss Denny should produce their guineas immediately. She did so, laughing, and the three younger members of the party raced into the house to discuss how they would spend their largess, while Miss Denny followed after with her father and mother.

"Indeed, I cannot like your cutting your visit short, my dear," said Mrs. Denny, surveying her daughter with concern.

"It seems a shame you had to sacrifice your pleasure on my account."

"To tell the truth, it was not entirely on your account that I cut my visit short, Mama," said Miss Denny, smiling back at her rather crookedly. "The plain fact is that I had had enough of London and was beginning to feel homesick for Winfield."

"Homesick for here, when you were living in luxury in that great house of Fanny's?" said her mother, looking pleased but incredulous. "That is one up for your father, as Kit would say. You know I was half afraid to let you go to London in the first place because I feared you would come home spoiled for Winfield society. But Thomas said we might depend on your good sense to hold you steady, and I see he was right."

"I don't know if it's so much good sense as want of taste," said Miss Denny, flashing her father a smile. "Fanny's house was very splendid, but I am afraid I am a hopeless rustic at heart. How good it is to be home!" She looked around her with a sigh of pleasure.

Winfield Rectory was a low, rambling, timber-framed house picturesquely set about by trees and flowering shrubs. Its rooms, though spacious, were a trifle shabby about the edges and boasted none of the luxuries which Lady Spicer's home possessed in such abundance.

Yet Miss Denny, remembering the discord that had reigned at the heart of the house in St. James's Square, felt at that moment as though there was more of true happiness to be found at Winfield Rectory than in her sister's luxurious home. Discord might reign here too, of course, from time to time; but when it did, it took the form of straightforward fraternal squabbles and good-natured raillery instead of smoldering resentment and silent brooding.

"It's good to be home," said Miss Denny again, simply.

She had no cause to contradict that statement throughout the rest of that day. Each member of the family, even her young brothers, found time to take her apart and tell her how much they had missed her and how glad they were to see her home again. And at dinner she found that the maid Susan, who was gradually being schooled in the intricacies of plain cooking,

had of her own initiative scrabbled together a cake in honor of
Miss Denny's homecoming. That it was a rather heavy cake
did not matter, nor that it was slightly scorched on its upper
surfaces. The thought was there, and Miss Denny was touched
accordingly.

After dinner, the whole family retired to the parlor, where
they listened eagerly as Miss Denny described her London
experiences. Her account was necessarily an abridged one, and
she could not help feeling sad that the Duke, who had played
such a large part in so many of her adventures, could not now
even be mentioned. But she put on a brave front and laughed
and joked with her brothers and sister as cheerfully as though
there were no ache in her heart or lump in her throat. She must
have given herself away in some fashion, however, or perhaps
Mrs. Denny's maternal instinct made her keener-eyed than the
others. Late that evening, as they were all taking up their candles
to go up to bed, she lingered behind to address a few words
to her daughter in private.

"You made only a brief mention of the gentlemen you met
in London, Judith. I don't mean to pry, but you know Fanny
hinted in her last letter that there was someone who was paying
particular court to you. She wrote as though he would be a
very eligible match for you—indeed, I was at a loss how to
interpret some of her hints. Do you know of whom she was
speaking?"

Miss Denny was silent a moment as she considered how
much she ought to say. "Yes," she said at last. "I know whom
Fanny was talking about, Mama. But I am afraid she may have
overstated the case a bit. You know you cannot always take
what Fanny says too seriously."

Mrs. Denny nodded. "No, and I did not do so in this case.
You yourself had made no mention of any particular gentleman,
and I made sure you must have written me if you were on the
verge of becoming engaged." She was silent a moment, then
sighed and gave her daughter a rueful smile. "Mind you, I
cannot help being a little sorry that the business did come to
nothing. If you had met some decent man in London whom
you could have loved and esteemed, I need hardly say how

happy your father and I would have been to see you well married.''

Miss Denny made a small noise of assent. After another brief pause, her mother went on again, with a touch of diffidence. ''I cannot help worrying a little about you, Judith. You have so few opportunities living here in Winfield. I do not place undue emphasis on worldly things, I hope, but I confess I do aspire to something better in the way of a husband for you than Stanley Hibbert or one of the Smith boys.''

Miss Denny smiled a little. ''Fanny said almost the same thing, when I first came to London, Mama. She told me it was my duty to make a good match if I could.''

''Not a duty, no, but I would have been glad if it could have been managed. But I do not mean to level any reproach at you, my dear. Indeed, we are very glad to have you back home for as long as you care to stay. It seems to me, however, that you are not entirely in spirits, and that I cannot like. I hope—I hope you were not much hurt that this gentleman did not offer for you?''

Miss Denny hesitated. ''As a matter of fact, he did offer for me, Mama,'' she admitted reluctantly. ''But I was compelled to refuse him. I have not spoken of it to anyone because I did not want to seem to be boasting. He was a very eligible gentleman and very much sought after in London. I did not tell Fanny, even. She would have been very upset with me for letting such a splendid opportunity slip through my fingers.''

Mrs. Denny's eyebrows went up, but she only said, ''I see. Well, you need not fear any reproach from me on that score, Judith. Of course, if you could not care for the gentleman, you did right to refuse him, no matter how eligible he may have been.'' She kissed Miss Denny lightly on the brow. ''And now that you are back among us, we will do our best to help you recover your spirits. Welcome home, my love, and I hope you will not soon leave us again.''

''No fear of that,'' said Miss Denny, with a lump in her throat.

The lump was still there as she went about her preparations for bed that night. As she lay once more in her old familiar

bed in her old familiar room, she tried resolutely to put all
thought of the Duke out of her mind, but in spite of her efforts
she could not help giving way to the weakness of a few tears.

Fatigue soon put an end to her sorrowings, however. When
she awoke the next morning and found the sun shining brightly
in a cloudless blue sky and all the birds caroling aloud the
glory of a spring day, she told herself hopefully that it was a
favorable omen. If being once more in the heart of her family
and the dear familiar home surroundings could not cure her of
her malady, nothing could. Hard work would probably assist
in the cure as well. With this in mind, Miss Denny rose, arrayed
herself in a pink sprig muslin dress rather past its prime, and
went downstairs to begin the process of trying to forget.

"What can I do for you today, Mama?" she asked, as she
seated herself at the breakfast table. "You know that is why I
am here: to help you with your work."

Mrs. Denny, who was helping her sons to generous helpings
of ham and boiled eggs, looked up with surprise. "Why, I had
not really thought of it, Judith. Let's see, what work could you
do? Sarah and Susan are to do the rooms while I finish hemming
my new dress—and Christopher is to gather the eggs, and Cecil
is going to run a message over to Mr. Harris at Long Elm for
your father. And Tilda is practicing her music—at least I hope
she is—and this afternoon I shall supervise her and the boys
at their lessons."

She pondered a minute more, then smiled at Miss Denny.
"Really, it seems as though the day's work is all arranged for,
Judith. I don't know that I need you for anything today. Perhaps
you could just take the day and rest? I'm sure you need it, after
traveling so far yesterday and the day before."

Miss Denny shook her head with decision. "No, I am perfectly rested now, and I want to work, Mama. In all this great
house there must be something I could do. Could not I help
you in your work in *some* way?"

Mrs. Denny shook her head doubtfully. "You could pick
the French beans, I suppose," she said. "Hodgkins usually
does that, but you know he will never pick them small enough

to suit me. I hate to ask you to do such a menial job, but if you would not mind—"

"I would be delighted," said Miss Denny firmly. "I'll go out and pick them right after breakfast."

Her mother gave her a worried look but said nothing. As soon as breakfast was over, Miss Denny tied on a wide-brimmed straw hat, collected a bowl from the kitchen, and went out to the garden to pick the French beans.

She remembered having disliked picking beans as a child, and it was not long after setting to work that she began to remember why. The sun beat down hot on her back; the earth was dry and dusty between her fingers, while the touch of the bean leaves on her skin made it itch furiously. Her mood, which had been martyred to begin with, became more so as she went down the rows, stooping and tugging at the stubborn beans.

She paused to wipe away the perspiration that had gathered on her brow. As she bent to work again, the sound of wheels on gravel caught her ears. She gave only a cursory glance in the direction of the drive, however, supposing it merely to be some visitor to see her father on parish business. The visitor was driving a curricle, she noted, harnessed to a team instead of a pair. She could not imagine who the driver might be. None of the local gentlemen had been wont to affect such a dashing mode of transportation prior to her departure for London.

"One of our local beaux aping the London smarts, no doubt," she muttered to herself as she went along the line of bean plants. "Perhaps it is Arthur Blalock. He always fancies himself a great whip. It would be just like him to try to drive a curricle-and-four when he can't even manage a one-horse gig. I'm surprised he hasn't overset himself long before now, the way he goes on."

She had enough curiosity to look again at the curricle-and-four standing in the Rectory drive. The driver of the curricle was leaning over in the seat, addressing some words to her brother Christopher, who was on his way back from the hen-house with a basket of eggs. In response to his words, Christopher nodded vigorously and pointed in Miss Denny's direction. The gentleman turned around to look, and Miss Denny's heart gave a great leap in her breast. There was no mistaking that silver-blond hair or aristocratic profile.

"It can't be," she whispered, rising swiftly to her feet and upsetting the bean bowl in her agitation. "It can't be!"

But she had no real doubt it was the Duke. Seeing her eyes fixed upon him, he smiled and raised his hat to her, then turned to address a word to the groom perched behind him. The groom hopped down and ran to the horses' heads. The Duke waited until he had taken the reins, then lightly swung himself down from the curricle with a swirl of his caped greatcoat. He paused to address another word to the groom, then began to stride toward Miss Denny with a radiant smile lighting up his face.

Miss Denny smiled feebly in return, but she had no strength to do any more. She stood among the bean plants, still clutching the empty bowl in a nerveless grasp and watching the Duke advance toward her.

When he was within a few feet of her, he stopped and stood looking at her without speaking. She looked back at him a moment, then sighed and pushed the hair back from her perspiring forehead. "You *would* come when I look like a perfect ragamuffin," she said.

"You look perfectly adorable," contradicted the Duke. With scant respect for the intervening beans plants, he came forward and took Miss Denny in his arms. She made no objection. The bean bowl joined the scattered beans on the ground as he crushed her against him. "Ah, Judy," he whispered, pulling off her hat and kissing her with a reckless disregard for any interested onlookers in the farm and stableyards. "What a chase you have led me! I think I've set a new record for land travel in the last twenty-four hours."

"Oh, James," said Miss Denny, laughing and crying at the same time and returning the Duke's embrace with mindless fervor. "Why did you come? I left London on purpose to get away from you."

"I know it," said the Duke, a smile twisting his lips. "But somehow I couldn't leave it at that, Judy. I was so unhappy— so miserable to think you had left without speaking to me. You can't know how unhappy I have been."

"Yes, I can," said Miss Denny emphatically, whereupon the Duke laughed and kissed her again. Miss Denny was seduced into returning this kiss, but an instant later she pulled away with an exclamation of dismay. "Oh, James, you mustn't. That's to say, *I* mustn't, because really I cannot—oh, dear, what a muddle I have made of things! No, indeed, James, you really must not. We must talk, of course, but not here. Why don't you go on into the house? I know Mama and Papa would be delighted to meet you. I'll come inside in a minute, after I finish picking up all these wretched beans."

"Let me help," said the Duke, leaning down to pick up a handful of spilled beans. Miss Denny protested violently and tried to shoo him into the house, yet he insisted on helping her pick up the beans and on carrying them into the house, too. It was only through the most strenuous efforts that she was able to keep him from carrying them on into the kitchen and depositing them in the scullery.

"No, indeed, I can take care of that, James. You must meet Mama and Papa first," she said, steering him toward the parlor.

As luck would have it, all her family were gathered there. Her father and mother were seated together on the sofa; her sister Matilda was at the pianoforte; and Cecil and Christopher were sprawled on the floor turning over the pages of an illustrated paper. All of them looked up in surprise as Miss Denny came in with the Duke. Christopher gave the Duke a piercing look, then turned to Mrs. Denny. "That's him, Mama," he said eagerly. "That's the man I was telling you about. Judy was kissing him in the garden."

These words made Miss Denny blush a vivid pink. The Duke only laughed, however, and addressed Christopher in a conspiratorial voice. "No, *I* was kissing *her*," he said. "The distinction is very fine, I will admit, but there *is* a distinction, however slight it may appear to an outside observer."

Miss Denny, blushing more deeply than ever, hastily made introductions. "Mama, Papa, this is his Grace, the Duke of Ashland. James, this is my mother and father, the Reverend Mr. and Mrs. Denny. And this is my sister Matilda, and these are my brothers Cecil and Christopher."

"I am very pleased to meet you all," said the Duke politely.

Mrs. Denny curtsied slightly by way of reply, but appeared incapable of speech. All three of the younger Dennys were likewise rendered speechless, and sat staring at the Duke with round eyes and open mouths. It thus fell to Reverend Denny to reply to the Duke's greeting, which he did with his habitual air of unruffled calm.

"Delighted to make your acquaintance, your Grace," he said, rising to shake the Duke's hand. "I suppose you must be one of Judith's London acquaintances. Are you staying in this neighborhood, or merely passing through?"

"Well, that rather depends," said the Duke, looking at Miss Denny. "I have taken rooms at the Swan, but I'm not sure how long I shall be staying."

"At the Swan!" exclaimed Mrs. Denny, galvanized into speech by this intelligence. "Oh, but your Grace cannot be comfortable at the Swan, I am sure. If you are staying in the neighborhood any length of time, you must come and stay with us here at the Rectory. There's no shortage of room, I assure you—and though I cannot promise you anything wonderful in the way of hospitality, I am sure we can do better for you than they can at the Swan!"

The Duke smiled. "I appreciate the invitation, Mrs. Denny," he said. "But I think my staying with you might not be quite convenient."

As he spoke, he looked again at Miss Denny. Miss Denny felt as though she must sink through the floor with embarrassment, but she forced herself to speak. "Indeed, your Grace, we would be very happy to have you here at the Rectory. You must not think of staying at the Swan while we can give you rooms."

Although her embarrassment was plain to see, the Duke was reassured by the smile that accompanied her words. He therefore gave way graciously to his hostess's urgings, and Mrs. Denny hurried off to instruct her servants about preparing him a room and fetching his bags from the Swan. While she was engaged on this errand, Reverend Denny and the Duke conversed easily about the weather, the prospect of the coming hay crop, and the recent fluctuation in corn prices.

Their conversation was interrupted from time to time by the younger Dennys, who had recovered from their stupefaction enough to question the Duke on various highly divergent subjects. Matilda wanted to know if he was acquainted with the Royal family; Cecil, who was to go to Eton that fall, was curious to learn whether he had been educated at that same, or a rival, institution; and Christopher, with the ease of a longtime acquaintance, commented favorably upon his horsemanship in driving a curricle-and-four.

Their questions, while ingenuous, were intelligent and put forward without the least trace of disrespect or impertinence. Listening to them talk, Miss Denny reflected with gratitude that though she might have many things to blush for in the present situation, her family was not one of them. If only the house was half as presentable! Miss Denny surreptitiously nudged a footstool over a stain in the carpet and settled herself to listen as the Duke smilingly endeavored to satisfy her siblings' curiosity.

Mrs. Denny came back presently and announced that the Duke's new quarters were ready whenever he cared to take them. "And of course you are invited to dinner, too," she told the Duke with a smile. "We dine at four o'clock—unfashionably early, I know, but Thomas prefers the old-fashioned custom of an early dinner, and I must confess that I do, too. Perhaps Judith can show you about the house and garden while I am busy in the kitchen. The church is well worth seeing, too, if you have the time."

This speech did not entirely suit Miss Denny, who would have liked to oversee the preparation of dinner herself. She felt in her bones that Susan's cooking would not be improved by knowing a duke was to partake of it. The prospect of sitting down to an ill-dressed meal in his company was a mortifying one, to say the least. She made no demur, however, but rose to her feet. "Certainly I will show you around," she told the Duke. "Shall we start with the house or garden?"

"The garden, I think" said the Duke, giving her a wicked

smile. "I have lately conceived a peculiar fondness for gardens—particularly of the kitchen variety."

Miss Denny blushed a little at this, but retaliated by taking him out to the kitchen garden and giving him an exhaustive tour of each individual plot of beans, asparagus, cabbage, carrots, peas, lettuce and cucumbers. He commented with grave approval on each, helped her and himself to a few strawberries from the strawberry bed, and then directed her steps toward the church, which stood apart from the rectory with the churchyard beyond.

"The nave is thought to date from the twelfth century," said Miss Denny in her best instructive voice, as she and the Duke entered the church. "And we have a fine example of a fifteenth century belltower."

"I see that you do. But though I normally find medieval architecture a fascinating subject, there are other subjects that are concerning me more at the present moment. I would like, for instance, to know if you are very angry with me for coming to you this way?"

Miss Denny turned to look at him. Her color was a little heightened, but she gave no other sign of discomposure. Having contemplated him a moment reflectively, she smiled, sighed and shook her head.

"No, James. It's very wrong and inconsistent of me, I know, but I can't help being glad you are here. How did you find out where I had gone?"

"From your sister, of course. I called in St. James's Square only a few hours after you had left and learned from her that you had suddenly decided to go home. Of course, I ought to have taken that as a hint that you weren't eager to see me again—but instead I dashed back home, threw a few things in a portmanteau, and set off in pursuit. I actually reached Winfield not long after you did, but thought it would be better to pass the night at the Swan and call upon you this morning rather than bursting in upon you when you were fatigued from your journey. I thought I would be more likely to get a positive reception that way," he explained, with a hint of a sparkle in his eyes. "And it turned out I was quite right."

Miss Denny, remembering the reception he had received, blushed all the deeper but shook her head. "I ought not to have let you kiss me, James," she said. "If I had known you were coming, I would have had a nice, polite, discouraging speech all ready for you. As it was, I was so overcome by seeing you so suddenly that I just acted on impulse."

The Duke looked at her pensively. "That ought to be a facer to me, oughtn't it? And yet—and yet, I find myself oddly encouraged. Call me foolishly persistent, if you will—even call me an overbearing nuisance—but I give you fair warning, Judith Denny. I came here to formally solicit your hand in marriage, and I intend to do so, no matter how many discouraging speeches you make me. What have you to say to that?"

Miss Denny's response was to make him a mock reverent curtsy. "Of course it shall be just as your Grace wishes," she said with exaggerated humility.

The Duke smiled ruefully. "If only that were true," he said. "However, *nil desperandum* is my motto. I shall formally solicit your father for your hand after dinner. Until then, we can occupy ourselves with medieval architecture or some other safe, neutral subject."

Miss Denny gave her tacit consent to this proposal by pointing out the unique design of the apsidal arches behind the altar. The Duke admired them gravely, and for the remainder of the period before dinner they discussed medieval architecture with the utmost propriety.

Chapter XVI

Dinner that evening went much better than Miss Denny had dared hope. The information that a real live duke was to partake of her cooking had naturally flustered Susan, the Rectory's novice cook, but it had also spurred her on to heroic efforts. Miss Denny, surveying the number of side dishes and corner plates flanking the central roast of mutton, feared indeed that she might have overextended herself, but everything proved quite edible save for a violently-colored molded jelly which Miss Denny adroitly whisked off the table while conversation was directed the other way.

The Duke behaved with his usual impeccable manners. He praised everything he ate, accepted second helpings of several dishes, and remained politely oblivious to the servants' awe-stricken scrutiny. When Sarah, who was waiting at table, insisted on offering him the potatoes with a deep curtsy and a reverent ''your Grace,'' he accepted them with a pleasant smile; when Susan popped her head through the kitchen door to inquire anxiously if the gravy would ''go round,'' he behaved as though it were quite an everyday thing for the cook to come among the company in such a fashion. And he seemed not to notice that Hodgkins, the outside man, made several unnecessary trips down the passage beside the dining parlor to gawk at his master's aristocratic visitor.

Reverend Denny finally put a stop to this last disturbance by getting up and closing the parlor door. "We seem to have an unusual amount of traffic in the house this evening," he observed with a twinkle in his eye. He then returned to his seat to resume his interrupted conversation with the Duke. Miss Denny sat listening to them talk while picking at her mutton and vegetables. She was nervously anticipating the moment when dinner would be over and the Duke should request an interview with her father.

The moment came not long after. As soon as the dessert, a rhubarb tart, had been eaten and cleared, Reverend Denny politely invited the Duke to take a glass of port in his study. "Thank you, sir, I should be glad to do so," was the Duke's calm reply. "Your invitation comes very opportunely, for it happens that there is a matter of importance I wish to discuss with you in private."

Reverend Denny received this speech quite as though it were nothing out of the ordinary but Mrs. Denny's eyebrows shot upwards. She looked across the table at her eldest daughter. "Shall we retire to the parlor, Judith?" she said. "The Duke and your father seem likely to be gone for some time."

"Yes, certainly, Mama," said Miss Denny, coloring vividly. Rising, she hurried across the passage to the parlor. Matilda, Cecil, and Christopher trailed after, their faces bright with interest.

"What's the Duke want to talk to Papa about?" Christopher wanted to know, as soon as they were seated in the parlor. "Why did he want to be alone with him, Mama?"

"Ask your sister," said Mrs. Denny, surveying her elder daughter with amusement.

Christopher at once repeated the same inquiry to Miss Denny, but got no very satisfactory reply. She professed herself as ignorant as he of the Duke's motives. "Perhaps he is indigent and in need of assistance," she suggested solemnly. "You know that since Papa is a clergyman, people are always expecting him to give them food, or fuel, or money enough to help them through to the next quarter day.''

Christopher looked incredulous, and Cecil laughed at the idea of a duke needing financial assistance. "Nonsense, Judy! He is a duke, after all. Why, I daresay he is rich enough to buy this whole village—this whole parish, perhaps.''

"Really?'' said Christopher, looking deeply impressed. "If he's that rich, it can't be money he wants, or food or firewood. Why does he want to talk to Papa, then?''

"*I* know why he wants to talk to Papa,'' said Matilda, shooting a sly look at her sister. "And so would you and Cecil if you have any brains at all.''

Cecil and Christopher turned a skeptical gaze on her and demanded to know, first, why she thought she was so vastly more intelligent than anyone else in the world; and second (almost as an afterthought), why the Duke had wanted a private interview with their father. Matilda gave them a superior smile. "Because he wants to marry Judy, of course. He is asking for her hand in marriage.''

"No!'' said Christopher incredulously.

"Judy?'' said Cecil, going off into paroxysms of laughter once more. Christopher did not join in his brother's laughter, however, but appealed to his mother, as to the ultimate authority.

"Mama, is that true? Does the Duke want to marry Judy?''

"I wouldn't be surprised,'' said Mrs. Denny. With a faint smile she looked over to where Miss Denny sat blushing on a corner of the sofa. "I must say, Judith, that you have kept all this very dark.''

Miss Denny merely shook her head. She was saved making any further answer by the entrance of Reverend Denny, who came into the room, carefully shutting the door behind him.

"Papa, the Duke wants to marry Judy,'' Christopher informed him in a voice of incredulity.

"Yes, I know,'' returned his father with admirable gravity. "His Grace has just made a formal offer for her hand.'' Looking at Miss Denny, he added, "Now it is necessary that I ascertain your sister's feelings on the subject. Perhaps you and Cecil and

Matilda could run upstairs and study your lessons while we discuss the matter.''

There were protests from the younger Dennys, but none of them attempted to argue. Rising, they reluctantly quit the room, shooting looks of mingled awe and respect over their shoulders at their elder sister. "Oh, Judy, this is so exciting," whispered Matilda as she went out of the room. "It's just like something out of a novel.''

"It is, isn't it?" agreed Miss Denny with feeling.

When Matilda and the others had gone, Reverend Denny looked again at Miss Denny. His expression was grave, but there was a quirk about his lips that suggested he was trying not to laugh. "I am inclined to agree with Matilda. Never did I expect to receive such a visitor in my home, intent upon such an errand. I must say, however, that I have been most favorably impressed with his Grace. He appears to be a man of sense and (I believe) character. What do you think of him, Judith?''

Although Miss Denny could not control the hue of her complexion, she could answer a question such as this readily enough. "I think just as you do, sir. His Grace seems to me a man of sense and character. I have always enjoyed his company very much.''

Reverend Denny smiled. "The feeling would appear to be mutual. Indeed, I may say that the sentiments his Grace has expressed do both you and him the greatest credit. It is true that he is not a suitor I would have anticipated for my daughter, but take it all in all I see nothing to dislike in the match—''

At this, Mrs. Denny was unable to contain herself any longer. "Nothing to dislike in the match! My dear Thomas! A duke of the realm, handsome as a prince, with I know not how many thousands a year! I should hope you would see nothing to dislike!''

Reverend Denny smiled, but his voice held a touch of reproof as he responded to his wife's words. "All that is very well, of course, my dear Sophia. But there are more than merely worldly considerations to be taken into account here. What I was going to say just now was that I see nothing to dislike in a match between Judith and the Duke apart from the dissimilarity of their backgrounds and positions. There, I must confess, I do see something to dislike—or if not to dislike, at least something which must cause me concern.'' He looked at Miss Denny. ''I must ask you, Judith, if this proposal of the Duke's has come as a surprise to you?''

''Not entirely, no,'' admitted Miss Denny, twisting her hands together nervously.

Reverend Denny gave her a sympathetic smile. ''Then you have had time to consider the situation—and no doubt you have already decided what your answer to his Grace must be. Please believe that I have the highest opinion of your understanding, Judith. I have no doubt that the concerns that have occurred to me will have occurred to you, too, and that in making your decision you will have given them a full and just consideration. That being the case, I see no need to belabor the subject further. The Duke is waiting in my study. When you are ready, you may go to him and tell him whether you mean to accept his very obliging offer.''

Miss Denny was both astonished and touched by this speech, but Mrs. Denny looked as though it did not entirely satisfy her. ''My dear Thomas, it is all very well to talk about 'concerns' and 'consideration' in that unworldly fashion, but you know as well as I do that such an opportunity as this will never come to Judith again,'' she said with a touch of asperity. ''To whistle a duke down the wind, when she might live in luxury all her life—''

''My dear, I am persuaded that you cannot wish your daughter to marry from such motives as that,'' said Reverend Denny, gently, but with an authority that silenced his wife. ''And I am equally persuaded that you do not wish to urge Judith into doing anything that is against her conscience. It is she who must live with this decision, after all, and I feel strongly that she ought to make up her mind uninfluenced by any opinion of ours.'' He looked affectionately at his daughter. ''She knows her own heart, I hope—and I hope she knows also that we will love and support her, whatever decision she may make.''

''Yes, of course,'' said Mrs. Denny, swallowing her rebuke with a good grace. She smiled ruefully at Miss Denny. ''Your father is quite right as usual, Judith. You must do what *you* think is right, and then you will never have cause for regret.''

Miss Denny embraced them both, quite overwhelmed by this display of parental support. ''Thank you,'' she said. ''I'm sure no one ever had such understanding parents as I do. I only hope I shall contrive not to disappoint you.'' She embraced them both a second time, then squared her shoulders and drew a deep breath. ''Now if you will excuse me, I must go and talk to the Duke.''

Miss Denny found the Duke standing at the window of her father's study. He was looking out at the neatly ordered garden and the green of the shrubbery beyond it, but turned around as she came into the room. For a moment he regarded her in silence, a faint smile playing about his lips. ''I suppose your father has conveyed to you the fullness of my intent?'' he said. ''I do like your father, Judy. In fact, I like your whole family. I never met with such a welcome in my life as they have extended to me this day.''

Miss Denny smiled back at him shyly. ''That is hardly surprising, James,'' she said. ''They are none of them in the habit of entertaining dukes, you see.''

''I never would have supposed it. Like you, they have a refreshing way of ignoring my rank and treating me as an ordinary human being.'' He came toward her as he spoke and took her hands in his. ''And Judy, I *am* an ordinary human being—a man who wants desperately to marry the woman he loves. I know you have refused me once. That probably ought to have dissuaded me, but though you refused my offer of marriage, you could not say you did not love me. Can you say it now?''

Miss Denny shook her head, a smile trembling on her lips. ''No, I cannot. I do love you, James. I have known it a long time, but I had hoped to conceal it, for your sake.''

''For my sake!'' said the Duke, looking incredulous. ''You have an odd idea of concern, if this is your way of expressing it! I've been worrying my head off these last six weeks, wondering if you weren't going to marry young Manville.''

At this, Miss Denny could not help laughing. "Oh, James, how ridiculous! Mr. Manville is nothing but a friend—a very good friend, to be sure, but I have no intention of marrying him.'' In a more sober voice, she added, "But the fact is that I ought not to marry you either, James. I cannot deny that I am tempted—oh, yes, very tempted—to accept you. But I am afraid that I am not the woman to make you happy.''

The Duke opened his mouth to protest this statement, but Miss Denny forestalled him. Laying her hand on his arm, she continued on quickly, looking up at him earnestly as she spoke. "You ought to marry a beautiful girl of noble birth who would be an ornament to your position. I know nothing of society, or next to nothing, and I have no experience in managing a great house or in performing any of the other duties that would fall to your wife's lot. You say you love me, but I am afraid I would be a disappointment to you, James, and that I could not bear. I love you so much that I would rather live without you than bring the least shame or embarrassment upon you. You must see, if our positions were reversed, that you would feel the same.''

The Duke was looking grim. "My cousins have been talking to you," he said, and the words were a statement, not a question. "It was that day they took you out driving, wasn't it? I was afraid of it at the time, but you denied it, and I was happy to be convinced otherwise. But I ought to have known Lou and Phil were at the bottom of this.''

"Louisa and Philippa did express some of the concerns I have just mentioned when we were out driving,'' admitted Miss Denny. "But that would have made no difference to me, if what they said had not been true. You must see it yourself, James. I hardly fit the conventional image of a duchess!''

"Certainly you do not,'' returned the Duke promptly. "There is nothing conventional about you. At the same time, however, I think you imagine the position to be more standardized than is really the case. The Dukes of Ashland have historically been quite democratic in their choice of brides. One of our duchesses started life as a cowman's daughter; one was a cast-off mistress of George I; and one I have strong reason to believe was a Jewess, though they gave her out to be of Spanish blood. I'll wager Philippa and Louisa did not tell you that!''

"Is this true, James?" said Miss Denny, looking up at him in astonishment.

"Yes, quite true," said the Duke, smiling down at her. "You see you would be quite a boringly conventional duchess compared to the ladies I have just mentioned. And as for your not being raised to perform a duchess's duties, that is (if I may say so kindly, my dear) complete nonsense. The duties of a duchess are probably no different from those which your mother daily performs. They would merely be performed on a somewhat larger scale. And since you would have more servants to assist you in performing them, I would not wonder if you found the job overall quite a bit easier than your mother's.''

Miss Denny laughed shakily. "Mama always says nothing could be more challenging than being a clergyman's wife,'' she said.

"And you ought to believe your mother, who is a woman of admirable good sense if I ever saw one. Indeed, I think you are letting mistaken reverence for my position cloud your judgment, Judy. You must recapture a little of that irreverence that led you to snub me the first time we met!''

Miss Denny smiled but looked indecisive. "I don't know,'' she said, twisting her hands together nervously once again. "If only I could be sure. But I don't quite dare take such a gamble, James. Marriage is such a serious business, and there's no going back if one makes a mistake.''

"True, but you must not let that idea cloud your judgment, either,'' said the Duke, recapturing her hands in his and carrying them to his lips. "Treat the matter as you would any ordinary day-to-day decision. Have confidence in your own intelligence and abilities, and put no reliance whatever on other people's opinions. That is how you have behaved from the first moment I met you, and I don't think it's too much to say that it was that, as much as anything, which made me fall in love with you.''

This speech earned him a tremulous smile, but still Miss Denny looked indecisive. "Oh, James, I wish I could, but I can't be quite as heedless about this business as I would about an 'ordinary day-to-day decision,'" she said, with a shake of her head. "I don't care about other people's opinions in the general way, but where marriage is concerned, there really are more people to be considered in this than you and I. If your family should take me in dislike—"

"They won't," said the Duke firmly. "Lou and Phil may kick up a dust, of course, but they'd do as much for any woman I wanted to marry. I don't care in the slightest what their opinions may be, and neither should you. As for my other relations—well, the plain fact is I don't have very many other relations. Most of the ones I do have I don't see once in a twelvemonth. The only relation on earth whose opinion I care about is my grandmother, and if I mistake not, she will like you as much as I do."

"Oh, James, I wish I could believe you," said Miss Denny, with a shake of her head. The Duke looked down at her wistfully.

"Cannot you believe me, Judy? It seems hard that I cannot have the wife I want only because I am a duke. I have half a mind to renounce the title here and now and see if plain Mr. Montfort wouldn't stand a better chance with you!"

"That isn't necessary, James," said Miss Denny, smiling a little. "If I could only be sure I wouldn't be a disgrace to you, I would marry you even in spite of your disadvantages of rank and title! But unfortunately I cannot be sure without actually committing myself. If only there were some way of knowing beforehand."

The Duke looked thoughtful. "Perhaps there is. I don't mean to make light of your scruples, Judy, for I can see how you would be intimidated by what is unknown to you. That is simple human nature, after all. But by the same token, if you were to gain some acquaintance with what you fear, I believe you might be reassured. If you were to visit me at my home and see for yourself what your duties would consist of, for instance—yes, I believe that might do the trick."

Miss Denny looked dubious. "I could not visit you in your home without it looking very particular, James," she said. "When it came to people's ears, they would naturally assume that we were engaged or about to become engaged. And if it turned out later that I didn't marry you, there would inevitably be a great deal of talk. I would rather avoid that if I could."

"Naturally," said the Duke, nodding. "Even though I have no doubt you will discover your fears are groundless, I can see how you would rather not commit yourself beforehand. How does this sound? I will invite a party down for the period of your visit, so you are merely one of twenty or thirty other guests. That will allow you to look about you and make up your mind quite inconspicuously, without being in any way committed."

Miss Denny drew a deep breath. "That sounds wonderful," she said fervently. "But will it not be a great deal of trouble for you, James?"

"Much less trouble than renouncing my title," he said with a glimmer of a smile.

"Then I'll do it," said Miss Denny, smiling back at him. "Invite your party, James, and I shall see for myself exactly what is involved in this duchess business."

Chapter XVII

The Duke took leave of the Dennys early the next morning. Reverend and Mrs. Denny had been apprised of the decision he and Miss Denny had reached, and while they both expressed perfect satisfaction with the idea of their daughter attending the ducal house party, in private Mrs. Denny grieved a little that there was no positive engagement to be announced. She was human enough to covet the distinction of having a daughter betrothed to a duke.

Fortunately, the same cheerful philosophy that had sustained Mrs. Denny through six pregnancies, a succession of half-trained servants, and thirty years of marriage to an unworldly man of moderate income enabled her to bear her disappointment with Christian fortitude. She bade farewell to the Duke with the appearance of complete satisfaction and urged him to return whenever he might be in the neighborhood, no matter what her daughter's eventual decision might be.

The Duke did not return to London but went directly to Ashland Palace, arriving there early in the second day of his travels. He was intent on assembling his house party as soon as possible. To this end, he requested immediate interviews with his chef, butler, and groom of chambers. He also imparted the news to his paternal grandmother, who was in year-round residence at Ashland Palace.

The Dowager Duchess of Ashland, a formidable-looking dame with a Roman nose and front of improbable saffron hair, received his tidings with her usual outspoken candor. "So you're thinking of getting buckled at last, are you?" she said, eyeing him with a cynical smile. "You've kept clear of the altar long enough, goodness knows, but I knew it'd be only a matter of time before some clever gel snared you."

The Duke smiled ruefully. "No, I assure you it isn't like that at all, ma'am. This particular young lady has not only not tried to snare me, but has evaded all my own attempts to snare *her* with the greatest perspicuity."

"She *is* clever," said the Dowager Duchess admiringly. "The clever ones always make you think it's you that's chasing them, not the other way around."

"Perhaps, but I believe that in this case the young lady's reservations are genuine, ma'am. Miss Denny fears her birth and background have not fitted her for a duchess's position."

"Oh, she does, does she?" The Dowager Duchess eyed her grandson shrewdly. "Mayhap she's right, James. Who is this Miss Denny? Is her birth respectable?"

"Perfectly respectable, ma'am. She is the daughter of a country clergyman, a very superior, scholarly gentleman. Both he and his wife are people of undoubted gentility, and they are tolerably well-connected, too. I first met Miss Denny at the home of her elder sister, who is the wife of a baronet."

"That's all right, then," said the Dowager Duchess with a dismissive nod. "Just so long as she's respectable, that's the chief thing. And so you plan to bring her here?"

"That is my plan, ma'am. I thought if she could see what a duchess's duties actually involve, she might not be so intimidated by the idea of taking them on. Dare I hope you will assist me in making her welcome and showing her the ins and outs of the place?"

"Well, that depends," said the Dowager cannily. "I'd rather wait till I meet the gal before I make any promises of that sort, James. If I like your Miss Denny, I'll do what I can to convince

her to have you, but if I don't, I tell you fairly that I'll wash
my hands of the whole business. I won't be a party to your
making a *mésalliance*.''

''You need have no fear of that, ma'am. I am quite sure you
will like Miss Denny extremely. Indeed, she reminds me very
much of you in some ways. The way in which she speaks her
mind, for instance, quite regardless of other people's opinions
and equally regardless of what violence she might be doing
my feelings!''

The Dowager appeared tickled by this revelation. ''Oh, she's
like that, is she? I must say, she sounds just the girl for you,
James. It wouldn't do for you to marry one of these toad-
eating, mealy-mouthed creatures that're always swarming about
underfoot.'' Grinning widely, she added, ''I tell you what,
James: I'll do what I can to help you win your Miss Denny,
if only to vex Louisa and Philippa. Won't they be wild when
they hear what's in the wind, though!''

On this point, the Dowager proved a true prophet. The Duke's
cousins arrived at Ashland Palace the following day, full of
concern over his sudden departure from London. And when
they learned what had prompted his departure, and that Miss
Denny was actually coming to Ashland Palace to inspect its
premises as a possible future mistress, their concern was ampli-
fied a hundredfold.

''You cannot have been thinking, James!''

Louisa made this statement in a hushed voice, regarding the
Duke solemnly from across the long dinner table in the Palace's
Marble Hall. She and her sister wore matching pale muslin
dinner dresses shrouded with shawls and scarves in deference
to the arctic temperatures which prevailed within the Hall. As
the footmen removed the dishes from the dinner's first course
and began to replace them with the second, Louisa leaned
forward to address her cousin again in a confidential tone.

''Indeed, James, I cannot think what could have prevailed
on you to do such a heedless thing. What is this Miss Denny,

after all? A country clergyman's daughter with no beauty, no breeding, and no accomplishments worth the mentioning."

"A nice girl, I daresay," interjected Philippa kindly, "but no fit bride for you, James. Louisa and I were shocked beyond words to hear that you had actually proposed to her."

"I wish you really had been shocked beyond words," said the Duke, irritably waving away a plate of Spanish fritters which one of the footmen was offering him. "I have already told you that I do not mean to discuss this matter with you. And particularly not at the dinner table." He looked meaningfully at the servants.

"But James, you must know it is only our concern for you that prompts us to speak," persisted Louisa. "You cannot have considered what you are doing. To take a young lady to wife whose antecedents are so distinctly inferior—can you really consider disgracing your ancient and honored name in such a way? You ought to marry a woman whose ancestry is as high and pure and untainted as your own."

She was interrupted by a coarse laugh from the Dowager. "Stuff and nonsense, Louisa. If the girl's a gentlewoman, that's all that matters. I've got no patience listening to you drivel on and on in that foolish fashion."

Louisa looked aggrieved. "But Miss Denny's antecedents—" she began.

"It's not as though you were in any position to talk about that," said the Dowager crushingly. "This Miss Denny's antecedents are likely as good as yours and maybe a sight better."

Louisa looked nettled, but managed an indulgent laugh. "Whatever do you mean, Grandmother?" she said. "Considering that my father was your own youngest son—"

"Aye, but your mother always had the morals of a stray cat," said the Dowager triumphantly. "For aught any of us know, you might be one of the footmen's daughters as easily as my poor Simon's."

The dozen or so footmen waiting at table were all too well-trained to betray any emotion at these words, but there was an imperceptible stirring among their ranks and a certain amount of coughing and exchanging of glances. Louisa threw a look of deep reproach at the Dowager. "Really, Grandmother!" she said. "I know you like to have your joke, but I consider that remark to be in extremely bad taste." Rising to her feet, she added with dignity, "My appetite is quite destroyed. I think I will go to my room and lie down for a while."

"And I, too," said Philippa. Giving her grandmother a smile that mingled reproach with martyred forgiveness, she rose from her seat. One of the footmen, his face wooden, opened the door for the two ladies, who acknowledged the action with a cold nod. Side by side they swept out of the room.

The Duke looked at the Dowager, who was grinning gleefully at the success of her joke. "I must say, ma'am, that I agree with my cousin," he said. "That remark was really not in the best of taste."

"She deserved it," said the Dowager unrepentantly. "Besides, she oughtn't to be such a ninny as to take what I said just now seriously. She and Philippa are Simon's daughters, right enough—no mistaking those whey faces of theirs." She winked at the nearest footman, then suddenly grew sober. "You'd better hope your Miss Denny has a thick skin, though. She'll need it, living here with those two. Hope she has a strong constitution, too." With a shiver, the Dowager hitched her shawl over her skinny shoulders. "This has got to be the coldest house in the four kingdoms. I swear my cattle are more comfortably housed."

"That goes without saying, ma'am," said the Duke with a smile. The Dowager Duchess was passionately devoted to her pet herd of milch cattle and had been known to personally assist in the breeding and lying-in of her favorites. "If you had your way, they would eat off gold plate and bed down at night with silken counterpanes."

"No, but they wouldn't dine in an ice house," retorted the Dowager. "I can't think why I continue living in this demmed uncomfortable mausoleum. Habit, I suppose—your grandfather brought me here when we were first married, and by this time I'm more or less used to it."

"It is an uncomfortable house, isn't it?" said the Duke, looking around him. He was so accustomed to the continual chill that permeated Ashland Palace that he scarcely noticed it anymore, but now it struck him with renewed force.

The Marble Hall, with its classic proportions and sumptuous furnishings, was a beautiful room, but so cold that any dish brought within its walls became immediately as chilly as the surrounding atmosphere. The sauce for the pigeons *en compote* which the footmen had just brought in was already congealing in its sauceboat, and the *omelette soufflée* had deflated to a sad-looking pancake. Only the jellies and creams stood firm, defying the cold by virtue of their own chilly natures. The Duke helped himself to a claret jelly and ate gloomily, while his grandmother regaled herself on Rhenish cream and chicken *chaud-froid* at the other end of the table.

When the meal was over, the Duke refused his butler's offer of port and left the Marble Hall. He strolled through the saloon, gallery, and other state apartments, looking around him and trying to see everything as Miss Denny would see it when she arrived on the following week.

What he saw made his gloom deepen further. The Palace was a magnificent place, rich in marble, murals, and ornate carvings and replete with treasures of art; but it had been designed with more consideration for showing off these treasures than for the human beings who inhabited it. The same marble that made it magnificent to look at also made it bitterly cold, and the rooms were arranged and furnished with a formality that was highly oppressive.

Nor had consideration been shown for anything like efficient household management. Nearly a quarter mile of passage separated the servants' quarters from their master and mistress's in the opposite wing, and it was impossible to go even from one sitting room to the next without traversing a length of bleakly splendid corridor ornamented with murals depicting the first Duke and Duchess in classical dress, being received by various Olympian deities.

The Duke, surveying them morosely, supposed that the egoism which could command such follies could also support life in a marble museum. For his part, he would have been glad to trade it for the humblest of his other dwelling places—his hunting box in Leicestershire, perhaps, or the small farmhouse attached to his Scottish property.

He wished now he had arranged to hold his house party in one of these other residences rather than Ashland Palace. But of course the Palace was the historic seat of the Dukes of Ashland, the place where tradition dictated that he spend the majority of his time. If Miss Denny were to gain a true idea of all that her future duties might comprise, she could do so nowhere more fitly and comprehensively than here. It struck the Duke with disagreeable force, however, that she might well balk when she saw under what conditions those duties must be performed.

"And I don't know that I would blame her. Really, I can't think why any sane woman would want to be a duchess," he muttered to himself as he strolled through one chilly, magnificent room after another. "It's a bit much, asking any young woman to take on a proposition like this. To live in a barracks of a house and be hedged about by pomp and tradition day in and day out . . . even if I were as handsome as Adonis, I'd find it hard to put across such a bargain."

With a grim smile, the Duke looked at a mural depicting his noble ancestor in that very guise, languishing in the arms of Venus. "And I'm not conceited enough to fancy myself an Adonis, God knows. The best I can hope is that the weather warms a little before Judith gets here, so the house isn't as miserably uncomfortable as it is today."

Unfortunately for the Duke's hopes, the weather during the ensuing days continued chilly and rather damp. The day of Miss Denny's arrival was chillier even than those that had preceded it, and an ominous gray sky gave witness to the likelihood of rain before the day was out.

The Duke was in a fret all that day, looking out for the Spicer's carriage (for it had been agreed that less comment would be aroused if Miss Denny returned to St. James's Square and attended the house party under the auspices of her sister and brother-in-law). When at last the long looked-for carriage made its appearance beneath the first of the triumphal arches that spanned the Palace's stately main drive, the Duke brushed aside Louisa and Philippa (who had been hovering about, trying in their languid way to distract him) and hurried to the entrance hall.

It was some minutes before Miss Denny made her entrance. Since she was preceded into the hall by her statuesque sister and burly brother-in-law, the Duke missed seeing her at first, and for a panic-stricken moment wondered if she might have changed her mind and decided not to come after all. Then he caught sight of the small figure that trailed behind Lady Spicer, and his panic eased somewhat.

Anxiously the Duke watched Miss Denny, trying to see from her face what impression the Palace was making on her. She was looking about at the statues on their pedestals; surveying the lofty domed ceiling overhead and the glossy marble floor underfoot with apparent interest, but her expression was rather reserved. When she caught sight of him standing at the foot of the stairs, however, a smile suddenly blossomed forth on her face.

"Good day, Lady Spicer, Sir Geoffrey," said the Duke, greeting the Spicers first, as etiquette dictated. As soon as he could, however, he turned to Miss Denny. "And so you are here at last," he said in a low voice, taking her hand in his. "Dare I ask what you think of it all?"

Miss Denny glanced around her once more, a little smile playing at the corners of her mouth. "I think I shall have to be very rude to you indeed, James, if I am not to be completely intimidated," she said. "It is all quite overpoweringly magnificent."

The Duke grimaced. "I suppose to the uninitiated eye it might appear so. But I beg you will reserve judgment until you have seen it more fully. I have already promised to give everyone a tour of the place after dinner, so that will give you a nice opportunity to get a first look at everything. For now, I suppose I ought to let you go to your room." In a lowered voice, he added, "I have given you the best bedchamber. At least, my grandmother claims it is the best—they all seem about equally bad to me. However, I have done the best I could, and if you need anything I've overlooked, please don't hesitate to ring for it. We dine in about an hour.''

Under the direction of the Duke's groom of chambers, a small, fussy-looking gentleman who was hovering nearby, the Spicers and Miss Denny were taken to their rooms along with their baggage and installed there with every comfort. Miss Denny was rather awed by the chamber assigned to her, a cavernous room equipped with a bed big enough to sleep a moderate-sized family. But she accepted it with a smile and word of thanks and set about dressing for dinner. "Wear a warm shawl if you've got one, Miss," advised the maidservant who had been assigned to wait on her. "The Marble Hall is mortal cold."

"Is that where we meet to go into dinner?" asked Miss Denny, smoothing the folds of her mulberry crepe dinner dress and giving her curls a final fluff.

"No, that's where you'll have dinner, Miss. You'll soon learn that everything's a hall in this house—everything that's not a gallery or a court, that is. There's the Great Hall, where you came in; the Marble Hall, where you eat; and the Little Hall, which you have to go through to get from one drawing room to the next (though little it is not, to my way of thinking). Then there's the Long Hall in the south wing, where they keep a lot of statues and pictures and such stuff; and the Upstairs Hall, just down the corridor from here; and the Servants' Hall downstairs—and the Octagonal Hall, of course, though that's by way of being a saloon.''

"Gracious, it all sounds very confusing," said Miss Denny, throwing a flowered silk shawl over her shoulders. "If you will show me to the room where we meet for dinner, I should be much obliged.''

The maidservant willingly conveyed her to this apartment, which happened to be the Little Hall. As the girl had said, the Little Hall was somewhat deceptively named, being some eighty feet long and (it seemed to Miss Denny's fancy) very nearly as high. Its muraled walls were lined with galleries, and on the ceiling high overhead, the figures of the First Duke and

Duchess frolicked in an Arcadian landscape with a troupe of nymphs and satyrs.

Miss Denny was relieved to see she was not the first to come down, nor yet the last. A group of guests was huddled at the far end of the hall, doing their best to laugh and chat gaily but looking nevertheless rather intimidated by their surroundings. Miss Denny was in the midst of exchanging greetings with those guests whom she was already acquainted with when the Duke arrived on the scene. He was accompanied by an elderly lady in black taffeta and Brussels lace whom he introduced to the party as his grandmother, the Dowager Duchess of Ashland.

The Dowager looked notably bored as one after another of the party was introduced to her. She received their civil greetings with an absent nod and half-smile and seemed to be thinking all the while of something else. When the Duke introduced Miss Denny to her, however, her manner changed.

"So you're Miss Denny," she said, surveying Miss Denny with critical interest. "You didn't tell me she was such a little thing, James. Not a beauty, either—but that's neither here nor there. I was never a beauty, either, and I've done well enough for all that. It ain't looks that count, it's spirit: that's what I always say. Have you got plenty of spirit, girl?"

"I hope so," said Miss Denny, laughing in spite of herself at this unconventional greeting.

The Dowager nodded with approval, then narrowed her eyes and leaned forward to address her young guest in a hushed voice. Miss Denny was sure it was some highly sensitive inquiry she was about to make and waited rather nervously to hear the Dowager's question. What actually came out, however, was: "Tell me, Miss Denny, do you know anything about milch cattle?"

"A little," said Miss Denny, a good deal taken aback. "My father raises Ayrshires back home in Derbyshire."

Again the Dowager nodded approval. "A good breed. Not so good as Jerseys, of course, but I daresay they do better up north than Jerseys would. Still, there's nothing like Jerseys for rich, creamy milk. I'll take you out to see my herd after dinner."

"I am giving Miss Denny a tour of the house after dinner,

ma'am," said the Duke. "You can show her your cattle tomorrow, if you like." To Miss Denny, he added with a smile, "You must know that my grandmother has devoted most of her life to the upbringing of milch cattle. The upbringing of her only grandson was, in comparison, a matter of minor interest to her. My doings always took a secondary position to the doings of Lady Belle and Queen Mab and her other pets."

"And very right, too," retorted the Dowager. "You were nothing but an ordinary scrubby boy, James, but Lady Belle was the best milcher I've ever had. Calved twenty-six times, she did," she informed Miss Denny with pride. "All heifers, and everyone of 'em a prize milcher, though none so good as herself. I've a painting of her by Stubbs hanging in my closet. Stubbs did a fair job of it, though I don't think myself it really does her justice. Still, it's a decent effort, and I must be sure to show it to you sometime when I get a chance. But I want to show you my present herd first. Tomorrow morning, after breakfast—shall we say seven o'clock?"

Here, however, the Duke intervened with an air of authority. "Seven is a rather early hour, ma'am," he told the Dowager. "Not everyone chooses to rise at the crack of dawn like you. And you know Miss Denny has spent most of this day traveling. It would be only polite to allow her to recuperate a little from her journey."

"Eight o'clock, then," said the Dowager, with the air of one willing to make a concession.

"That's still very early," protested the Duke. Miss Denny smiled, however, and said that eight o'clock would suit her very well, as she never lay abed late. This speech made the Dowager look upon her more approvingly than ever. The Duke, for his part, gave her a rueful smile; and as the last of the party had just come into the hall, he turned to his butler with word that dinner might be served any time. The butler presently announced that all was ready, and two by two the party filed into the Marble Hall.

Miss Denny soon saw that the maidservant had not exaggerated in describing the Marble Hall as "mortal cold." It was a magnificent room in the classical style, proportioned on double cube lines and floored in the finest Sienese marble. Urns, friezes, and Grecian statuary abounded, furthering the theme of classicism; but since its designer had not seen fit to mar its antique splendor by introducing the anachronism of fireplaces, the room was as cold as it was magnificent. Gooseflesh stood on the ladies' exposed arms and shoulders, and the hot dishes which the footmen laid on the table smoked furiously for a moment or two, then settled down to congeal with all speed.

Miss Denny passed the meal in a state of bemusement, eating almost nothing and taking little part in the conversation that was going on around her. She could not converse with the Duke in any case, for the formality of the setting had obliged him to cede the places on either side of him to ladies better born than she.

She would not have minded talking to the Dowager, to whom she had taken a fancy; but that lady, at the foot of the table, was almost as distant to her as the Duke. She might have talked to Sir Geoffrey, who was seated across the table from her, but he appeared to be sulking; and since he had sulked more or less continuously since they had left London that morning, Miss Denny judged it futile to try to engage him in conversation now.

As for Lady Spicer, she was too busy flirting with a young cabinet minister whom she had engaged in lieu of her usual flirt, Lord Henry, to observe her sister's preoccupation. Miss Denny was not sorry for this, nor was she sorry to find Lord Henry had not been included among the Duke's guests. With no immediate disaster threatening her sister's marriage, and no one to engage her in conversation, she could give her full attention to looking about her and taking stock of her surroundings.

"And I might be mistress of all this if I chose," she marveled to herself, watching the footmen moving swiftly and silently about the table. "Could I possibly fill such a role?"

For a moment Miss Denny was overawed, imagining all the pomp and splendor that must attach itself to the title of Duchess of Ashland. Then her practical self reasserted itself. "I don't know if I could be a grand lady ordering people about left and right, but I know I could never endure to sit freezing through dinner seven nights a week," she told herself. "I'd find some way to bring heat into this place if I had to put braziers under the table! And while I was at it, I'd put cushions on the chairs, too, and make things that much more comfortable. It's ridiculous to spend all this time and money on an elaborate meal and then suffer while you eat it."

The meal dragged to an end in due course, and the ladies filed shivering out of the Marble Hall, across the equally inclement Little Hall, and into the principal drawing room. For such a prosaic room as this, the house's designer had granted the concession of a fireplace, and the ladies gathered gratefully about its warmth. They were very soon joined by the gentlemen, who, given the temperature of the dining parlor, had not cared to linger over their port. The Duke accepted a cup of tea from his grandmother, then maneuvered over to Miss Denny, who was surveying the view from the drawing room window with a meditative air.

"I trust you are not contemplating an escape," he murmured, taking a sip of his tea.

Miss Denny looked at him in surprise. "No, not at all, James. Why should I want to escape?"

"Well, I could hardly blame you if you did, now you have seen the kind of hospitality we inflict on our guests here at Ashland Palace. Although I don't know if hospitality is the right word. It's really more of a form of torture—'ordeal by cold,' if you will."

"Oh, that!" Miss Denny laughed. "Yes, it was dreadfully cold in that Hall, James, no doubt about it. Why do you not eat in some other room?"

"Tradition," said the Duke gloomily. "The Dukes of Ashland have always dined in the Marble Hall; *ergo,* they must continue to do so until overtaken by death—probably a premature death brought on by exposure to cold! We do have a smaller dining room where we occasionally eat on informal occasions, but it isn't much of an improvement as regards comfort. Besides, it's even farther from the kitchens than the

Marble Hall, so the food ends up even colder than if we just went ahead and dined in the Hall.''

"I see,'' said Miss Denny. She pondered for a minute. ''Could not some other room be made into a dining parlor?'' she ventured at last, in a timid voice. ''Some room, perhaps, that is *closer* to the kitchen?''

Looking more gloomy than ever, the Duke shook his head. ''All the rooms on that side of the house are state rooms,'' he explained. ''Not only are they crammed with works of art, they've been sanctified by the visits of various exalted personages over the years until now they're more shrines than mere rooms. That's the problem with this whole place, when you come right down to it. Everything's so imbued with tradition that there are shrieks of outrage if one so much as moves a table out from the wall.''

Miss Denny nodded, but was prevented from speaking by Louisa and Philippa, who came trailing over in their light muslin frocks. ''I hope we're not interrupting, James, but your conversation sounded too fascinating to resist,'' said Louisa. She gave him a honeyed smile which became tinctured with vinegar as her gaze shifted to Miss Denny. ''What's this about moving a table? Has Miss Denny suggested altering the furnishings?''

Her tone implied that it was premature, not to say impertinent, for Miss Denny to suggest any such thing. The Duke answered calmly, however, forestalling Miss Denny's response. ''No, not at all, Lou. I was merely apologizing to Miss Denny for the temperature of the Marble Hall at dinner tonight and explaining why, though rich in every other luxury, we cannot offer our guests comfort when they dine at Ashland Palace.''

Louisa afforded this witticism a perfunctory smile. ''Although I am something of an invalid, I do not find the Marble Hall at all uncomfortable. I suppose it is because it is so very beautiful and historic. Whenever I sit at table there, I am so overcome by reflecting on all the great men and women who have dined within its walls that I forget everything else. Do you find the Marble Hall cold, Miss Denny?''

''Yes, very,'' said Miss Denny frankly. ''I can't think why it hasn't any fireplace.''

Louisa gave an indulgent laugh, which was echoed by Philippa. "Oh, my dear! A fireplace in the Marble Hall! But you must see how that would mar the room's classic beauty. Or perhaps you cannot see—but I assure you such a thing is impossible. A fireplace would be utterly out of place in such a room as the Marble Hall. It would be like putting a fireplace in a great cathedral."

Philippa nodded, her face solemn. "It would be sacrilege. The room is a perfect thing as it now stands."

Miss Denny regarded her with some amusement. "Yes, but it's a dining room, Miss Montfort," she pointed out gently. "I can't think any room is perfect as a dining room if it's not comfortable to dine in."

"I suppose you would put fireplaces on all four walls if it belonged to you," said Louisa, with an ill-concealed sneer. At the same time she threw a look at the Duke that said as plainly as possible, "You see what a Philistine she is? She wants to desecrate the Marble Hall with fireplaces!"

Miss Denny ignored the sarcasm and considered the question quite soberly. "No, I don't think I'd put fireplaces," she said. "That would be difficult to do after the fact, and it would, as you say, spoil the looks of the room. I think if it was mine, I'd do what we did in my father's church and heat it with stoves."

"Stoves!" said Louisa, in the same tone she might have exclaimed, "Rats!" or "Blackbeetles!"

"They need not *look* like stoves," said Miss Denny patiently. "For my father's church they were made in a Gothic style to imitate some of the ornament on the capitals. I expect for here, they could be made in a classical style—perhaps to imitate urns, or something of that nature. It would have to be done very artistically, of course, so as not to spoil the room, but I am sure it *could* be done, if one had the funds to pay for such a project."

She looked inquiringly at the Duke. He did not respond, but merely looked back at her, a curious expression on his face. "I don't think—" began Louisa, in a haughty voice.

"I do," said the Duke, finding his voice. "Judy, that is a

magnificent idea. I shall call in a builder this very week and see what it would take to have stoves put in.''

Louisa said nothing, but twitched her shoulders in an expression of disgust and walked away. Philippa followed after her with a similar disgusted twitch of her shoulders. The Duke watched them go, then looked down at Miss Denny. "You really will have to marry me, you know," he said in a low voice. "It has just become clear to me that all my comfort depends on it, as well as all my happiness.''

Miss Denny smiled at him. "We shall see, James. It's still very early to be speaking of that." In a mock-stern voice, she added, "No pig-in-a-poke bargains for me! I shall have to see the rest of your house, sir, before I commit myself.''

Chapter XVIII

Obedient to Miss Denny's dictum, the Duke spent the next couple of hours showing her and the other guests around the Palace. Miss Denny said little during the tour—much less than the other lady guests, who were wont to "Ooh" and "Ahh" at the slightest provocation. Yet the Duke, covertly watching her, found himself growing more and more encouraged. She seemed awed but not intimidated by her surroundings, and when she did speak, it was not only to admire but to interpose an occasional suggestion for making life at the Palace more livable.

"You were quite right, James. Your Palace does remind me a bit of my father's rectory, though your cousins would no doubt call it presumption for me to say so," she whispered to the Duke, as the party solemnly filed through the Great Gallery. "It's much bigger and grander than Winfield Rectory, of course, but you've got most of the same disadvantages, including the disadvantage of not being able to make any major changes while you're living in it. Still, I daresay there are some little things you could do here and there to make it more comfortable. I wonder that your mother or grandmother didn't think of them already."

The Duke smiled. "By all accounts, my mother detested Ashland Palace and refused to come here more than she was absolutely obliged to. As for Grandmother—well, you've seen what she is like. As long as her milch cattle are comfortably housed, she isn't one to bother her head about the comfort of mere humans!"

Miss Denny nodded thoughtfully. "Of course. I suppose it's natural that everyone should have his or her own preoccupations. But if I lived here—" She stopped short, with a quick, self-conscious look at the Duke.

"If you lived here, it would be a paradise on earth, and I would cheerfully dine on cold food and sit in drafty rooms for the rest of my life," said the Duke, smiling down at her. "But I wouldn't have to. You would single-handedly reform all the petty discomforts and inefficiencies about the place, and future generations of duchesses would revere your memory as the woman who turned Ashland Palace into a livable residence."

"How you do go on," said Miss Denny, coloring noticeably but laughing nevertheless. "As I said before, it's early days yet for that, James. When I've been here a week or two, I will be happy to discuss the matter with you, but for now you'd better devote yourself to Lady McKearney and Mrs. Fulbright. I can see them looking at us very curiously, and I have no doubt they are wondering what we are talking about so confidentially."

The Duke, obedient to his beloved's behests, spent the rest of the evening chatting with Lady McKearney, Mrs. Fulbright, and his other guests. He could look at Miss Denny, however, even while he talked to the others, and so he was happy. What made him happiest of all was the way Miss Denny had received his remarks about marriage—with an indulgent smile, as though the idea of marrying him were quite a possible one.

True, she had not committed herself in speech. But it was obvious from her remarks that she was now considering the idea seriously—more seriously than she had done before. And if what she had seen of Ashland Palace thus far had not been enough to dissuade her, he could not imagine that anything she saw during the rest of her visit was likely to do so. The first and greatest hurdle had been passed, and he trusted that a greater familiarity with the Palace would vanquish any doubts she still entertained about being unfit to rule there as mistress.

The days that followed were in the main enjoyable ones for the Duke. He chafed now and then at having to play host to several dozen guests when he wished to devote himself to one alone, but even with all the demands of hospitality he generally found time each day to slip away for an hour or two with Miss Denny. The weather had improved so that he was able to take her for walks and drives about the estate, and he also made sure that she had every opportunity to acquaint herself further with the interior of Ashland Palace and the workings of its staff. One day, when the others of the party were busy playing battledore and shuttlecock in the garden, he took her to see the portraits in the portrait gallery.

"This particular corner is devoted to portraits of our past duchesses, you see. There is my mother—and there is Grandmother, looking only a little different than she does now. And here is our Jewess that I was telling you about. A handsome creature, isn't she?"

"Very handsome," said Miss Denny, surveying with interest the dark beauty he had indicated. "I think she is the loveliest of all, save perhaps for your mother." She looked pensively at the portrait of the smiling, fair-haired woman the Duke had identified as his mother. "You resemble her a great deal, James. Is there a portrait of you anywhere about?"

"Yes, but I don't care for it. It's tucked away in a closet somewhere, I think. I suppose I shall have to sit for another one, one of these days, so there will be something to hang in the gallery along with my forefathers." The duke turned his head to smile at Miss Denny. "And we shall have to arrange a sitting for you, too. I am looking forward to seeing your portrait here with Mother and Grandmother's."

Miss Denny glanced again at the portraits on the wall and shook her head dubiously. "I'm afraid I should look terribly out of place in such company, James. I don't dislike my own looks, but I am under no illusion that I am a beauty. These other ladies would shine me down entirely."

"I don't think so." The Duke looked down at Miss Denny meditatively. "Mind you, it would take a good artist to do you justice. We might have to try several before we could find one who could really capture you on canvas. But if I could make him see you as I see you, I would imagine that you would outshine every other lady here, my late mother not excepted."

Miss Denny regarded him a moment, her lips a little parted. Finally she drew a deep breath. "Really, James," she said, "that is a very remarkable speech!"

"I meant every word of it, I assure you," said the Duke.

"I know you did. That is what makes it so remarkable," said Miss Denny. Her eyes were sparkling with laughter, but there was a deeper emotion in them as well as she looked up at the Duke. "Upon my word, I don't believe anyone ever paid me such a pretty compliment before, James. Almost I am tempted to kiss you."

"Then by all means allow me to help the temptation along a little," said the Duke. Miss Denny submitted to his embrace without demur and raised her lips most willingly to his. Their kiss was not of long duration, however, for a moment later a clatter at the far end of the gallery announced the arrival of a troop of housemaids with mops, brooms, and dusters, come to perform their daily cleaning of the room. The Duke and Miss Denny drew hastily apart and were assiduously admiring portraits again by the time the housemaids noticed their presence.

Although the Duke could not help regretting this untimely interruption, he was nevertheless quite happy with the way his interview with Miss Denny had gone. He felt sure that her kissing him in that way signified a tacit acceptance of his suit and that when he asked her once more to marry him, she would accept him. Accordingly, he began to make plans for proposing formally to her, at the grand ball which was to be the climax of the house party festivities.

Although he was fairly certain that Miss Denny would accept him, he did not dare take her acceptance for granted and so gave a great deal of thought to choosing the most favorable time and place to put forth his proposal. On the whole, he thought the rose garden at midnight would be the best and most romantic setting. By way of a contingency plan, he also selected an alternate indoor setting to be used if the weather should prove unsuitable for an outdoor one.

Having settled these points, the Duke went on to plan out the other details of the party with the same anxious care. He engaged the best orchestra in the county to provide music for dancing, made certain that a tempting array of sweets figured among the refreshments served, and arranged for a fireworks display timed to go off at more or less the same moment in which he had received what he hoped would be Miss Denny's whole-hearted acceptance.

Miss Denny, being female and reasonably intuitive, could not help sensing the intent behind the Duke's preparations. His anxiety to have every detail of the party absolutely perfect amused her, even as it touched and gratified her. She still had moments when she looked around her and wondered in a panic what she was doing at Ashland Palace, but those moments were growing increasingly rare. It might be temerity of the worst kind, and doubtless there would be those who would criticize and others who would wonder at the Duke's choice, but she had made up her mind to accept him if he asked her to marry him again.

In making this decision, she had been influenced by several factors. One of these was the Dowager, who had been amazingly kind to her, showing her her cattle and her model dairy, introducing her to the servants, and generally putting her at her ease in her surroundings.

"I cannot help being rather worried about having the care of such a large house and so many servants," she confided shyly to the Dowager one day. "I am not sure I am capable of managing it all."

"Oh, you needn't bother your head about that," said the Dowager, dismissing Miss Denny's concern with an airy wave of her hand. "*I* don't, I assure you. Housekeeping bores me to tears, so I just leave it all to the servants to manage among themselves. It answers very well, I assure you."

Miss Denny, who had observed the often inefficient management that prevailed behind the scenes at Ashland Palace, forbore to contradict the Dowager, but one of her concerns was eased, at least. Whatever she did in the way of household management could hardly help being superior to the *status quo*.

Nor, when she considered it, could she believe her own capabilities in that regard were inferior to any other young woman's. It had occurred to her one day, watching Louisa and Philippa languidly attempting to monopolize the Duke's attention, that neither of them would have hesitated to marry him had the opportunity come their way. And yet they were plainly the most ineffectual creatures, capable hardly of any exertion more strenuous than lying on the sofa.

Neither would the Misses McKearney have hesitated to marry the Duke, or (to judge from their flirtatious behavior toward him) any of the other young ladies at the house party. What abilities could they possess that she did not? What accomplishments could they bring to marriage which she could not, in time, acquire?

"None, that's what," was Miss Denny's rational conclusion. "I am a reasonably intelligent being, and I don't mind working hard. If James doesn't care about my birth being inferior to his, then I shan't either. I always did think it was the greatest nonsense to suppose one person was superior to another merely because he or she had the luck to be born into a particular family. Not that James isn't superior to most people—but it's not his birth that makes him so. It's simply what he is himself. He would be superior even if he wasn't the Duke of Ashland." And she reflected with fond pleasure on the superior character of her lover.

Altogether, Miss Denny was a very happy girl at this period. She had the pleasure of daily seeing and conversing with the Duke, and the prospect of a more intimate congress to anticipate in the future. Almost the only cloud on her horizon at present was the rift that seemed to be daily widening between her sister and brother-in-law.

This rift was very marked. For the past few weeks Sir Geoffrey and Lady Spicer had scarcely spoken to each other, and they spent almost all their waking hours apart. Sir Geoffrey's mornings were generally passed in the billiard room or library, and his afternoons out-of-doors with those gentlemen who shared his taste for sport. Lady Spicer gossiped, played cards, and went for walks and rides with the other ladies during the day; and in the evenings she flirted by turns with all the best-looking gentlemen of the party.

It could have been worse, however. Miss Denny could only rejoice that the Duke had not included Lord Henry among his guests. It seemed to her that her sister's extramarital flirtations were less noticeable (and less exceptionable) when they were divided among a variety of objects, as on the present occasion. But her rejoicing proved premature, for one day, when she had been out walking with the Misses McKearney, she returned to find her sister seated alone in the Palace's lofty Saloon with Lord Henry Nathorp.

The two of them were sitting side by side on one of the cushioned benches fitted into the window embrasures along the far wall. Lord Henry had hold of Lady Spicer's hands and was saying something to her in a low voice. Lady Spicer listened to him, shaking her head now and then with a dubious air. On her face was a curious mixture of guilt and pleasure, excitement and uncertainty. She started violently when Miss Denny and the others came into the room. Miss Denny could tell she was embarrassed, but she recovered herself quickly, smiling and unobtrusively withdrawing her hands from Lord Henry's as she addressed her sister.

"Oh, Judith, only see who is here," she said, indicating Lord Henry. "You did not expect to see Henry again so soon, did you? No more did I, to be sure. But it seems that Henry's brother has a house in the neighborhood where he is visiting for a few weeks. And since he knew that we were staying at the Palace, he decided to drive over to pay his respects."

"It is a pleasure to see you again, Lord Henry," said Miss Denny, albeit without any real pleasure in her voice.

Lord Henry's pleasure in seeing her again appeared to be equally spurious. With a sardonic smile, he rose and sketched a bow to her. "The pleasure is mine, Miss Denny," he drawled. Turning to Lady Spicer, he added, "I must be going now,

Fanny. Give my respects to Ashland when you see him, and tell him I am looking forward to the ball tomorrow night.''

He laid a certain emphasis on these last words, which caused Lady Spicer to color slightly. ''Certainly I shall tell him, Henry. Good afternoon.''

Lord Henry returned this greeting with another bow and left, nodding in a perfunctory way to the Misses McKearney as he went out. As long as there were others in the room, Miss Denny said nothing, but when presently her walking companions excused themselves to go and change for dinner, she confronted her sister. ''Why was Lord Henry here, Fanny? And what did he mean by saying he was looking forward to the ball tomorrow night?''

''Why, exactly what he said, I suppose,'' said Lady Spicer, avoiding her sister's eye. ''As for why he is here, I told you that already, Judith. His brother has a property in the neighborhood, and Henry is visiting there for a few weeks.''

''Yes, I heard you say that. But you don't really mean that Lord Henry will be at the ball tomorrow night, Fanny?''

''Yes, I do. Why should he not be?'' Though struggling for a light tone, Lady Spicer gave the question an air of defiance. ''The Duke sent him an invitation, after all.''

''Did he?'' said Miss Denny, rather grimly. ''I must ask him about it, the next time I see him.''

She did ask the Duke about it, that very evening. The party had just finished dining in the Marble Hall, an experience which was rendered less trying than usual by the recent warming of the weather. The Duke, on entering the drawing room, had been temporarily waylaid by his cousins, who wished to show him some sketches of the Palace which they had done earlier that day. Successfully disengaging himself at last from Louisa and Philippa, he made his way to Miss Denny's side.

''Good evening, Judy,'' he said. Having surveyed her thoughtfully for a moment, he added in a quiet voice, ''Something is troubling you. Is it something you want to talk about, or would you rather I pretended not to notice?''

Miss Denny smiled wryly. "How transparent I must be. You seem to read me so easily, James. Yes, something *is* troubling me, and it happens that it was something I was wanting to discuss with you anyway." Lowering her voice, she added, "Lord Henry has been here. He was with Fanny in the saloon when I came back this afternoon. And he says he has an invitation to the ball tomorrow night."

The Duke looked startled. "Yes, I suppose he would have. The Nathorps have a house in this neighborhood, and since our families have always been on good terms with each other, Henry's name is automatically included on the guest list whenever we send out invitations from the Palace. I didn't even think of it, Judy." He looked with concern at Miss Denny. "I'm sorry if it worries you. If I had remembered about your sister, I might have had Henry's name omitted from the list—though it would have been an awkward business, I'm afraid. Still, I daresay something might have been contrived."

Miss Denny shook her head resolutely. "Don't give it another thought, James. I quite see how it was. Of course you could not omit Lord Henry's name from the guest list when his family and yours are so close." She sighed. "I must say, however, that it is rather unfortunate. Fanny and Geoffrey have hardly exchanged a word since we got here. Now that Lord Henry is here, too, I daresay things will only get worse."

"I'm sorry," said the Duke again. "I wish there was something I could do. I hate to see you worried about anything, especially if it keeps you from enjoying yourself at the party tomorrow night."

Remembering how much time and effort he had spent to secure her enjoyment on that night, Miss Denny was moved to compunction. It was unfair that the Duke should be troubled by her own private concerns, much less those of her sister and brother-in-law. Laying her hand on his arm, she smiled up at him warmly.

"Oh, but nothing could spoil my enjoyment in your ball, I am sure, James. This business is merely an annoyance, that is all." With a rueful air, she added, "Sometimes I could shake Fanny for the way she is behaving. There are times when I wouldn't mind shaking Geoffrey, too. All this trouble between them is so foolish and unnecessary. If only they would talk to each other, I am sure it could all be set straight.'' Again she smiled at the Duke. ''I think that is one of the reasons I enjoy your company so much, James. You are such a sensible, rational person. One always knows where one stands with you, and there is never any equivocation.''

''As you say,'' said the Duke, deliberately lifting her hand to his lips. Miss Denny blushed, and for the rest of the evening forgot all about her sister's marital difficulties.

Chapter XIX

The day of the ball dawned bright and sunny, to the Duke's exceeding relief. He felt the rose garden was much the best setting for a romantic proposal and was glad he need not now resort to an inferior, indoor setting.

He was busy throughout that day, supervising the party preparations as well as seeing to the entertainment of his guests. But in the back of his mind lurked the awareness that tonight was the night on which, if all went well, Miss Denny would finally consent to become his wife.

Since he was impatient for evening to come, naturally the morning and afternoon dragged by with intolerable slowness. Miss Denny found the hours dragged slowly, too, but she was more fortunate than the Duke, for she could occupy herself with preparing for the ball. For such an important occasion as this, of course, no amount of preparation could be considered excessive, and she retired to her bedchamber early in the afternoon to bathe, wash her hair, do her nails, and attend to all the other minutiae of her toilette.

She had communicated nothing of her hopes for the evening to her sister. For a wonder, Lady Spicer had not asked her about them, though the Duke's recent behavior would have justified sisterly speculation far more than on previous occasions. Ever since coming to Ashland Palace, however, Lady Spicer had been unusually subdued. Miss Denny had earlier found it necessary to tell her about the Duke's first proposal, but whereas previously Lady Spicer would certainly have berated her for not accepting such an advantageous offer, on this occasion she had received Miss Denny's communication with unnatural quiescence.

Miss Denny, reflecting on this phenomenon now as she laid out her dress and slippers, felt there was something unnatural altogether about her sister's behavior in the last few weeks. Lady Spicer had been much quieter than usual and curiously self-absorbed. Miss Denny had frequently found it necessary to address a question to her two or three times before getting any response. This behavior had been particularly noticeable since Lord Henry's visit on the previous day.

Miss Denny would rather not have associated the two events, but her mind persisted in drawing a connection despite her wishes. She could not help remembering, with a feeling of disquiet, Lord Henry's expression when he had spoken the words, "I am looking forward to tomorrow night," and her sister's blushing and self-conscious reply.

This dimmed a little the mood of happy anticipation which Miss Denny had been feeling all that day. Making a determined effort, she set her worries aside to concentrate on dressing her hair. This occupied her for some little time; and finding presently that she required the help of Lady Spicer's dressing woman to achieve the proper fashionable effect, she wrapped herself in her dressing gown and stepped across the hall to her sister's room to beg the loan of Françoise for a moment.

"Who is it? Oh, it's you, Judy." Lady Spicer, with a harassed expression, looked around at her sister's entrance. She was standing in front of her wardrobe, and on the floor around her were drifts of rainbow colored tulle, satin, and crepe: balldresses which she had been examining and discarding. Françoise was standing at the wardrobe, too, her expression one of long-suffering as she presented her mistress with yet another dress, this one of lilac silk. Lady Spicer took it from her, examined it a moment, then cast in on the floor with its fellows.

"No, not that one, either, Françoise. That color makes me look positively haggish. I can't think why I ever purchased the beastly thing in the first place." With a pettish expression, she gave the lilac-colored dress a little kick. "Take it away when you go, if you please, Françoise. I never want to see it again."

"Certainly, Madame," said Françoise, deftly whisking away the offending dress. As she turned again to the wardrobe, Lady Spicer stooped to re-examine a white lace gown already lying on the floor. Having subjected it to a second examination, she cast it aside once more with a despairing expression. "I have nothing to wear—nothing, nothing. I don't know what I shall do for a dress tonight."

"Why not wear your cerulean moiré?" said Miss Denny, observing a dress still hanging within the wardrobe. "You looked very elegant in that, I thought, when you wore it to the Havilands' ball last month."

Lady Spicer gave the cerulean moiré an unenthusiastic scrutiny. "It will do, I suppose. As I have nothing else, I suppose it will *have* to do. Ah, well, it doesn't matter anyway." In an abrupt change of mood, she smiled brightly and turned away from the wardrobe and heap of discarded dresses. "How is your toilette coming, Judy? You were wearing your gold brocade tonight, were you not?"

"Yes, and I need a bit of help arranging my hair. Might I borrow Françoise for a few minutes?"

"Oh, certainly, certainly," said Lady Spicer, with the same bright smile. "Now my dress is decided, I'm in no hurry here. She can attend to me whenever you are finished."

Miss Denny, accompanied by Françoise, went across the hall to her room. As she took her place at her dressing table and handed Françoise her brush and comb, she ventured a comment. "I appreciate your coming to me this way, Françoise. It appears that you already have your hands full this evening."

"Madame is *exigeante* tonight," agreed Françoise, her fingers moving skillfully through Miss Denny's golden-brown curls. "First her hair could not be made to satisfy her, and then her dress—*oh la la, c'est déraisonnable, ça!* But me, I do not mind. I understand well that Madame is in a mood, and the moods, you comprehend, are a thing which one must endure. My last mistress, when she was in a mood, was accustomed to scream and cry and throw the furnishings about. I am thankful that Madame your sister does not behave thus. Very unpleasant it was for the staff, and for *le pauvre* husband of Madame also, without doubt.''

"Yes, so I should imagine," said Miss Denny, smiling at this Gallic understatement. Nonetheless, she had been disturbed by what Françoise had said about her sister. There might be any number of reasons for Lady Spicer's mood, but Miss Denny still felt this one had something to do with Lord Henry Nathorp, and the vague sense of disquiet that had plagued her earlier returned in an intensified form.

"Blast Fanny," thought Miss Denny, in a burst of sisterly irritation. "I have enough to think about tonight without worrying about her, too. Even if she is contemplating doing something foolish, I don't know what I could do to stop her. She always was the most willful creature. If I were to say something to her about Lord Henry now, it would probably only cause her to plunge ahead with whatever she is planning rather than drawing back. Much better to put the whole business out of my mind and trust to Fanny's own good sense to keep her out of trouble."

Miss Denny did her best to follow this eminently sensible plan as Françoise helped her into her balldress and assisted her with the finishing touches of her toilette. Since she did indeed have plenty of her own concerns to occupy her, she succeeded fairly well, and when at last she was ready to go down for dinner, she had all but forgotten her sister's travails.

With pleasure she surveyed her reflection in the glass. Her gold brocade balldress was the very latest style, a short-sleeved closed robe with a square neckline and scalloped flounce. Its rich color set off to perfection the glossy coils of her hair, which had been dressed in loose curls about her face and in a low knot at the back of her head. Flat gold slippers adorned her feet, and her sister had lent her a set of topazes whose amber glow exactly matched the color of her eyes.

"I don't think it would be possible for me to look any better," she said aloud. "I'm no beauty and never shall be, but I think I shall do. Yes, certainly I shall do." And she turned away from the mirror with a smile.

Downstairs the guests were assembled in the Little Hall, waiting to go into dinner. The Duke, splendid in austere black evening clothes, was occupied with Lady McKearney, who was as usual attempting to draw his attention to the Misses McKearney, bejeweled and beribboned and very ready to be admired.

So voluble was Lady McKearney in her maternal endeavors that the Duke was prevented from saying any word to Miss Denny when she entered the Hall. The look he cast her way spoke volumes, however. Miss Denny colored prettily, swept him a smiling curtsy, and devoted herself to her dinner partner, Mr. Ormand, who likewise seemed very struck by her appearance and who took the opportunity of paying her a very pretty compliment as he escorted her into dinner.

The dinner itself passed quickly, despite its numerous courses and removes. As usual, Miss Denny's position at table prevented her from making conversation with the Duke, but she felt his eyes on her frequently throughout the meal. At the dinner's conclusion, when she was rising to leave the table with the other ladies, the Duke caught her eye and raised his wineglass in a wordless salute. Miss Denny smiled at him and hurried out of the room, her heart bursting with joyous anticipation.

The ball was scheduled to begin at nine o'clock. For some time previous to this, the steady rumble of carriages could be heard in the drive outside, and a steady stream of guests were admitted to the hall by the butler and his attendant footmen.

The Duke strolled in just as the clock was striking nine. He exchanged greetings with several guests who happened to be standing near the door, then looked around him. Miss Denny, watching him from her seat beside her sister, felt her heart swell with pride to see how distinguished he looked. His height made his silver-blond head clearly visible above the crowd, while the perfection of his tailoring and his easy, unconscious air of authority set him apart even more than his height and coloring.

The orchestra had begun tuning their instruments for the opening dance. Several ladies approached the Duke, ostensibly to thank him for inviting them to the ball, but really to hint broadly for invitations to dance.

"I am so glad you could come. Forgive me for not conversing longer, but I must collect my partner for the first dance," was his smiling response to one and all. No more could they get out of him, try as they would; and a battery of jealous, disappointed, and resentful feminine eyes watched him stroll unhurriedly across the room to where Miss Denny was sitting. And when he had bowed to her, and exchanged a few smiling words with her and Lady Spicer, the disappointed ladies had presently to endure the spectacle of seeing him lead her onto the floor.

Miss Denny, aware of the scrutiny of those around her, caught the faint collective gasp that arose when the Duke led her out for the first dance. He had distinguished her in London, and during the previous weeks of the house party, but never to this extent.

"You know, James, by rights you should have led out Lady Anne Deveril instead of me," she told him with an unsteady laugh. "She looks quite affronted, and I am sure I do not blame her. I'm afraid we are causing a tremendous scandal."

"That's what I'm depending on," said the Duke cheerfully. "The only thing that could justify such scandalous behavior is an incipient engagement. Now that my reputation is ruined, I am trusting your sense of honor will impel you to make an honest man of me."

Miss Denny colored, but tried to respond in a manner as insouciant as his. "You are taking a tremendous risk," she said. "Now you have alerted me to your motives, I might retaliate by leaving you in the lurch."

"Not at all," countered the Duke. "I know by now that you're clever enough to divine my motives, no matter how well I try to conceal them. By revealing them openly, I hope to win you over with a show of candor and open-dealing.''

"I see," said Miss Denny with a little smile. She said nothing else for a considerable time. The Duke was quiet, too, content to watch her and enjoy the pleasure of partnering her in the dance. At last she sighed and smiled up at him. "This is all so perfect, James. I wish this evening could never end."

"You are happy?" he said, looking down at her.

"Happier than I have ever been before, I think," she said simply.

"Then you don't find all this a bar to happiness anymore?" he said, indicating the baroque splendor of the hall around them.

"No, oddly enough I don't. I seem to have forgotten all about it. Those outside things really don't matter, do they?" Miss Denny looked pensively at the Duke. "All that matters is that I am with you—and I am happy."

The Duke pressed her hand, too pleased by the sentiments she had expressed to be able to respond to them effectively. They were both silent for so long after this that one elderly dowager, watching them keenly, leaned over and whispered to her neighbor, "I must say, my dear, that it appears to me to be all a hum. Only look at them! Why, they have not a word to say to each other."

When the dance was over, the Duke was obliged to do his duty by his other guests. He exchanged greetings with his friends and neighbors, made conversation with dowagers and chaperones, and danced resignedly with a series of flirtatious young ladies.

Meanwhile Miss Denny flitted gaily from one partner to the next. She looked what she was—happy and in a glow of spirits—and this being the case, her partners one and all found her irresistible. Mr. Ormand, who stood opposite her for a couple of country dances, found himself envying his friend's position; Sir Stephen Willis, who partnered her in the quadrille, was so captivated by her charm that he began to calculate whether it might not be too late to set up as a rival to the Duke and win her for himself; and Captain Lord Robert DeVere, who was in attendance with his sister Lady Emily, irritated that young lady very much by saying that Miss Denny was a jolly nice girl who was far too good for that stuffed shirt Ashland.

Miss Denny was quite oblivious to these undercurrents, however. Her happiness was of a kind to make her see everything around her through a rose-colored haze. Even the sight of Lady Spicer dancing with Lord Henry Nathorp did not cause her more than a momentary concern. Of course Fanny ought rather to be dancing with her husband, but Sir Geoffrey appeared to be nowhere about, so she could not be held too culpable in choosing another partner. With a passing wonder that other couples could not manage their affairs as well as she and the Duke, Miss Denny fell to thinking of happier subjects.

When it came time for the last dance before supper, the Duke once more sought out Miss Denny. He found her just coming off the floor after an exuberant reel with Mr. Manville. That young gentleman, along with his mother, had been invited to the house party as a special concession to Miss Denny, but Mr. Manville had been at first so overwhelmed by his surroundings as to render him (so the Duke had confided to Miss Denny) a virtual mute. Of late, however, he had seemed to be losing some of his shyness, and this evening he showed himself quite amazingly urbane, not only greeting the Duke with a fair semblance of ease, but even venturing to make some remark beyond a simple "Hello" or "Good evening."

"I say, but this is a bang-up party, your Grace," he told the Duke impulsively. "Don't know when I've had a better time. Your orchestra there's first class. I gave the head fiddler a guinea to play a reel, and Miss Denny and I've been showing everyone else the way out on the floor."

"Indeed," said the Duke with a smile. "Then I have no doubt you are both in need of rest and refreshment. And if I were a truly polite and conscientious host, I should doubtless counsel you to sit down while I hurried off to the refreshment room to procure you both some champagne. But—" he raised his hand as Mr. Manville opened his mouth to protest. "The sad truth is I am not a polite and conscientious host, Mr. Manville. My object on this occasion is to basely deprive you of your partner. Therefore, I recommend that you go fetch your own champagne, while I abscond with Miss Denny.''

''Fair enough, your Grace,'' said Mr. Manville, grinning at him shyly. ''If your champagne's as good as your fiddlers, at least it'll be some consolation.''

''You see how fortunate you are that your choice is fixed on me rather than young Manville,'' said the Duke, as he led Miss Denny away. ''My champagne is, I flatter myself, as good as anyone's, but I should be ashamed to consider it any consolation for the loss of your company.''

Miss Denny shook her head with pretended despondency. ''It is very lowering to be so little esteemed. I had not thought Mr. Manville would have relinquished me so easily. Why, he did not even offer to fight a duel for my sake!''

''A sad want of spirit on his part,'' said the Duke, also shaking his head. ''But that is the way with these younger men. It takes an older gentleman to properly render a lady those little attentions that mean so much. If you marry me, I shall make it a point to demand satisfaction of any gentleman who looks at you twice—or perhaps you would rather that I make the invitation indiscriminate and call out everyone, regardless of the number of times they look at you. You will have to let me know what you prefer in that line.''

''Well, I don't know,'' said Miss Denny, looking at him quizzically. ''I confess I hadn't thought that far ahead, James. Must I give you an answer tonight?''

''*An* answer, but not that one,'' said the Duke, returning her look with a meaning one of his own. ''Let me get you a glass of champagne, and then we will go somewhere and discuss the matter in private.''

The Duke fetched champagne for Miss Denny and himself, then led her out on the south terrace. The rose garden lay beyond and was reached by way of a broad alley bordered on either side by stately rows of limes. Normally at this hour the alley would have been plunged in darkness, but the Duke had caused small colored lanterns to be placed in the trees, and the effect was all he had hoped for.

"Oh, James, how lovely," said Miss Denny, looking around her with awe. "It all looks quite magical—a perfect fairyland."

"Thank you," said the Duke, gratified by her response. "It would look even better if it were moonlight. But since the moon wasn't obliging enough to be at the full tonight, we had to make do with what we could."

Miss Denny said solemnly that she thought lamplight was nicer than moonlight, being more exclusive. "And your champagne is very nice, too, James. I like it much better than the Winchcombs'—almost as well as lemonade, in fact."

The Duke gave her a look that made her laugh out loud. "On my honor, James, I like it even better than lemonade," she assured him with a smile. "It is as perfect as everything else tonight."

The Duke smiled back at her but did not speak. They were approaching the rose garden now, a circular plot of ground that formed the natural termination of the lime alley. A sundial stood at the center of the garden with pathways radiating outward like the spokes of a wheel. Meticulously-tended rosebushes bloomed in the wedge-shaped beds between the pathways, and a low stone wall formed the garden's outermost boundary. Beyond it, just visible in the shadows, was a small temple dedicated, appropriately enough, to the Goddess Flora.

The Duke led Miss Denny to the center of the rose garden, where the sundial stood on its ornate pedestal. The scent of roses hung deliciously in the air, and a soft light was diffused over the scene by the lanterns hung in the surrounding trees. The Duke felt once again that it was a perfect setting for a romantic proposal. He cleared his throat. "I suppose you know what I wished to talk to you about, Judy," he began in a low, self-conscious voice. "Some weeks ago I made you a proposal of marriage. Since then—"

He was interrupted unceremoniously by Miss Denny. "Listen, James," she whispered, gripping his arm. "Do you hear something?"

The Duke was mildly affronted by his beloved's inattention at such a moment, but he was nevertheless willing to humor her. He listened intently but heard nothing apart from the stirring of leaves in the surrounding trees. "It was probably just the wind," he was beginning to say, when he became aware that it was not the wind. What he heard was the sound of voices, and they seemed to be coming from the Temple of Flora.

"*Now* what's wrong?" The words, spoken in an impatient-sounding masculine voice, came drifting across the garden. Another voice responded to the unknown speaker's words, but it spoke too low for the listeners in the rose garden to hear what was being said. A brief pause followed, and then quite suddenly the second voice spoke again. This time it spoke quite audibly, in tones that were both agitated and unmistakably feminine.

"Ah, no, I can't. I'm sorry, but I can't. It's no use."

There followed another pause in which the masculine speaker could be faintly heard, apparently arguing or expostulating with his companion. Then the feminine voice rose again, sharper this time. "I said I can't, and that's all there is to it. I have changed my mind, Henry."

A lengthy murmur followed, in which the masculine speaker appeared to be disputing this statement. His voice was too low for the Duke and Miss Denny to make out his words, but it was apparent that he chose to couple his speech with a more physical form of persuasion, for the female speaker's next words were an angry, "How dare you?" followed by the sound of a slap. A scuffling noise was heard, and then the female speaker let out a high-pitched scream. The Duke waited to hear no more. He set off at a run for the Temple of Flora, and Miss Denny was right behind him.

The Temple was a small square stone building fitted up to serve as a summerhouse. It was dark inside, but not too dark to distinguish the couple who lay struggling atop an upholstered couch. Lady Spicer, her dress and hair in disarray, was biting, scratching, and kicking with the fury of a cornered animal. Lord Henry sought grimly to restrain her thrashing limbs, gasping out a stream of singularly filthy invectives as he did so. The Duke did not hesitate, but strode across the room, hauled Lord Henry to his feet by the collar of his coat, and slammed him against the wall of the Temple.

"Leave her be, Nathorp," he commanded in an icy voice. "You forget yourself, I think."

Miss Denny, seeing that Lord Henry was out of the way, lost no time in hurrying to her sister. "Oh, Fanny, did he hurt you?" she said, kneeling beside the couch and possessing herself of her sister's hand. Lady Spicer lay still on the couch, her breath coming in gasps and the tears flowing freely down her cheeks. When she spoke, however, her voice was unexpectedly clear and firm.

"I am not hurt at all, only shocked and disgusted, Judith. If you will help me away from that—that beast over there, I should be very grateful." She shot a look of loathing at Lord Henry.

"That is not necessary, Lady Spicer. I'll take the beast outside and deal with him," said the Duke, also looking with disgust at Lord Henry. "You stay here and recover yourself."

Miss Denny, turning her own eyes on Lord Henry, thought he looked rather discomposed by his predicament. He responded, however, with a creditable imitation of his usual manner. "I have no quarrel with you, Ashland," he told the Duke. "Of course I will name my friends if you insist, but surely it is foolish that we should meet over such a business as this."

"I have no intention of meeting you over this business," said the Duke calmly. "That method of settling disputes is for gentlemen, and your behavior tonight proves you are no such thing. If you behave like a cur, you deserve to be beaten like a cur, and that is what I propose to do to you. If you would please to step outside?"

Lord Henry gave him a look of venomous dislike. "Fine words, Ashland, but don't think you'll have it all your own way," he snarled. "I will meet you outside with the greatest pleasure."

As he stalked out of the Temple, Miss Denny was struck by a sudden inspiration. Hurrying over to the Duke, who was preparing to follow Lord Henry, she whispered in his ear, "James, I know you want to punish Lord Henry, and I must say he deserves it. But instead of beating him, do you think you could keep him occupied for ten minutes or so without really hurting him? Just play around with him, so to speak?''

"Why, yes, I think so,'' said the Duke, regarding her with surprise. "I have sparred with Nathorp before at Jackson's, and though he is a pretty fair pugilist, I think I'm more than a match for him. But why should you want me to spare him, Judy? I would think after what he did to your sister, you would want to see him punished.''

"Oh, I do,'' Miss Denny assured him. "It's only that I've thought of a better way to punish him—at least, I think I have. But it all depends on your holding him here for a little while. Can you do it, James? I don't mind if you hit Lord Henry, you know; just don't hurt him *too* badly.''

This speech made the Duke laugh. But seeing that Miss Denny was in earnest, he promised to damage Lord Henry as little as possible during their coming engagement. Miss Denny turned next to Lady Spicer. "Fanny, I must leave you,'' she said. "I don't know for exactly how long, but I'll be back as soon as I can.''

"Where are you going?'' asked Lady Spicer, half sitting up on the bench to regard her with surprise. Miss Denny did not answer, but only patted her hand reassuringly. She then gathered up her skirts, hurried out of the Temple, and began to run up the alley toward the house.

She had counted on having to re-enter the house, but luck was with her. She found her quarry on the terrace, smoking a cigar and staring moodily out at the lantern-lit trees. "Oh, Geoffrey,'' she cried, hurrying up the steps. "You must come with me right away, Geoffrey. The most dreadful thing has happened! I don't know what we shall do.''

Sir Geoffrey turned to regard her in surprise. "What's that?'' he said. "What's happened, Judy? Somebody taken ill?''

"Not taken ill, exactly, but a most unfortunate incident. Poor, poor, Fanny! I am afraid she is quite prostrated with shock.''

Observing her brother-in-law closely, Miss Denny was satisfied to see him straighten suddenly and his face grow tense. "Fanny?'' he demanded. "What's wrong with her, Judy? Where is she?''

Miss Denny, hastily reviewing her options, decided a modi-fied form of the truth would suit the situation best. It would be for Lady Spicer to make a fuller explanation later if she so desired. "I don't know exactly what happened, Geoffrey. As nearly as I can find out, Fanny and Lord Henry Nathorp were dancing and decided to go out for a breath of fresh air. And it seems that once they were outside, Lord Henry tried to—well, to attack her."

Sir Geoffrey drew in his breath sharply. Miss Denny went on quickly, before he had time to speak. "She is not at all injured, Geoffrey. Fortunately, the Duke and I were in the garden at the same time and came to her rescue. But she is naturally upset, and—and I think she wants you."

Sir Geoffrey's reaction was all she could have hoped for. Flinging away his cigar, he started down the alley at a run. Miss Denny had hard work to keep up with him, but followed after as best she could, panting out additional information between breaths. "Lord Henry tried to call the Duke out, but the Duke said dueling was for gentlemen, and that Lord Henry deserved beating like a cur," she told Sir Geoffrey. "They were getting ready to fight when I left. I do hope the Duke will be all right. Lord Henry looked a regular wild man and sounded one, too. If you had heard the language he was using—"

"I'll settle him," said Sir Geoffrey grimly. "I'm much obliged to Ashland for his assistance, Judy, but this is between Nathorp and me. And I only hope I'm not too late to have a hand in punishing him as he deserves."

Miss Denny hoped so, too. But as they approached the Tem-ple of Flora, she saw she need not have worried. The Duke and Lord Henry, both stripped to their shirtsleeves, were grimly circling each other, their fists raised and their breath coming hard. There was blood streaming from the Duke's aristocratic nose, but he appeared otherwise unhurt. Lord Henry's clothing, however, bore signs of an encounter with the earth, and his face, too, looked rather the worse for wear. He swung out wildly at the Duke and missed, just as Sir Geoffrey came hurrying up.

"Stand aside, Ashland. This is between Nathorp and me,"

he ordered. The Duke looked around in surprise. Seeing who it was, he lowered his fists and reluctantly stepped aside.

Lord Henry looked around, too, and when he saw his new opponent, a smile of contempt appeared on his lips. Sir Geoffrey was a big man, but indulgence and advancing years had thickened his waist and softened the once solid muscularity of his frame. With the contemptuous smile still on his lips, Lord Henry raised his fists and started forward. He was met with a single blow from Sir Geoffrey's fist that sent him reeling senseless to the ground. "Get up, Nathorp. I'm not done with you yet," snapped Sir Geoffrey, looking menacingly down at Lord Henry's prone figure.

"Perhaps not, but I think you will have to wait to administer any further retribution," said the Duke, stooping to examine Lord Henry. "I doubt Nathorp will be up to anything more tonight."

"That's all right, then," said Sir Geoffrey dismissively. Brushing off his hands, he looked around the garden. "Where's Fanny?" he demanded. "Judy, did you say Fanny was here?"

Miss Denny pointed mutely to the Temple of Flora. There in the doorway stood Lady Spicer, her hands clasped in front of her and her eyes fixed on her husband's face.

"Oh, Geoffrey," she said with a catch in her voice. "That was magnificent, Geoffrey. I am so glad I saw it. It was exactly what I would have liked to do to Henry myself, if only I could have."

"At least you boxed his ears for him," said Miss Denny consolingly. Lady Spicer gave a little gasp of laughter, then burst into tears. Sir Geoffrey hurried forward, a look of concern on his face.

"Here now, Fanny, there's no need to cry," he said. "It's all right now, little girl. I'll make sure that blackguard never sets foot in society again—"

He got no further, for Lady Spicer had thrown herself into his arms, weeping uncontrollably. As she wept, she sobbed out a series of disjointed apologies. "Oh, Geoffrey, I am so sorry. I've been such a fool. Please try to forgive me, Geoffrey. I am so sorry, upon my word."

"Nothing to be sorry about," said Sir Geoffrey, patting her tenderly on the back. "Daresay I ought to be the one apologizing, if it comes to that. I should have been taking better care of you this while instead of running off to my club every minute. But we'll see it doesn't happen again, won't we, Fanny?"

"Oh yes, Geoffrey," said Lady Spicer, with redoubled sobs. Sir Geoffrey patted her on the back once more and advised her not to take on so.

"I think you really ought to take her inside, Geoffrey," suggested Miss Denny helpfully. "She has had a trying evening and will want to rest now."

Sir Geoffrey instantly approved this suggestion. Taking his wife by the arm, he began to lead her back toward the house. At the same moment, Lord Henry let out a groan and opened his eyes, looking around him with a dazed expression.

"I believe he's coming around," said the Duke, looking down at him critically. "It's a good thing he waited till Spicer was gone, or I daresay he'd have gotten another dose of home-brewed. I wonder what the deuce I ought to do with him?"

"Put him in his carriage and send him home," said Miss Denny promptly. "His family lives nearby, you said, so it stands to reason his carriage must be somewhere hereabouts. And if he has a carriage, presumably he must have servants, too. They can help carry him out to the carriage and see he gets home safely. After that, he will be someone else's responsibility, and I wouldn't worry about him any longer, James. If Geoffrey wants to punish him further after tonight, that will be between him and Lord Henry."

"You have a solution for every difficulty, don't you?" said the Duke, regarding her with a mixture of admiration and amusement. "And as usual, your solutions are wonderfully practical. I shall do just what you suggest, Judy. Do you care to come with me while I see about ordering around Nathorp's carriage?"

"I would be delighted to," said Miss Denny.

The Duke bent down to address Lord Henry. "You wait here, Nathorp," he said in heartening tones. "I'm going to call your carriage. Don't assault any more of my female guests while I'm gone, there's a good fellow.''

Lord Henry's response was to groan faintly and turn his face away. Leaving him where he lay, the Duke picked up the topcoat and waistcoat he had discarded previous to the fight and put them on. He then offered Miss Denny his arm. As they started toward the stables, she looked up at him meditatively. ''There's blood on your nose,'' she said.

The Duke touched his nose gingerly. ''Yes, Nathorp managed to work a left in under my guard,'' he said. Pulling a handkerchief from his pocket, he dabbed cautiously at the afflicted member. As he folded the handkerchief away, he added in more cheerful tones, ''But I ought not to complain. I landed a few good hits, too—in fact, I'm fairly certain I blacked both Nathorp's eyes for him, which is a decent revenge. And I am quite sure that if we had been left to ourselves, I could have finished him off quite as well as Spicer did, if not quite so quickly.''

Miss Denny nodded. ''Yes, but it was better that Sir Geoffrey should do it, James,'' she said seriously. ''It allowed him to relieve his feelings about Lord Henry for one thing, and for another it impressed Fanny with his capability. I shouldn't be surprised if they didn't get on quite well together now, at least for a little while,'' she added in a voice of satisfaction.

The Duke looked down at her, a quizzical smile playing about his lips. ''And I suppose that was exactly what you intended should happen,'' he said. ''I wondered what you were doing when you went haring off that way—but I should have guessed you had your reasons. And so you actually managed to reunite the estranged lovers and dispose of the unwanted suitor, all in one blow! What an eye for opportunity you do have, after all.''

''Oh, I don't know about that,'' said Miss Denny, looking modest. ''It was all a gamble, really—but the thing was, you know, that I couldn't see that anybody had much to lose. Things between Fanny and Geoffrey were already about as bad as they could be, and there was bound to be a big emotional scene between them once Geoffrey learned about this business tonight. So I thought I might as well turn it to account. I have frequently observed that emotional scenes do often draw people together.''

"Is that so?" said the Duke, quizzing her. She responded quite seriously, however, with a vigorous nod.

"Oh, yes. When Henry Smith was courting a friend of mine in Winfield, he would come and sit with her for hours and hours on end and yet say hardly a word, until poor Beatrice was beginning to think he never meant to declare himself at all. But when she fell off her horse at the New Year's Meeting and everyone feared she had done an injury to her spine, Henry was beside himself. And the moment the doctor said she was only stunned and would be well again directly, he asked her to marry him.''

"Ah," said the Duke, and seemed to fall into a reverie. He and Miss Denny continued on a little way in silence. At last the Duke spoke again. "All the same, I don't know that I think much of your Mr. Smith. By delaying so long, he put himself in jeopardy of losing the thing he wanted before he ever had a chance to win it. Surely it would have been more sensible to speak up as soon as he was sure of his own mind.''

"Well, of course it would have been more sensible," said Miss Denny, regarding the Duke with amusement. "But you know not very many people *are* sensible, James. Take Fanny and Geoffrey and this business tonight, for instance. If they had been really sensible people, they never would have become estranged in the first place. And even though they do seem to be back on good terms now, I wouldn't bet a ha'penny against the chance that this whole business won't have to be done over again a year or two hence." She shook her head forebodingly.

"You dismay me," said the Duke, his voice choked with laughter. Recovering himself presently, he added in a thoughtful voice, "I am glad you and I are sensible souls, at least. There will be no such foolishness between us after *we* are married.''

"No, certainly not," agreed Miss Denny. She would have gone on walking after making this statement, but the Duke pulled her to a stop.

"Judy, do you mean it?" he demanded, putting his hands

on her shoulders and looking down at her. "You are saying you will marry me?"

Miss Denny smiled up at him. "Well, of course, James," she said. "Do you have to ask?"

The Duke let out his breath in a long sigh. "Thank God," he said devoutly. With a touch of asperity, he added, "And yes, Miss Denny, I did have to ask. It didn't seem to me that there was any 'of course' about it. This evening hasn't exactly gone according to plan, you know. I meant to propose to you in the most romantic fashion possible—in the rose garden, at midnight, with me on bended knee and everything as neat and decorous as possible. And instead, here I am, torn and blood-stained and looking thoroughly disreputable, offering you my heart and hand in that most romantic of localities—" he looked around him with a grimace—"the stableyard."

Miss Denny laughed. "I don't care a penny for that, James," she said. "Stableyards are very good and useful things, you must know—a good deal more useful than rose gardens when all is said and done. I should think myself foolish to refuse your proposal for such a reason as that."

"And of course you are never foolish," said the Duke, smiling down at her tenderly.

"Not very often, at least," Miss Denny temporized. A sky-rocket burst overhead, and she looked up with surprise that turned quickly to enchantment. "Oh, look, James! Fireworks!"

"Well, at least one thing tonight is going as planned," said the Duke, regarding the sky with satisfaction. Putting his arm around Miss Denny's shoulders, he addressed her in a smiling yet serious voice. "What you see in the sky above us, my dear, are not merely Roman candles and Congreve's rockets, but the visible expression of an overflowing heart. By accepting my proposal of marriage, you have made me the happiest man on earth. I only hope that one day I will be able to make you equally happy."

"You already have," said Miss Denny, smiling at him. Growing serious in her turn, she added, "But you know, James, you must not be expecting everything to be plain sailing between us from now on, merely because I have agreed to marry you. I have not been brought up to be a duchess, and it stands to reason that I shall make a great many mistakes, especially at first.''

''My dear, I beg you won't fret yourself about that,'' said the Duke. He bent to kiss her lightly on the lips. ''I have complete confidence in your abilities, and I am sure you will make no mistakes worth the mentioning.'' With a hint of mischief in his voice, he added, ''Besides, you must remember the position you are marrying into. It is a widely known and generally accepted fact that a duke can do no wrong. And so, by extension, neither can a duchess. You may do just as you please after we are married, and the world will automatically assume you are right, merely because you are my wife.''

Miss Denny burst out laughing. ''Oh, James, what an odiously conceited speech!'' she said. ''Why if I really thought you meant all that, I should be obliged to give you the most crushing set-down!''

The Duke pretended to look apprehensive. ''And are you going to?'' he said.

Miss Denny pretended to consider, then shot him a sideways smile. ''Not this time,'' she said.

''Good,'' said the Duke, and kissed her again.

ABOUT THE AUTHOR

Joy Reed lives with her family in the Detroit area. She is the author of five Zebra Regency Romances: AN INCONVENIENT ENGAGEMENT, TWELFTH NIGHT, THE SEDUCTION OF LADY CARROLL, MIDSUMMER MOON and LORD WYLAND TAKES A WIFE. Joy's newest Regency Romance will be published in November 1998. Joy loves to hear from her readers and you may write to her c/o Zebra Books. Please include a self-addressed stamped envelope if you wish a response.

BOOK YOUR PLACE ON OUR WEBSITE AND MAKE THE READING CONNECTION!

We've created a customized website just for our very special readers, where you can get the inside scoop on everything that's going on with Zebra, Pinnacle and Kensington books.

When you come online, you'll have the exciting opportunity to:

- View covers of upcoming books
- Read sample chapters
- Learn about our future publishing schedule (listed by publication month *and author*)
- Find out when your favorite authors will be visiting a city near you
- Search for and order backlist books from our online catalog
- Check out author bios and background information
- Send e-mail to your favorite authors
- Meet the Kensington staff online
- Join us in weekly chats with authors, readers and other guests
- Get writing guidelines
- AND MUCH MORE!

**Visit our website at
http://www.zebrabooks.com**

WATCH FOR THESE ZEBRA REGENCIES

LADY STEPHANIE   (0-8217-5341-X, $4.50)
by Jeanne Savery
Lady Stephanie Morris has only one true love: the family estate she
has managed ever since her mother died. But then Lord Anthony Rider
arrives on her estate, claiming he has plans for both the land and the
woman. Stephanie soon realizes she's fallen in love with a man whose
sensual caresses will plunge her into a world of peril and intrigue . . . a
man as dangerous as he is irresistible.

BRIGHTON BEAUTY   (0-8217-5340-1, $4.50)
by Marilyn Clay
Chelsea Grant, pretty and poor, naively takes school friend Alayna
Marchmont's place and spends a month in the country. The devastating
man had sailed from Honduras to claim his promised bride, Miss
Marchmont. An affair of the heart may lead to disaster . . . unless a
resourceful Brighton beauty finds a way to stop a masquerade and
keep a lord's love.

LORD DIABLO'S DEMISE   (0-8217-5338-X, $4.50)
by Meg-Lynn Roberts
The sinfully handsome Lord Harry Glendower was a gambler and the
black sheep of his family. About to be forced into a marriage of con-
venience, the devilish fellow engineered his own demise, never having
dreamed that faking his death would lead him to the heavenly refuge
of spirited heiress Gwyn Morgan, the daughter of a physician.

A PERILOUS ATTRACTION   (0-8217-5339-8, $4.50)
by Dawn Aldridge Poore
Alissa Morgan is stunned when a frantic passenger thrusts her baby
into Alissa's arms and flees, having heard rumors that a notorious
highwayman posed a threat to their coach. Handsome stranger Hugh
Sebastian secretly possesses the treasured necklace the highwayman
seeks and volunteers to pose as Alissa's husband to save her reputation.
With a lost baby and missing necklace in their care, the couple embarks
on a journey into peril—and passion.

*Available wherever paperbacks are sold, or order direct from the
Publisher. Send cover price plus 50¢ per copy for mailing and
handling to Kensington Publishing Corp., Consumer Orders,
or call (toll free) 888-345-BOOK, to place your order using
Mastercard or Visa. Residents of New York and Tennessee
must include sales tax. DO NOT SEND CASH.*

WATCH FOR THESE REGENCY ROMANCES

BREACH OF HONOR   (0-8217-5111-5, $4.50)
by Phylis Warady

DeLACEY'S ANGEL   (0-8217-4978-1, $3.99)
by Monique Ellis

A DECEPTIVE BEQUEST   (0-8217-5380-0, $4.50)
by Olivia Sumner

A RAKE'S FOLLY   (0-8217-5007-0, $3.99)
by Claudette Williams

AN INDEPENDENT LADY   (0-8217-3347-8, $3.95)
by Lois Stewart